RAVE REVIEWS FOR *USA TODAY* BESTSELLING AUTHOR ROBIN T. POPP!

IMMORTALS: THE DARKENING

"In book two of this spine-tingling series, Popp demonstrates her deft characterization and plotting ability as she propels the story forward while enriching the romance. Make a place on your keeper shelf for this outstanding series!"

—*Romantic Times BOOKreviews*

"Ms. Popp does a fine job of continuing this truly charming and titillating series with her latest release, *The Darkening*. Her characters are enchanting, the story line fast-paced and intriguing. All in all, *The Darkening* is one that shouldn't be missed."

—Romance Reviews Today

"Excellent and well worth the read."

—Once Upon a Romance

"Robin T. Popp provides the audience with a delightful romantic fantasy."

—*Midwest Book Review*

TOO CLOSE TO THE SUN

"Robin T. Popp blazes onto the scene and delivers a truly unique, fast-paced, thrilling and sexy adventure."

—*Romantic Times BOOKreviews*

"A powerful futuristic tale that subgenre fans and those who appreciate a delightful speculative fiction story will enjoy."

—*Midwest Book Review*

MESSAGE IN THE MIRROR

"I am *not* hallucinating," Mai said, hoping the sound of her own voice would make it more convincing. What had happened to her was real. She hadn't imagined it. She hadn't.

She headed to the bathroom, moving with a weariness brought on by worry more than fatigue. She started the water and while she waited for it to get hot, she stripped off her clothes.

Stepping beneath the stream, she let it beat down on her until the heat slowly stole past the chill of her doubts. After what seemed an eternity, she snapped out of her inner reflections. It was time to get out.

Shutting off the water, she left the curtain closed to trap the warm air inside with her and snaked a hand out to grab a towel. She rubbed her skin and hair briskly until she was dry enough to get out and then pulled the shower curtain aside.

As soon as the warm air hit the mirror, it fogged over— and a single word appeared in the glass.

Remember.

ROBIN T. POPP

IMMORTALS: THE HAUNTING

LOVE SPELL NEW YORK CITY

To my fans—I appreciate you all.

LOVE SPELL®

November 2008

Published by

Dorchester Publishing Co., Inc.
200 Madison Avenue
New York, NY 10016

ISBN 10: 0-505-52766-9
ISBN 13: 978-0-505-52766-0

The name "Love Spell" and its logo are trademarks of Dorchester Publishing Co., Inc.

Printed in the United States of America.

10 9 8 7 6 5 4 3 2 1

Visit us on the web at www.dorchesterpub.com.

ACKNOWLEDGMENTS

I would like to thank...

Marlaine Loftin— for being a steadfast friend, a fantastic plotting partner and proofreader.

Mary Baxter—for sharing with me a moment of creative genius which became the Well of Lost Souls.

Leah Hultenschmidt—for being such a terrific, hands-on editor.

Jennifer Ashley and Joy Nash—for all their hard work and effort on this project, which extended beyond the writing of their respective books.

Immortals:
The Haunting

CHAPTER ONE

The elevator car shuddered as it slowly rose. Mai Groves had a vivid image of thick cables, stressed beyond their tolerance, snapping one by one. When the last cable broke, the car would plummet six stories to the basement, where the force of impact would crush it like an empty beer can—killing everyone inside, of course.

The ringing of her cell phone interrupted the gruesome daydream.

"Hello?"

"Mai, it's Tom. Are you all right?"

She glanced around the empty car. "For now, why?"

"Where are you?"

"In an elevator. A really old, really small elevator." Belatedly, the urgency of her editor's tone registered. "What's the matter?"

"So you're not at your therapist's?"

"No," she replied, not bothering to hide the irritation sparked by his question. "I told you last week that I'd stopped seeing him. I'm cured. No more seeing things that aren't there." She kept her tone light and wondered whether he was buying the "I'm as normal as the next wood nymph" argument she was trying to sell him.

Ever since she'd helped a coven of witches, four drop-dead-gorgeous Immortal warriors and a cast of other magical beings take on an ancient demon in a battle that almost destroyed the world, Mai had been having problems. Specifically, she'd been having hallucinations brought on by what her therapist had diagnosed as post-traumatic stress disorder. Mai didn't think that seeing demons everywhere she looked necessarily meant she was looney tunes. After her previous near-apocalyptic experience, Mai knew that demons looked like everyone else. Of course, the fact that no one else saw them tended to undermine her claim to sanity.

"There was a break-in at your therapist's office today," Tom went on. "I was afraid you might have been there at the time."

"You're kidding? Is everyone okay?" As a therapist, Ken Barbour was draining, but as a person, Mai liked him well enough.

"No. Dr. Barbour, well . . . he was found dead at the scene. Shot to death."

Mai's heart gave a lurch as the elevator stopped and the doors opened. For a second, she stood there in shock. Finally, she forced her feet to move. She automatically started walking down the hall toward her apartment. "Do they know who did it?"

"They have suspects—thirty of them. All patients."

Indignation pierced the shock that had kept her numb until that point. "I hope you're not suggesting *I* killed him."

"No. Of course not, but generally speaking, Dr. Barbour's patients were . . . disturbed. The police found patient records strewn about the place, so they think one of the patients might have had something to do with the killing."

Mai didn't even ask how Tom knew so much about

what had happened. He had contacts on the police force and at all the television news stations. Besides, even if she asked him, he wouldn't tell her.

"You all right?" Tom asked after she'd been silent for too long.

"Yeah. It's just such a shock."

"I know. Do you have someone you could call to come stay with you?"

Mai bristled at the implication that she was too fragile to deal with this horrible news. "Tom. He was my therapist, not my friend and not my lover. Obviously, I'm upset to learn he's dead but I don't need someone to babysit me."

She heard Tom sigh. "I'm just worried about you," he said. "I'm ready for my ace reporter to come back to work."

"Is that why you fired me?"

"Mai, you know I couldn't keep you on staff when you weren't writing."

She sighed. "I know." She paused. "Speaking of writing—I'm working on a new story."

"Really? Another one? Are you sure that's wise after what happened at the training station?"

"Please, Tom. That was ages ago."

"Mai, it was last week."

"I told you, I didn't hear them announce the flash fire demo. When it flashed, I wasn't prepared. It . . . startled me." Actually, it had scared the hell out of her. She'd been instantly transported back to the big battle with the ancient demon—an experience she was already reliving entirely too often in her dreams.

"You almost killed three firemen before they tackled you to the ground. By then, the fire had grown considerably larger than planned."

"But it all worked out. No one was hurt. They didn't

press charges and I apologized. Plus, you got a great story out of it. Happy ending."

"Only because I made a sizeable contribution to the training station on behalf of the paper."

Oh. She hadn't known that, but she sensed he was weakening and she didn't want to give up. "Listen, I think this story I'm working on now is going to be big." She patted the folded piece of paper burning a hole in her jeans pocket. It held everything she needed to nail Bill Preston, the leading mayoral candidate. Her source had been very forthcoming with information about the politician's involvement with mob boss Tony Perone. Mai only had to verify a few facts and get some corroboration to piece it all together.

"Great. What's this one about?" he asked with a decided lack of excitement.

"Right. I'm going to tell you so you can have one of your staffers scoop me? I don't think so, but tell you what? Because I like you"—*and because you bailed me out of the fire station disaster*, she silently added—"when I'm done, I'll give you first dibs."

He agreed and they said good-bye. A story as scandalous as this one would make big headlines and sell a lot of papers. She might no longer have a regular position on staff, but she'd still come a long way as a journalist, she thought as she dropped her cell phone into her bag and rummaged for her keys.

There was a time when she wouldn't have dared do an article of this nature for fear of the ramifications. That had been before she'd gone up against an ancient demon to save the world. Almost dying tended to change one's perspective on things. When one realizes there might be no tomorrow, today becomes pretty damn important. Mai had always had a zest for living and that hadn't changed. What *had* changed was the way she chose to live each of those days.

She no longer spent her work time pursuing lightweight stories, and she didn't spend her personal time pursuing meaningless one-night stands. Of course, such lifestyle decisions made for many lonely nights.

She unlocked her apartment door, thinking how she missed her best friend. Lexi was a witch, werewolf and retired bounty hunter now living in Ravenscroft, the Immortal dimension, with her husband and infant son. Not that Mai blamed her for never being in New York City. If Mai were married and had a child, maybe she—

She cut off the thought as she walked into the kitchen, letting the door fall shut behind her. She dropped her purse on the counter as she passed through the kitchen and continued the short distance to her bedroom, which also served as her home office. She flipped on the light switch and the click echoed loudly in the unrelieved darkness of the room.

Damn it, she thought. *Burned-out bulb.* Not wanting to take the time to change it, she continued over to the desk. There, she fumbled with the knob on the lamp, turning it several times before finally leaning over the shade to see why the light wasn't coming on.

The tiny hairs on the back of her neck began to prickle. Something wasn't right. She stood still, making an effort to quiet her breathing so she could listen. From outside came the distant rumble of traffic and people passing from one destination to the next. Mai was barely conscious of it. She was listening for a sound that shouldn't be there.

Everything seemed normal.

Still feeling a little spooked, she reached over to turn on her laptop—and stopped with her hand still suspended in air. The cord to her phone jack had been severed, with one short end dangling off the desk while the other lay curled like a snake on the carpet.

Her breath caught in her throat. She knew she should run, but she was too scared to move.

A noise drifted to her. The merest whisper of sound over the hushed thrum of activity outside. She held her breath and cocked her head, straining to hear; willing the sound to come again, praying it wouldn't.

It did—soft footsteps muted by the thick carpet. Tension shot along her nerves. She might have stood with the Immortals and others to battle an ancient demon over a year ago, but Mai was neither a hero nor a fool. She wasn't waiting around to find out who was there or what they wanted.

Summoning her magic, she closed her eyes and willed herself to the Blood Club, a bar owned and operated by vampire and close friend Ricco.

She waited for the deafening drone of people to tell her the teleportation had been successful, but heard only her own rapid breathing and the rustle of fabric. *Damn.* Her magic hadn't been working right ever since the battle.

A cold fear settled over her as she realized she was alone with her intruder. The hallway light snapped on. Mai blinked at the sudden brightness that revealed a masked figure dressed all in black.

He filled the doorway, cutting off any hope for escape.

"What do you want?" She hated the small tremor in her voice. "I have money, in my purse."

"I'm not after money." His voice sounded harsh and raspy.

When he stepped into the room, she automatically backed up, trying to keep some distance between them. "Get out."

"I have a message for you: *Forget the story.*"

So her investigation had touched a nerve. That meant she'd really stumbled onto something big. "Who sent you?"

"Still asking questions? That's what got you into trouble in the first place." He began to close the distance between them.

Mai forced herself to hold her ground. "Fine. You've delivered your message. Now get out."

"That wasn't the message. This is."

Pain exploded in her jaw before she'd even registered his hand moving. Her head snapped to the side and tears sprang to her eyes. The inside of her lower lip split against the edge of her teeth, and the coppery taste of blood filled her mouth. With the room spinning around her, she fell to her knees. She tried to crawl away but couldn't. Her vision started tunneling and she felt consciousness slipping away.

She wasn't lucky enough to pass out, though. Spitting out the blood that filled her mouth, she looked up.

"Who's your source?" her attacker growled.

Lenny Brown. The name skittered through her head and she fought to keep from blurting it out. How easy it would be to just give it to him. Make him—and the pain—stop. But it was Lenny's death warrant if she did, so she bit back the words and said nothing. Instead, she thought about revenge. If she could survive this, she would use the paper in her pocket and all the information on it to crucify Preston, because he was behind this. He was the only one with a reputation to protect.

"Start talking," he demanded.

"Fuck you."

She cried out in pain when the man grabbed her hair and jerked her head back. Too dazed to stand on her own, she was hauled to her feet. "Remember that you brought this on yourself." Blinding pain shot between her eyes when he punched her in the face. As she gasped for breath, her hands automatically rose to protect her broken nose. It was a tactical mistake. With her arms raised, her stomach was unprotected and the man took advantage of her vulnerability by punching her—hard.

"Remember," he growled again.

She crumpled to the floor, unable to draw a breath.

Through the nausea, she thought, *This is it. This is how I die.* All the things she'd wanted to accomplish but hadn't flashed through her mind. Unfulfilled dreams. Unfulfilled love. There was someone out there for her, the man she could have given herself to completely, loved unconditionally. *Where are you?*

Her vision tunneled to black and the ringing in her head grew louder. Death, she thought. Coming for her. Longing for a love she'd never known—and now never would—filled her with despair. *I'm sorry.*

She wondered how death would feel. Would it hurt?

She waited. Slowly, air seeped into her lungs and the will to survive pushed her to drag in more. The air burned when it hit her throat, and she coughed uncontrollably while tears and blood ran unnoticed in commingled streams down her face. When she dared to open her eyes, she found her vision blurred and distorted, as if she were looking at the world through textured glass.

It hurt to move her head, but hope flickered. Was the attack over?

Suddenly, hands grabbed her about the throat and squeezed. Bitterness rose even as the energy to fight ebbed. It was as if her attacker had only been waiting for her to recover before finishing her off.

Then, from out of nowhere, a huge form shot across the room straight into her attacker, knocking him back.

It hurt to turn her head, but Mai had to know what was happening. Through her impaired vision, the images of two fighting men were nothing more than blurs of movement. She tried to rally the strength to get up and help her rescuer, but even that effort seemed beyond her.

Then she saw the dark form of her attacker race out the door and she was left alone with her rescuer.

He came over to her and laid his hand on her shoulder. The warmth of his touch immediately spread through her.

She stared up into his face, wishing she could make out the details of his features. "Are you all right?" His voice was tender.

She looked around, staring hard in the direction of the doorway. Her rescuer seemed to understand her fear.

"You're safe now. He's gone."

"Thank you." She struggled to sit up and did so only with his help. Peering at him through swollen lids, she thought she recognized him. Perhaps he was a new tenant and she'd seen him around the building. She wished her vision weren't so blurry so she could see him better. "How did you know I needed help?"

"I heard your call."

She must have cried out when her attacker grabbed her hair, Mai thought. "Lucky for me you were home." She held out her hand. "I don't think we've met."

"No. I would remember you." His voice, deep and sensual, sent a ripple of awareness through her. He brushed the hair from her face in a gesture that was oddly intimate for someone she didn't really know. She found herself compelled by his face even though she couldn't really make out his features. It was like looking at him through a thick film, but even so she felt drawn to him.

When he slowly bent his head to hers, it never occurred to her to pull away. The touch of his lips was gentle, tentative. All pain faded into the background, and the longing she'd felt earlier swelled to raw, hot desire.

Then, as suddenly as he'd appeared, he vanished and Mai was left lying on the floor alone.

She felt so bereft, she wanted to cry. She didn't understand how he could have left so quickly unless maybe she'd passed out. It was the only logical explanation, yet if that was the case, why had he run out on her? To call an ambulance perhaps?

She waited for him to return.

And waited.

It seemed she lay there with her eyes closed for hours. Finally, though, she knew he wasn't coming back.

As she summoned the energy to move, she thought back over the attack. If Preston had hired the man who'd attacked her, he'd made a huge mistake. Not only was she going to call the police and report him, but she was going to finish her story. She wasn't going to let these guys intimidate her. By God, she'd faced demons before. Did they really think she'd be frightened by humans?

Feeling better, she pushed herself to all fours and crawled to the bathroom. Once there, she collapsed into a sitting position, leaning back against the bathtub. She needed a breather. The room was dark and she glanced up as best she could, considering one eye was swollen shut. The light switch was out of reach.

Pushing herself to a standing position, she held on to the countertop for balance and stared into the mirror. With the lights out, her reflection didn't look that awful. There wasn't nearly as much blood as she'd been afraid there'd be. In fact . . .

She peered closer. Something wasn't right. She reached out and flipped on the light switch. What the hell was going on? There was no blood—anywhere.

She gently pressed her fingers against either side of her nose. Yes, it was a little tender, but it wasn't broken. Furthermore, there was only one slight bruise across her face. Not even her eye was swollen. And her vision was completely back to normal.

What was going on? How could she have been beaten so severely and yet look as if nothing had happened? She'd been bleeding like a sieve—

She hurried into her office to check the carpet. It was as spotless and clean as it had been that morning.

Desperation built inside her as she looked around. Her

phone cord was no longer severed. Even before she switched on the overhead light, she knew what to expect. She wasn't surprised at what she saw. She was terrified.

There were absolutely no signs of forced entry and nothing out of place in her entire apartment. It was almost as if she'd imagined the entire attack.

"I am *not* hallucinating," she said with conviction, hoping the sound of her own voice would make it more convincing.

It didn't—and neither did knowing that none of her previous hallucinations had ever been this bad.

She covered her mouth with her hand and tried to suppress the cry that escaped. What had happened to her was real. She hadn't imagined it. She hadn't.

What had her therapist said? That there is no cure for post-traumatic stress disorder and she could suffer from hallucinations the rest of her life. She hadn't wanted to believe it, and denial of the problem had been working so well for her lately.

Apparently her PTSD had come back with a vengeance.

Rubbing her head, she thought about poor Dr. Barbour. What would he have told her at a time like this? *You must look within yourself for the key to your hallucinations. Fear is what attacked you. It beat you down until you thought you could not continue. But there is an inner strength fighting to save you from your fear, fighting to save you from yourself.*

With crap analysis like that, it was no wonder somebody offed the good doctor.

Regretting her disrespectful thoughts, Mai went to lock the front door. Then she headed back to the bathroom, moving with a weariness brought on by worry more than fatigue. She started the water and while she waited for it to get hot, she stripped off her clothes.

Stepping beneath the stream, she let it beat down on her until the heat slowly stole past the chill of her worries and doubts. After what seemed an eternity, she snapped out of her inner reflections. It was time to get out.

Shutting off the water, she left the curtain closed to trap the warm air inside with her and snaked a hand out to grab a towel. She rubbed her skin and hair briskly until she was dry enough to get out and then pulled the shower curtain aside.

As soon as the warm air hit the mirror, it fogged over—and a single word appeared in the glass.

Remember.

CHAPTER TWO

Terror hit Mai with the force of a Mack truck. She stared at the word, struggling to decide whether she was hallucinating again—or if someone had actually written on the glass in anticipation of the word appearing as soon as steam from the shower hit the mirror.

Panicked, she wrapped the towel tightly around her, while looking all around for signs of an invisible attacker—as ludicrous as that might seem. She was fairly certain she was alone. But what might be lurking on the other side of the door?

She searched the bathroom for a weapon. She'd be damned if she was going out there unarmed.

Her gaze fell on her Lady Shaver, but she quickly dismissed it. Next she spied the toilet bowl cleaning wand. Useless. Feeling desperate, she looked at the collection of beauty products on the counter. Foundation? Eyeliner? Hair spray? Yes—the hair spray. Maybe she could blind him by spraying it in his eyes.

Armed with the aerosol can, she crept to the bathroom door. For all she knew, someone could be standing on the other side, waiting. With her heart pounding in her chest and holding the hair spray in front of her defensively, she snatched open the door.

There was no one there.

Bracing herself, she moved out into the hallway, creeping along until she reached her bedroom. She flipped the wall switch and was relieved when the light came on. She quickly scanned the room to make sure no one was there, then hurried to the kitchen and pulled a butcher knife from the cutlery block. Turning to face the living room, she looked over the small open counter that divided the rooms and saw—nothing.

Torn between relief and confusion, she returned to the bathroom. The steam had dissipated and the word had vanished, along with her only evidence that the attack might have been more than her imagination.

She went into her bedroom and with a heavy sigh, put down the knife and hair spray, though she left them within easy reach. After dressing, she was about to toss her dirty clothes into the hamper when she remembered the notes she'd made talking to Lenny. She couldn't afford to lose them because they *were* the story.

She pulled the paper out of her pocket and was about to set it on her dresser when it struck her that it was the wrong color. The paper she'd written her notes on had been white, not yellow. With a growing sense of panic, she unfolded it—and stared at the blank page.

Seconds later, she had her purse in hand and was racing out of the apartment with no particular destination in mind. Either she was going crazy or Preston was far more dangerous than she'd anticipated.

Nick drifted in a sea of black nothingness and was content. There was no pain, no worries. Chirping crickets provided a backdrop for a symphony of other twilight noises: the skittering of mice, the deep-throated croaking of frogs, the gentle stirring of leaves overhead. The sound of labored breathing. His.

With more effort than he would have thought necessary, Nick Blackhawk opened his eyes. He had to blink several times before he realized his vision wasn't failing. The sun was going down and less light was filtering through the trees.

How long had he been out? His recollections of the man he'd fought were shadowy and distant, but the woman—that was something else. She'd seemed so real—and the way he'd been drawn to her, like she was a part of him. He hated like hell to think she'd been nothing more than the product of a delirious mind. He longed to surrender to the nothingness he'd just awakened from, longed to find *her* again, but knew he couldn't. Time was running out.

With the renewed sense of urgency came the rush of memories of why he'd been in the forest in the first place.

Representative Stan Gentry sat on the House Appropriations Committee and his current investigation was making someone very nervous. So nervous, in fact, that they were willing to kill.

When the first attempt was made on Stan's life, he knew he needed protection. The problem was he didn't know whom to trust. His enemies were men of power whose friends were also men of power. Stan needed someone the government couldn't control—and so he'd hired Nick.

Nick taught survival training to the military's toughest. Both hunter and strategist, he enjoyed pitting himself against Mother Nature's fiercest challenges. The more rewarding challenges, however, he found in the city—protecting the innocent, tracking the missing and hunting the criminal. That was why he'd started his own security agency in New York City.

After weeks of trying to keep Stan safe by thwarting

various attempts, Nick came up with a plan to lure the would-be assassin out into the open by means of a well-publicized hunting trip in Nick's own backyard—the four hundred acres of wilderness in upstate New York owned by Nick's village—Los Paseantes de Espíritu, the Spirit Walkers.

Being a member of a race of human chameleons whose abilities, among other things, included assuming the shape of almost any living creature made Nick specially qualified to lure Gentry's would-be assassin on a merry chase. The plan had worked, too, because right now Nick was lying on the forest floor slowly bleeding to death. The first bullet had lodged in his shoulder while the second had pierced his side.

He'd had enough sense to hide in the surrounding woods before a third shot found him, but he'd paid a high price for his effort. His head pounded in tempo to his racing heart, which was currently working overtime to make up for the blood spilling out of his body. After assuming Stan's likeness, Nick had expected to get shot at, but he thought he'd be able to avoid actually getting hit. He'd been wrong. Gentry had been right to worry. The assassin after him was a true pro. But as long as the bullet missed Nick's head and vital organs, his enhanced abilities gave him a good chance of recovering.

Nick closed his eyes and focused on the space outside his body. The transition to the spiritual plane took more effort than usual, but soon he felt his essence leave his body to hover overhead. He took a quick moment to assess the damage to his physical form. It was serious, but not fatal. Not if he hurried.

He turned his attention to scanning the spiritual plane around him. Like ever-widening concentric ripples in a pond spreading out from a single point, his senses touched the surrounding forest.

The first sign of the assassin showed up like a mottled red light off to the northeast. Behind it, fading light trailed off in the distance, evidence of the shooter's progress through the forest. He was closing in. Time for Nick to execute the rest of his plan.

Nick focused on finding his father, letting instinct guide him.

"I heard shots." His father's image appeared before him and Nick heard his concern.

Emotion, more than words, were the mode of communication here; therefore Nick tried to project calm assurance. "My plan worked a little too well. I made it as far as the fallen tree where Dave shot his buck last season. From the aural imprints, I'd say this guy's about 150 yards northeast of there."

"Okay. Hold on, son. We're on our way. Go back and slow your heart rate. This will be over shortly."

Half a dozen specks of lights, each representing the aural imprint of a state policeman, began moving. If Nick were to look around, he'd see the other lights representing members of his tribe closing in from the other side.

Nick put a lot of stock in well-laid plans.

He returned to where his body lay and noted how weak his own energy light had become. He hoped the cavalry arrived in time.

He let his spirit be reabsorbed into his body. Searing pain shot through his shoulder and side, causing him to suck in a breath.

He levered himself into a sitting position, fighting a wave of dizziness as he braced his back against the closest tree. He hoped he had enough energy to see this thing through to the end.

The snap of a twig alerted him to the presence of the assassin.

Nick propped the barrel of the rifle on his bent knee.

"Hold it right there!" he shouted. The approaching foot-steps didn't even slow, and a second later a man dressed in camo stepped into view.

"Gentry, aren't you dead yet?" The man aimed his rifle steadily at Nick.

"Put your gun on the ground," Nick ordered, glad that his voice, at least, sounded strong.

"I don't think you're in a position to tell me what to do," the man replied confidently.

"You're right." Nick pulled the trigger.

The bullet slammed into the man's shoulder, knocking him around so that his own shot went wide.

Come on. Where are they? Nick thought as the forest spun around him. Through vision that was starting to blur and tunnel, Nick saw the man recover his stance. His heart slammed against his chest, trying to pump enough blood to his brain. The roaring in his ears was so loud now that he heard only a couple of the gunman's words. ". . . kill you, mother fu . . ."

Nick felt himself fading, knew that in a matter of sec-onds he'd be dead. As time slowed, his vision suddenly grew sharp. He saw the instant the gunman's finger started to squeeze the trigger, and Nick used the last of his strength to pull his first.

The roar of both guns was deafening—and then there was nothing.

"I thought you loved that apartment."

"I needed a change," Mai said, stepping off the elevator. "I've lived at this old place so long, I just wanted some-thing different." *Something safe.* "Besides, the new one has a much better location."

"One that's costing you twice the money for half the space."

"I can afford it."

Heather Barnes didn't look like she was one hundred percent convinced, but she didn't press the matter. Heather, who belonged to the Coven of Light, was one of the witches who had helped summon the Immortals to vanquish the ancient demon. That's when Mai had met her and they'd been friends since.

"I really appreciate your help." Mai was feeling a little nervous as they walked down the hall to her old apartment. Since the hallucination two days ago, she'd been staying at a hotel. This was the first time she'd been back. "There's no way I could move all my stuff by myself," she continued as she found her key and inserted it in the lock of her door.

"I hope you won't mind, but I thought we might need more help," Heather said. "So I made a call."

Mai pushed open the door and saw a tall, slender woman with long black hair and light gray eyes. Beside her stood an even taller, muscle-bound man with shoulder-length dark hair and a sleeveless long black duster. His well-defined bare chest and arms were covered in tattoos.

"Lexi! Darius!" Mai rushed forward and embraced her friend. She might have hugged Lexi a little too tight and there might have been moisture in her eyes when she finally pulled away, but Lexi was nice enough to ignore it. "What are you two doing here?" She gave Darius a quick hug thinking again how lucky they both were to have found each other.

"Heather called and told us what was going on," Lexi explained.

Mai looked at Heather in disbelief. "I thought the Calling spell was only supposed to be used in cases of real emergencies. Like the-world-coming-to-an-end-as-we-know-it kind of stuff."

Heather and Lexi laughed. "That's not how she called me," Lexi explained. "She used her cell phone."

Mai was sure she looked as confused as she felt.

"We weren't in Ravenscroft," Lexi continued. "We were upstate—at my parents' place."

"Sekhmet let you go?" Mai asked, knowing how protective the goddess was of her grandson.

"Not without some persuading," Darius admitted.

"She means well," Lexi put in.

Mai knew that Lexi had a fondness for her ultracontrolling mother-in-law.

"Anyway, we were already planning to drop by for a visit when Heather called."

"But where's Zach?" Mai looked around for her godson. She hadn't seen him since his birth and wondered how big he'd grown.

"We left him with my folks." At her frown, Lexi smiled and gave her arm a pat. "Don't worry. When we're done here, I'll bring him by for a visit. Now, let's talk about your move. Heather said you wanted out fast, so Darius and I started packing a few of your things while we waited. Come on, I'll show you."

Lexi took her arm and led her into the bedroom.

"I can't believe it," Mai exclaimed, looking around. "This is amazing." The entire room was bare except for her stripped-down bed, her dresser and a dozen or more boxes. The doors to the closet stood open to reveal a lone twisted wire hanger dangling from the rod. "You packed everything? When did you get here?"

"A couple of hours ago." At Mai's look of disbelief, she shrugged. "What's the point of having access to all of Darius' superpowers if I don't ever get to take advantage of them?"

"But even I can't move all of this to the new place without help," Darius added, coming in to join them. "So Lexi called a couple of people she knows and we've got a truck with movers showing up any minute, so let's finish packing the kitchen. Tonight, you'll be sleeping in your new apartment."

Mai felt almost giddy with relief. Starting tonight, she'd finally feel safe once again.

Six hours later, Mai was standing in the kitchen of her new apartment pouring cold drinks. There was nothing left at her old place now but some bad memories and a bag of trash that the landlord had promised to take out.

She picked up the glasses and carried them into the living room where Lexi and Darius waited. Heather had already left for the airport to catch a flight to Seattle for a Coven meeting.

After handing out the drinks, Mai sat in her oversized chair and took a swallow of Diet Coke. For several seconds, no one said anything. It was Lexi who finally broke the silence. "Do you want to tell me what's really going on?"

Mai almost spilled her drink. "What do you mean?"

Lexi set her glass down on the coffee table and gave Mai one of those looks. "I've known you a long time. You can be impulsive at times, but suddenly changing apartments? In the middle of a lease? Come on. Something's up. Why don't you tell us about it? Maybe we can help."

Mai considered what to say. She could tell them about Preston and Perone, but she didn't even know whether the attack on her had been real.

"You're not alone, Mai. You have friends who care what happens to you."

They might care what happened to her, but they didn't live here anymore. They weren't around all the time. Besides, Mai didn't like the thought of not being able to deal with this problem herself.

But she knew Lexi and Darius would never be satisfied if she didn't tell them something. "All right. I think someone broke into my apartment. The only thing they took were some notes on a story I was doing, nothing else." She took a deep breath. "I couldn't go to the police because I have no real proof, but it freaked me out a bit." She didn't have to fake the quaver in her voice. "So I decided to move."

Lexi studied her closely for several seconds. "Okay. I can understand that. Are you sure there's nothing else going on?"

No, nothing much—other than my getting beaten to a bloody pulp by an imaginary man. You can't see the bruises because . . . well, I don't know why. Maybe because they're not really there. I'm still trying to decide if this is some form of death magic at work or a recurrence of my PTSD problem. Yeah, that sounded much better, didn't it? "Really, that's all it was," Mai said, shrugging as if to dismiss the entire thing, hoping Lexi wouldn't press.

She looked like she wanted to, but then her cell phone rang. With a muttered oath, she gave Mai an apologetic smile, mouthed "I'm sorry," and answered the phone.

"Hi, Mom, wh—" Lexi started, and then fell silent as she listened. Lexi's mother began ranting loud enough that even from where Mai sat, she could almost make out her words.

"But, Mom, he's a werewolf," Lexi said patiently when she finally got a chance to break in. "He's supposed to shift."

There was another long silence and then, "I can't help that my son is more advanced than the rest of the kids, Mom. No, I don't think it's unusual that he can shift at nine months when the others don't shift until they're toddlers. Okay, so maybe it's a little weird, but Darius' side of the family has lots of early developers."

The voice on the other end grew louder, more frantic.

"I'm sorry if he's frightening the other kids." Lexi rolled her eyes and lightly punched her husband, who had started laughing out loud. "I do take this seriously, Mother, but I'm not sure this is as big a problem as you're making it out to be. I mean, he's immortal, so how much trouble can he get into?" She sighed. "Really? That much. No, I think that's a bad idea. It's probably best not to make her mad." She paused and listened. "I know. Nobody worries about making you mad, you're right, but, Mom, you're not a goddess. You didn't make the Nile run red with the blood of those who pissed you off." This was followed by an even longer silence. Then, "Fine. We'll be there shortly."

Lexi disconnected the call and put her phone back in her pocket. "Sorry," she said. "I guess we won't be staying as long as I'd hoped."

"What was that bit about my mother?" Darius asked, looking amused.

"My mother doesn't think it was smart of Sekhmet to give Zach his own set of tattoos. Apparently, when he's not shifting into a wolf and running after the other kids, he's playing with the knives or freeing his dragon to fly around."

Mai smiled, imagining the home life Lexi must have. She was sorry that Lexi's mother was having so much trouble with Zach but hoped the baby would distract Lexi enough to stop her from asking any more questions. No such luck.

Lexi grew serious and turned to Mai. "I still think there's something else going on, but if you don't want to talk about it right now, that's fine. I just want you to know that I'm here for you if you need me."

"Sounds like you have your hands full," Mai said, hating the note of bitterness that crept into her voice. She smiled to take the sting out of her words and added, "I'm fine."

"We'll just go get Zach and come right back."

Mai wasn't sure that was a good idea under the circumstances. "I'd really love to see him, but do you think you could bring him by in a couple of weeks? After I've had a chance to unpack and get settled?"

Lexi regarded her like she wasn't sure if Mai was making excuses or not. Finally, she nodded. "I want you to call if you need me."

"Riiight." Mai sighed. "Does Ravenscroft have telephones these days?" The offer to help was nice, but how the hell was Mai supposed to get in touch with them?

"Oh," Lexi said, finally understanding. "What if you just try summoning me? I know you can't do a full Calling, but I'm sure I'd hear a simple summoning spell."

"Normally that wouldn't be a problem, but it seems my magic is still on the fritz."

"Really? Damn." Lexi's brow furrowed in concentration. "I guess if things got bad, you could always go stay with your folks."

Mai stared at her, horrified. "I'm not even sure where my parents are. But even if I found them, it would be so embarrassing to have to move back in. It's not just Mom and Dad, you know. I'd be living with two sets of grandparents, forty-four uncles and aunts, at least fifty cousins and goddess knows what kind of pets. They all live in a roving caravan of travel trailers where the biggest concern is making enough money from homemade goods and 'services' "—she put air quotes around the word—"to fund the next big party."

Darius smiled. "They sound like fun."

Mai shot him a withering look. "These are grown people trapped in a teenager's mentality. I moved to the city so I could do something more with my life. Just because things have gotten a little tough doesn't mean I should tuck tail and run home."

Lexi held up her hand to stave off the rest of a familiar tirade. "I know. I'm sorry. Bad idea."

Mai shook her head. "Look, don't worry about it. I'm fine." She said it with more confidence than she felt.

Lexi looked at Darius, who gave her arm an affectionate

squeeze. "I think I've got an idea," he said, reaching his left hand up to his right shoulder to touch one of the two lightning bolts tattooed there. When he lowered his hand, he was holding a small bolt of brilliant light.

Touching his left forearm with his right hand, he lifted off the dagger and, using the tip, cut a small hole at the base of the bolt. "Lexi, I need something to hang this from. Something that won't come off until Mai wills it to."

She smiled and lifted her hands to the chain she wore around her neck. "Use this," she said, undoing the clasp and holding it out to him.

Mai watched in fascination. "No, I can't take that," she said as Darius strung the lightning bolt onto the necklace. "Sekhmet gave that to you."

"Mother can give her another," Darius said. He held the necklace out so he could put it around Mai's neck. "Right now you need it more."

Mai worried that the bolt of lightning would burn, but the second it touched her skin, it turned into a brilliant gleaming diamond.

"When you need us, pull this from your neck and throw it against the floor—or against your attacker. It will turn back into a lightning bolt as soon as you let go of it, so be sure of who or what you're throwing it at. Once the energy is expended, the bolt will return to my arm. When it does, I'll know you need us and we'll come right away." He turned to Lexi. "Will that work?"

The love radiating from her face was almost embarrassing. "Brilliant. Thank you."

He gave her a quick kiss and it seemed to take Lexi a second to collect her wits when he let go of her.

"Okay, I guess we should go," she said finally. "Did Heather put protective wards on the apartment before she left?"

"I think so," Mai said, though she couldn't be sure. She remembered Heather muttering something before she left, but it had sounded more like a list of errands than the words to a magic spell.

Mai saw Lexi hesitate. She glanced at her watch and then looked around the room. Mai knew she was about to put off leaving again in order to add her own wards. Mai instantly felt guilty. No amount of wards would help if the problem was all in her head. "Lexi, I'm fine. Go take care of my godson." She gripped the diamond bolt hanging from her neck. "I'll be sure to call if I need you."

CHAPTER THREE

Later that night, Mai tossed and turned in bed, trying to get comfortable. She felt lost and alone—and wanted someone to give her answers to her problem. She needed someone . . .

Her thoughts turned to her mysterious rescuer. As the movers had carried boxes from her old apartment, she'd lingered first in the hallway and then in the lobby, hoping he'd happen by so she could meet him; maybe get his name; give him hers. She never saw him, though, and when the last box was carried down, she knew she never would again.

The thought had filled her with such sadness and longing. It was ridiculous, she scolded herself. She didn't even know him. Yet she couldn't stop thinking about him and when she finally fell asleep, he was there in her dreams.

"I wasn't sure I'd see you again," she told him as he came to her.

"I couldn't stay away. You're all I've thought about."

His admission warmed her and she smiled. "I'm glad."

"Walk with me," he said, holding his hand out to her.

She felt a thrill of excitement race up her arm as his large hand enveloped hers. He pulled her close to his side and they began walking. In her dream, they walked along a garden path, surrounded by fragrant flowers and trees. The crystal-blue sky was clear except for a couple of billowy clouds that seemed softer than cotton.

They were content to walk along in silence and simply enjoy being together on a cool, spring day.

They reached a grassy meadow where they stopped and spread out the picnic blanket that conveniently appeared. Lying side by side, they stared up into the sky. Mai had never known such peace.

"Are you happy?" he asked, rolling onto his side to face her.

"Yes."

The wind stirred her hair and he moved a strand out of her eyes with his fingertip, which then trailed lightly down the side of her face and across her cheek to brush across her lips. "You are so beautiful," he whispered.

She looked up at him, hardly daring to breathe. His gaze centered on her lips like he wanted to kiss her, and every fiber of her being wanted him to. The moment of uncertainty seemed to last forever before he finally—slowly—lowered his head.

The first touch of his lips seared her to the center of her being. It was as though with each touch he was claiming her and she wanted nothing more than to be his forevermore. Wrapping her arms around his neck, she pulled him closer. He needed no further urging to deepen the kiss.

Her pulse quickened, and she felt the stirrings of a primitive hunger deep inside her. She ran her hands along his broad shoulders and back, reveling in the feel of his bare skin. She savored every taste, every touch.

Then, as in the way of dreams, she, too, was suddenly nude and while one hand cupped her head to hold her a willing captive to his kiss, his other hand caressed the curve of her waist, moving upward until he found her breasts. He molded each one in turn until her nipples tightened beneath his intimate touch.

"Please," she begged, not sure what she was begging for. But he knew.

He lowered his head to caress each budded nipple with his tongue. Instinctively, her body arched into him and she buried her fingers in his hair to hold him there.

She thought she might die from the pleasure of his touch and felt deprived when he tore his lips away. Then he was kissing a path up the side of her neck, stopping beneath her earlobe.

"Let me make love to you," he whispered, his hot breath fanning across her ear.

With her senses under such attack, Mai found it hard to focus on anything other than the feel of his hand skating over her hip to find the sweet spot between her legs. He slipped a finger between her soft, slick folds.

She felt a tension building deep inside her, increasing with each stroke of his nimble finger.

"Tell me what you want," he whispered.

"You," she gasped, her body trembling while she teetered on the brink of her release. "I want you."

He withdrew his finger and moved his body to fit himself between her legs. His rigid shaft teased her sensitized flesh. She waited in anticipation, aroused to the brink of climax, knowing it wouldn't take much to send her over the edge.

As he pushed himself into her, she felt every nerve in her body tighten until she thought she would explode and then—

Mai's eyes flew open and she was suddenly wide-awake, her entire body still humming from a dream that had seemed so real she was having a hard time believing it wasn't.

The room was dark—and she was alone.

Reality hit her with crushing disappointment. She'd

been so happy. Even more than that, she'd finally felt she was no longer alone. She had found the man she could spend the rest of her life with.

A man who doesn't exist, she chastised herself with a fair amount of disgust. She climbed out of bed and ambled to the bathroom, where she proceeded to rub a cold, wet washcloth over her heated face and neck.

She understood why she'd had the erotic dream. Wood nymphs needed sex as much as they needed oxygen. Her decision after the big battle to abstain from recreational sex was taking its toll, especially since now she was living like a friggin' nun. No doubt this was her body's way of compensating for the loss. And since she wasn't finding Mr. Right in reality, it made sense she would find him in her dreams—and who better to play the role than the man who'd rescued her in her hallucination? He was strong, mysterious, heroic and totally imaginary.

The cold cloth wasn't doing much for her, so Mai jumped in the shower to help cool down. As she toweled off afterward, she couldn't resist checking the mirror for messages. Nothing. She breathed a grateful sigh.

But her sense of relief was short-lived as she thought about her article. As scared as she was, she refused to back down. She could write up what she remembered from Lenny's notes, but without the actual documents, she'd have no way to back up her story. She'd need another copy—and that's why she was going to have to track down Lenny again.

She was going to expose Preston for the piece-of-slime politician he was. She *would* do this. If necessary, vanquishing all foes that stood in her way—even if it turned out those foes were only in her head.

"Morning, sunshine. You look like hell."

"Bite me," Nick said, giving his best friend a nasty look

before heading directly to the coffeemaker and filling a mug for himself.

Dave Runningbear chuckled, but his tone was serious when he asked, "Those wounds still bothering you?"

I wish it were that simple, Nick thought. Thanks to his magical nature, his wounds were almost entirely healed and the whole episode was quickly fading into a bad memory. "I didn't get much sleep last night," he admitted, knowing Dave expected some kind of answer. "Bad dreams." Actually, they'd been great dreams. Erotic dreams. But not the kind of dreams he normally had when he slept, which begged the question: had he inadvertently participated in someone else's dream? While it was possible for spirit walkers to move about in the dreams of others, it wasn't Nick's habit of intruding on another's privacy. Especially someone he didn't even know.

"Want some breakfast?" Dave asked. "I was about to make some eggs."

Nick nodded and took a seat at the kitchen table. They were staying with his father at the Los Paseantes Compound. Generations of Nick's people had been living in the compound for over a hundred years. Only a few from each generation ever chose to live on the outside. Dave and Nick spent two-thirds of their time there and the other third living in New York City, where Nick operated his security business.

Nick let the coffee burn its way down his throat as his thoughts turned to his last job.

Stan Gentry was back in Washington, D.C., and the papers were calling Nick a hero—even though Nick considered it to be all in a day's work.

"I hear Grindal and his people are back," Dave said with ill-concealed interest.

Nick shook his head. "You have a half-track mind."

Dave grinned. "Why? Because I enjoy the pleasure of a lady's company?"

Nick laughed. "Like you'd know a lady when you saw her."

"Maybe not," Dave agreed. "But I know a nymph when I'm lying between her legs and let me tell you, there's nothing better than sex with a wood nymph. You should try it. All this work is making you old before your time. Tell you what? Come with me next time I run out to the gypsy camp. Grindal will set you up with one of his hottest girls."

"Are you sure you aren't half wood nymph yourself? I swear, sex is the only thing on your mind."

"Enough," Nick's father said, walking into the kitchen and interrupting the two of them. "We have a bigger issue than Grindal and his band of wood nymph gypsies to discuss. The Lampson Corporation wants to book ten different survival courses for its corporate executives. There are several families in the compound who need money and with a deal this big, we could afford to hire additional guides. The sooner we close this deal, the better. Only problem is, I have to stay here because Don Halfacre needs the services of the shaman."

Don had taught Nick how to track deer through the woods when he was just a boy. It was hard for Nick to think such a strong man was growing old and frail. Of course, Nick had seen the elder the day before and "old" and "frail" were not words he would have used to describe him. "What's wrong with Don?" Nick asked.

His father shot him a look. "You know that's privileged information—unless, of course, you're asking as the new shaman?"

Nick felt the weight of both Dave's and his father's stares on him. His father had been trying to get him to take over as shaman for some time now, but Nick wasn't interested in having his every action dictated to him by the demands of his people. He'd seen what such dedication to a job could do to a family. He'd seen what it had done to his. "You stay—I'll go."

His father's face fell a little before he nodded. "All right."

"I'll go with you," Dave offered. Nick knew it was as much for a chance to have fun as to help him, but he didn't mind. Maybe Dave was right. What he needed was a little more fun and a little less work. After all, wouldn't it be better to have real sex than dream sex?

It was midmorning when Mai took a break from her work. She made herself breakfast and then stood leaning against the kitchen counter as she ate, looking over the open divider into the living room. One of the things she liked best about her new apartment was that even though it was small, it felt spacious and open.

The front door opened into a short foyer from which she could either walk straight, and run into the small dining table that took up one corner of her living room, or turn left into the kitchen. The archway on the far side of the kitchen led to another short hallway off which were the bathroom and bedroom.

There were no walls separating the kitchen from the living room—only the half counter. It might have felt cramped except for the huge mirror hanging on the wall behind the dining table, which made the room seem that much larger.

Like her old place, this one had only a single bedroom, so her computer was set up on a desk in the left corner of the living room. She'd lined the rest of the left wall with bookcases, which held an assortment of reference books, popular fiction and mementoes from places she'd gone and things she'd done.

The main attraction of the room was the huge picture window on the far wall. Looking out across the city, it opened up the room and made it feel larger than it was. She put her favorite oversized chair in the corner next to it, opposite her desk, so she could sit and read books or enjoy the view.

Her TV was located against the right wall, with her couch in the center of the room facing it. She'd already managed to unpack several boxes, finding places for dozens of books and framed pictures. Unfortunately, she still had several boxes left to unpack and she hadn't even started on the kitchen or her bedroom.

A knock at the door brought her out of her musings. When she opened it, she found Will Johnson, the building's super, standing there. He was thirty-something and fairly attractive, but the two times she'd talked to him before, he'd looked at her as if he were disrobing her—and she was so not interested.

"Hi. I thought I saw you were back," he said. "All moved in?"

"Hello. Yes—I believe so."

"Good." His gaze dropped to her breasts. "I just came by to make sure everything was working."

"I think everything's fine." Mai crossed her arms over her chest, forcing his gaze back to her face. She wanted to smack the knowing smile off his face.

"I let the cable guy in yesterday to hook up your Internet," he told her, looking past her shoulder into her apartment. "I should probably check to make sure it's working." He pushed past her and moved into the room before Mai could protest. "I see you already have your TV plugged in."

He grabbed the remote off the set and turned on the TV. She considered ordering him out, but the last thing she wanted to do if she ever wanted leaky faucets or anything else fixed around the apartment was make the super hate her. So instead, she stood there fuming.

"Nice picture," he said a short while later. "Be good for watching the game."

Mai had no idea what "game" he was referring to, but she did know he wouldn't be watching it here. "I'm not really into sports."

"That's too bad." He said it like she was missing out on a great opportunity.

Afraid he would try to stick around, she was surprised when he suddenly turned off the TV and replaced the remote control where he found it. "You need help setting up your wireless router?" he asked, gesturing toward her laptop.

"I can handle it." She went to the door and opened it. "Thanks for coming by. I'm sure you're busy, so don't let me keep you."

He shrugged but took the hint. "Okay, then." He reached into the top pocket of his blue-gray coveralls and pulled out a business card. "Here's my number." He handed her a card with a number scrawled on it. "I'm available, day . . . or night, depending on your needs." He put particular emphasis on this last bit, leaving Mai to hope she never had to use the card.

She waited until he stepped out, then closed the door with a huge sense of relief. Looking out the peephole, she saw that he didn't immediately leave. She found that a bit odd—as well as unnerving—so as quietly as she could, she turned the dead bolt and slipped the chain across the door.

After another couple of seconds, he finally started moving down the hall. She watched him until he disappeared behind the elevator doors. Only then did she leave her door to go back to unpacking boxes.

Not ten minutes later, another knock sounded on the door. The thought that Will had returned brought a twinge of anxiety.

Looking out the peephole, she was surprised to see a young woman standing there.

"Hi. My name is Sarah Renfield," the woman said when Mai opened the door. She was maybe in her early twenties, about Mai's height—which wasn't much over five feet— and, also like Mai, had shoulder-length, straight dark hair. "I saw you moving in yesterday. I live down the hall, in 14-A."

"Oh, hi." Mai held out her hand. "Mai Groves. It's nice to meet you." You could tell a lot about a person by her handshake and Mai was glad Sarah's was firm and not of the limp "dead fish" variety. "So—you live alone?"

"No, I share a place with my older sister, Jenna. She's at work right now, but then again, she's always at work." She shrugged as if to say "whatever." "What about you? You live here alone?"

"Yep, just me, I'm afraid." She gestured toward the living room. "I've been slowly digging out from under all the boxes and could use a small break. Want to come inside and visit for a while?"

Sarah smiled. "Thanks. Maybe for a few minutes. I can't stay long. I have to go back and study." At Mai's confused look, she hurried on. "I'm taking classes at Hunter."

Mai stood back to let the girl come in and then watched as she idly walked around the room. "What's your major?"

"Education. I want to teach high school."

"Wow—tough age group."

Sarah smiled. "Only because kids that age are easily bored. The key is to make it interesting. Nobody likes a lecture. Besides, kids these days can handle a lot more stimuli coming at them than kids could a generation or so ago—thanks to video games, computers and cell phones. It's a whole new era of learning." Sarah's eyes lit up as she spoke.

"You sound like you're really into it."

"I am." Her excitement shone on her face. "What do you do for a living?"

"I'm a freelance reporter." Mai was getting more used to the sound of it each time she said it.

"Really? Any chance I've read your work?"

"Maybe," Mai said. "I used to write a regular column for the *New York Voice* before I . . . decided to go freelance." She saw no point in sharing the specifics of her situation with Sarah. Instead, she rattled off the titles of a couple of her pieces to see if Sarah recognized any of them. She didn't.

Mai didn't let it bother her. She had something else she wanted to talk about. "What can you tell me about Will Johnson?"

Sarah gave her a sharp look. "You're not—interested—in him, are you?"

"Uh—no." She said it with conviction.

Sarah smiled with relief. "That's good because if you were, I'd try to talk you out of it."

"Because you're interested in him?"

Sarah laughed. "Yeah, right. The guy's a jerk. He's got an ego as big as the day is long—as the saying goes. Thinks he's all that with the women. Me? I think he's just plain creepy, but he does a good job of fixing things." She shrugged. "I think he's harmless."

"Good, I'm glad to hear it."

There was another knock at the door making Mai feel as if she were living at Grand Central. Excusing herself, she went to answer it. Standing at the door was a woman who bore a striking resemblance to Sarah.

"Hi. I'm going to guess that you're Jenna," Mai said, holding out her hand. The woman looked a little worried and eyed Mai's outstretched hand suspiciously before reluctantly shaking hands with her.

"Is Sarah here?"

Mai stood back in tacit invitation to the woman. "Yeah. Come on in."

Jenna moved forward cautiously, her gaze darting around the room until she spotted Sarah. "There you are. I was worried."

"Sorry, Jen," Sarah apologized.

"Sarah came by to welcome me to the building," Mai explained.

"I tend to be a little overprotective sometimes," Jenna said to Mai, offering an apologetic smile. "Sarah and I lost our parents several years ago, so all we have left is each other. But Sarah's right—welcome to the building. As you already guessed, I'm Jenna."

"Thanks. I'm Mai. Mai Groves."

"The reporter?" Jenna asked, her eyes seeming to brighten. "Didn't you write for the *New York Voice*? I read your article on the vampire clubs. I found it very interesting—and amazingly detailed. Well written."

Flattery will get you everywhere, Mai thought, warming to the woman in spite of herself. "Sarah and I were just chatting about her schoolwork."

"Speaking of which"—Sarah looked at her watch—"I'd better get back to it." She turned to Mai. "It was nice meeting you. I hope to see you around."

Mai smiled. "Me, too."

Jenna echoed her sister's sentiment and Mai watched them leave. Once they were gone, Mai looked around at the boxes waiting for her. Procrastination was a skill that required practice, she thought, ignoring the boxes and going to the desk instead to turn on her laptop. The unpacking could wait.

As she waited for her laptop to boot up, she thought back to her hallucination. It had been four days now since she'd had it, but it still felt so real.

She logged on to the Internet and went to Yahoo. She

searched "hallucinations" and was taken to several medical Web sites that discussed hallucinations as a symptom of various psychological disorders, including post-traumatic stress disorder. "Yeah, already know that one," she muttered to herself. She clicked on Wikipedia and read its definition of hallucinations. The mention of the "related phenomena of dreaming" had her wondering if what she'd experienced had been some type of waking dream. She supposed it was possible. She'd been working hard and not getting much sleep.

Curious, she did a new search on dreams—and then yet another search on nightmares. It was here that she found an article about Los Paseantes de Espíritu—who could enter the dreams of others to help them put an end to their nightmares.

The author of the article wrote about his own experience with a "spirit walker" and described how Nicolas Blackhawk, the tribe's shaman, had helped him face and conquer his own inner demons.

Nicolas Blackhawk.

The name seemed familiar and Mai tried to remember where she'd seen it before. Then it came to her. It had been in the paper.

Hurrying into the kitchen, she grabbed the nearest box and opened it. Working carefully, but quickly, she pulled out each plate, one by one, unwrapped it and set it on the counter so she could scan the newspaper it had been wrapped in.

She was halfway through her third box when she found it. Eagerly, she read the story. Nick Blackhawk of Blackhawk Securities had saved Representative Gentry from a would-be assassin. There was no mention in the article of Nick Blackhawk being either a shaman or a spirit walker, which made her wonder if this was the same Nick Blackhawk.

She went back to her computer and did a search on Nick Blackhawk. This time she found a story from eighteen months ago about how Nick Blackhawk traced two missing teenagers to a graveyard where demons were performing a death magic ritual to honor the same ancient evil Mai had helped vanquish. To track the teens, he'd had to enter the spirit realm.

Bingo, Mai thought. Only a spirit walker could go into the spirit realm, so this must be the same Nick Blackhawk who was shaman. Maybe, if she asked him, he could help her fight the inner demons causing her to hallucinate. She looked up the Securities Web site and saw they were located right here in New York City. It was well after 9:00 AM Someone should be in the office.

A young woman answered Mai's call, sounding very professional. "Blackhawk Securities, may I help you?"

"Yes. I'd like to speak to Mr. Blackhawk, please."

"I'm sorry, he's not in the office. May I take a message?"

Disappointed, Mai improvised. "My name is Mai Groves. I'm a reporter and I'm interested in doing a story on Mr. Blackhawk."

She heard the secretary sniff. "Mr. Blackhawk doesn't normally do interviews. However, if you'll give me your name and number, I'll tell him you called."

Mai gave the woman her information. "I really need to talk to him," she said, injecting her voice with genuine sincerity. "If I could have just a few minutes of his time, I'd really appreciate it."

She must have sounded as desperate as she felt because the woman said, "I'll see what I can do."

Mai thanked her and hung up the phone. Then she spent the rest of the day washing the dishes she had unpacked and going through the boxes in her living room. When she got tired of unpacking, she called the number Lenny had given her, but to no avail. She considered leaving him a message to call her back, but that was dangerous and she wasn't that desperate—yet.

By the end of the day, she was dog tired. Making herself something to eat for dinner, she carried it into the living room to watch TV while she ate.

Last night, she'd been too tired to think about anything other than going to bed. Now, sitting by herself in her new apartment, she found herself listening for strange noises. Hoping a wine cooler would help calm her nerves, she grabbed one from the refrigerator and carried it back into the living room to drink while watching a movie.

Two movies and four wine coolers later, she was feeling pleasantly mellow.

She'd just started to doze when a flicker of light in the mirror distracted her. Fighting the haze of alcohol, she looked around the room, but couldn't find the source of the strange light. She looked back at the mirror—and saw it again.

She walked over to take a closer look. The glass seemed strangely translucent and insubstantial—as if it weren't there at all. Unable to resist, Mai reached out to touch it. Instead of stopping at the hard surface of the mirror, her hand passed straight through.

CHAPTER FOUR

With a small cry, Mai snatched back her hand. She backed away from the mirror, her heart racing because she half expected something to jump out at her.

It wasn't possible for her hand to have gone through like that. Was this another figment of her imagination? She had to know the truth.

Gathering her courage, she reached out again, slowly. Her fingers stopped when they touched the hard, cool glass and went no farther. She felt all around the surface just to make sure, but everything was back to normal.

Mai let her hand drop to her side and backed away from the mirror, her troubled reflection staring back at her. She wasn't crazy. It was the wine coolers. All she needed to do was sleep it off.

Making her way into the bedroom, she climbed into bed and closed her eyes. Sleep didn't come right away—but it did, eventually, come.

Nick held the woman in his arms and trailed kisses along the side of her neck, working his way to the base of her throat. There he gently sucked on the skin before quickly soothing the spot with his tongue. He felt her shudder beneath him and reveled in the effect he had on her.

"I want you," he told her, his voice husky with desire. "And I mean to have you."

He peered into a face he couldn't really see, yet knew it to be beautiful. He felt her smile at him as her arms stole about his neck and pulled him close for her kiss. The touch of her lips teased his senses and sent blood pumping to that part of him that was already throbbing with the need for release.

He moved between her legs, careful to keep from crushing her beneath his weight. Her hips lifted in invitation and when he pressed into her, tight muscles sheathed him, held him, and squeezed him until he thought he might explode.

Soon, his breath was coming in hard gasps and the tension inside him built until he thought he could take no more.

Nick came awake, his body drenched in a cold sweat. His need for release was a physical ache and he turned to the woman lying beside him, only to find a stranger sharing his bed.

He stared at the tangle of blond hair against his pillow and knew that this wasn't the woman he ached to make love to. That woman didn't exist—except in his dreams.

This was someone he'd picked up the night before, after he and Dave had flown into New York City. In his attempt to lighten up and do less work, Nick had let Dave talk him into hitting his favorite clubs.

Dave was well-known at these places and it didn't take long before they had all the female company they could want. As far as Nick could remember, they'd all enjoyed the night.

Hoping to regain his dream, Nick sighed and rolled

over, quickly falling back asleep. When he woke again, the woman was gone. Only the lingering scent of her spicy perfume and a stray blond hair remained. At least he wouldn't have to deal with the awkward morning-after moment.

As he went through his morning routine, he mentally reviewed the day ahead. There was the luncheon with the Lampson group at noon, which could easily run well into the afternoon. Nick needed to be ready to make a presentation if asked.

He searched his pants pockets for the flash drive with their PowerPoint presentation that detailed the various survival training courses available to corporate clients. When he couldn't find it in any of his pockets, he searched the dresser where he'd put his watch and cell phone. Still not finding it, he went to ask Dave.

The apartment he stayed in when he was in New York City actually belonged to the Survival Training Company. It consisted of four suites coming off a common family/kitchen area. He and Dave, as the two who regularly came to New York City, each had his own permanent suite while the other two were available as needed for other members of the company who happened to be traveling to the Big Apple.

As soon as Nick stepped out of his suite, he knew from the rhythmic pounding coming from Dave's that he didn't have to worry about waking Dave up. Nick had never known anyone to have sex as much as Dave did. The man never stopped. Which was why Nick didn't bother to wait until Dave was finished before knocking on his door.

"Be out in a sec," Dave shouted. Nick went into the kitchen to put on a pot of coffee. About the time the coffee was finished brewing, Dave came out of his bedroom, naked except for the sheet wrapped around his waist. He was escorting a small but buxom brunette who looked very much like a wood nymph. The outfit she wore looked uncomfortably tight to Nick, but he had to admit that it showed off *all* her assets.

Nick pulled two cups from the pantry and filled them both with coffee while Dave walked the woman to the front door.

"Thanks, love," he told her, giving her a quick peck. "It's always a pleasure."

A second later, she was out the door and Nick was handing Dave the second cup of coffee. "Did you have a good night?"

"As always." He looked around. "Did Darcy already leave?"

"Oh, was that her name?"

"You didn't even bother to get her name?" Dave shook his head in disbelief. "What's with you these days?"

"Nothing. I—" He tried to think of a way to explain his confusion, but couldn't. "I didn't get much sleep last night, that's all."

Dave gave a boisterous laugh and slapped Nick on the back good-naturedly. "Neither did I. Ain't New York great?" He took a swallow of coffee. "Happy birthday, by the way."

Another year older. Nick didn't want to be reminded. "Thanks."

"Wait till you see what I got you this year."

"Please. You know I don't like surprises."

Dave laughed. "Don't give me that. As I recall, you enjoyed the hell out of last year's surprise. And the year before that, too, if memory serves."

Nick couldn't argue with that. The year before, Dave had rented a belly dancer to perform for him on his birthday. Afterward, Nick and the dancer had disappeared behind closed doors so she could give him a few private lessons. The year before that, Dave had hired a woman to dress like a policewoman. She'd come to the office to "arrest" Nick and then proceeded to conduct a highly erotic strip search. Afterward, it had been Nick's turn to play cop.

In truth, both instances had been wild times and Nick couldn't help but look forward to this year's treat. Still, he couldn't spend the day playing. "You do remember that we have the Lampson luncheon today?"

Dave poked through the pantries, looking for food. He opened a pack of Pop-Tarts and put two into the toaster. "Of course, but don't worry. This won't interfere with the luncheon."

"Speaking of which—do you have the flash drive with the presentation on it?"

The toaster popped and Dave grabbed both pastries. "Here," he said, handing one to Nick. "I thought you had it."

"Nope." Nick took a bite and chewed thoughtfully. "Maybe Joe can e-mail the presentation to us." He pulled out his cell phone and made the call.

"Don't tell me you're in trouble already," Joe said by way of answering. "You haven't even been there twenty-four hours."

Nick heard a woman's voice shouting in the background. "What's that?" he asked.

Joe laughed. "Gina wants to know if you need bail money."

"Why does your wife think that all Dave and I do is get into trouble?"

"I don't know," Joe said, pretending to be confused. "Maybe it's because the last two times you two went to town, I had to bail you out of jail before your old man found out."

"It wasn't our fault the police raided those places," Nick

said, smiling. The truth was that he and Dave did tend to get into trouble when they went out to have fun.

"I just don't get the attraction of those vampire clubs," Joe went on.

"Oh, but you should see the women who go there. Why don't you come with us next time?"

"Thanks, but I have no interest in being with anyone but Gina."

"I suppose that's what having a spirit mate will do to you. No more sense of adventure, no more variety."

Joe was one of the rare members of Nick's village who had searched the dream realm and found his true spirit mate, the one woman who was his perfect match. It was little wonder to Nick that Joe opted to stay home with his wife rather than accompany him and Dave to the city, where they spent their nights going to clubs and picking up women.

Nick, on the other hand, liked his independence and having a good time. He wasn't interested in finding his spirit mate. If he ever did get married, he'd be loving and loyal—and most likely miserable. "Listen, Joe. The reason I called is that I need you to e-mail me the Lampson presentation. Do you mind?"

"No problem."

"Great. Thanks." They talked for a few minutes more and then Nick said good-bye. "So, we're all set," Nick told Dave. "I'm going to the office. You coming?"

Dave grinned. "You bet. I wouldn't miss today."

Nick watched Dave take his time eating the Pop-Tart and then proceed to put two more in the toaster. "Are you coming *now?*"

"Nah. You go on. You'll want to get a little work done before . . ." He let his words trail off and gave Nick a knowing smile. "This is going to be great."

Nick rolled his eyes and left the apartment, filled with a mixture of excitement and dread.

Mai woke up late. Her mouth was dry and her head hurt. It had been a long time since she'd had a hangover and usually she'd at least had a wild night of fun and great sex to offset the pain. Okay, well, she'd had the wild sex if erotic dreams counted.

She dragged herself into the bathroom, showered and afterward, felt a little more human. Going back to her bedroom, she looked at the multitude of boxes stacked along the wall, waiting to be opened and their contents put away. The clothes she'd worn for the last two days were definitely in need of washing and she couldn't stand the thought of putting them on again.

Staring at the first box, her hand absently sliding the lightning bolt charm back and forth on the necklace, she wished now that Lexi would have labeled the boxes.

Puffing out a breath in resignation, she grabbed the closest one and hefted it to the bed. There was no point in putting it off any longer.

She had just opened it when her phone rang.

"Hello?"

"Ms. Groves?" a polite female voice asked.

"Yes."

"This is Mr. Blackhawk's secretary. As it turns out, Mr. Blackhawk has had a change of plans and will be in the office this morning. If you're still interested in talking to him, I believe he might have a few minutes."

"Great. I'm definitely interested. Thanks. What time?"

"Can you come now? He'll only be here for about an hour."

Oh, shit, Mai thought. "Yes. Absolutely. I'm on my way."

"Fine. We'll see you shortly. Do you have the address?"

A minute later, Mai hung up the phone and tore through the contents of the box. *Please let there be something in here to wear*, she silently pleaded. Unfortunately, it held shoes. She went to another and opened it. This one was filled with lingerie. She grabbed a bra and panties and then tore into a third box, aware that she was wasting precious time.

The third box held her party clothes: the short skirts, flashy tops and body-hugging dresses she usually wore to the nightclubs. She quickly pulled out each item, making snap decisions on what might be respectable enough to wear to an interview. As the pile of discarded clothing on the bed grew, Mai started to grow desperate. If she didn't leave her apartment in the next five minutes, she might as well not even bother to go.

Midway through the box, she came across a possible outfit. The skirt was still too short and the blouse showed too much cleavage, but it was positively conservative compared to her other choices. Besides, she was out of time. This would have to do.

She dressed in record time, grabbed her makeup bag, purse and notepad—and left her apartment.

As luck would have it, Will was in the lobby when she exited the elevator. The minute she stepped into view, his eyes nearly popped out of his head. Which meant her outfit was definitely unsuitable for this interview. Well, she'd have to apologize to Mr. Blackhawk and hope he'd understand. Maybe he would. Maybe he wouldn't. She didn't care at this point.

"Going someplace?" Will asked, immediately coming over to her with a smile. His gaze never quite reached her eyes as it lingered far south of her chin.

"Yes, very astute of you." She smiled, hoping to soften her waspish tone as she continued past him without slowing.

Outside, the sun was shining but there was a chill in the air that snuck up beneath her skirt. It made Mai that much more conscious of her outfit. At least when she raised her hand to hail a cab, she didn't have to wait long to be noticed.

Climbing into the backseat, she gave the driver the address of Blackhawk's building and then set about putting on makeup while the driver split his attention between the street and eyeing her in the rearview mirror.

Will watched the cab pull away with the tenant from 14-B inside. Mai, he silently corrected himself. Her name was Mai. He rolled the word around in his head, enjoying the sound of it. Her name didn't fit her, he thought. She should have a name that matched her looks. Something like Sophia or Esmeralda.

She was so hot—and she wanted him, that was obvious. She was shy, though, and Will was growing impatient. He'd have to do something to speed things along. Fortunately, he knew just what to do.

Returning to his apartment, he stood before the large mirror hanging on the wall. "Mirror, mirror, on the wall. Who's the fairest of them all?" he intoned good-naturedly.

"Not you, asshole," the genie in the mirror growled back. "Now, if you don't mind, I was in the middle of something."

Will frowned at the show of disrespect. "Like you have anything more important to do than serve me."

"What do you want?" the genie asked, clearly not happy.

"I want her—Mai—the new tenant in 14-B."

"No way. She's way out of your league. Why waste your one wish on her?"

"Wrong." Will spoke in a firm tone. "I get as many wishes as I want."

"I told you before—it doesn't work that way. There are rules."

"To hell with your rules," Will snapped, his good humor vanishing to be replaced with a white-hot rage. He was in charge here—not the genie. *He* was the one who'd found the ancient spell book among his grandfather's possessions when the old man had finally kicked the bucket. And *he* had conjured the genie. It was time the genie learned who was in charge. "Your only job," he said loudly, jabbing his index finger in the air at the mirror, "is to make sure that *my* wishes come true."

"Not for long, you pathetic excuse for a man."

A hand shot out of the mirror and grabbed the collar of Will's shirt. He was jerked forward, off his feet. His head was almost halfway through the mirror before he thought to fight back.

Uttering the words of the spell he'd found in his grandfather's book, Will braced one hand against the wall beside the mirror while he desperately reached with the other for the ritual blade on the nearby table. For several—long—seconds, his fingers sifted through thin air before finally finding the cold metal of the blade. Spurred on by this small victory, he fought the genie's pull and dragged the knife closer.

When he was able to grab the hilt, he raised the knife and, turning the hand braced against the wall enough to expose his palm, dragged the blade across it.

Pain sliced through him followed by the warm ooze of blood. Chanting louder, he slapped his bloodied palm against the mirror.

Suddenly, he was free and the hand that had grabbed him disappeared back into the mirror. The portal that never should have been opened, closed once more. Will fell silent, his mind numb with shock. When had the genie become so powerful? From now on, Will was going to have to be much more careful.

Mai was late by the time she arrived at the Blackhawk Securities office. The receptionist was busy answering a barrage of phone calls, which gave Mai a moment to collect herself while she waited.

"May I help you?" the receptionist finally asked, greeting Mai with a smile and a curious look.

"Yes, I'm here to see Mr. Blackhawk. My name is Mai Groves."

"Oh yes. I'm glad you could make it on such short notice. Please follow me."

She got up from her desk and led Mai down the hall. Stopping at the second door, she knocked once and then opened it. "Ms. Groves is here to see you, sir."

At her gesture, Mai walked through the door and heard it close behind her.

The man behind the desk looked up, and Mai felt she finally understood the meaning of "stunningly good-looking." His coffee-brown hair was styled short but looked in need of a cut and there was a rakishness about him that left her feeling breathless. But it was his sparkling golden brown eyes that captivated her.

"May I help you?" he asked, sounding amused. It was no doubt because she was staring at him like some schoolgirl.

"You're Nicolas Blackhawk?"

"You can call me Nick. I've been expecting you." He stood and went to her, towering over her five-foot frame. "Come in."

"I appreciate you seeing me on such short notice." She took several steps into the room but felt she should wait for him to gesture to a chair before she sat.

Instead of making that gesture, he stood smiling and Mai had the distinct impression that he'd been studying her outfit. Imagining what he must think of her made her inwardly cringe. She debated whether to explain herself.

"You're a wood nymph, aren't you?"

She didn't see the relevance but answered, "Yes, I am."

He nodded and went to the closed door. "Happy birthday to me," she thought she heard him say. The sound of the lock turning was more pronounced. Her face must have shown her confusion because when he turned and saw her watching him, he said, "I don't want any interruptions while you're here."

She supposed she appreciated the gesture, though it did make her a bit nervous to be locked in the room with him.

"Where do you want me?"

"Excuse me?" Mai asked, confused.

"I didn't know if you had a preference," he explained. "We could do this on the couch, which will be more comfortable than the floor. Or, hell, we could use my desk. You pick because I'm game for anything."

"How about the chairs at your desk?" Mai suggested, wondering why he could possibly think she'd want to sit on the floor to conduct an interview. And because he was making her uncomfortable with his odd behavior, the couch was out of the question.

"The chair it is," he said, gesturing toward his desk. "This should be interesting." He went around to the far side while Mai went to take the chair closest to her. "Not that one," he told her just as she was about to sit. "It's too small. Let's use mine."

He was standing beside his chair, hands at his neck, loosening his tie. "Mr. Blackhawk, what are you doing?"

"Nick, please. I apologize for rushing things, but I have a luncheon in an hour. We should be finished by then, don't you think? Anyway, I don't want to get this shirt wrinkled, so I thought I'd take it off now. You look surprised. I'm sorry—did you want to do it?"

Mai knew she was in shock because she was having a hard time putting two thoughts together. There was a misunderstanding here somewhere and she felt on the verge of piecing it together, but damn it, he was taking off his shirt and she just couldn't think.

When he reached for his belt, she finally found her voice. "Stop, please. This is all wrong."

He smiled seductively and closed the distance between them. "The only problem I see here is that you're still wearing clothes."

"Wh-what?"

"You heard me. Take off your clothes."

CHAPTER FIVE

"Who the hell do you think you are?" Mai was outraged. She shoved at his chest and then headed for the door. Her fingers fumbled uselessly with the lock because she was upset, more so because he was someone she might have been interested in under other circumstances. "How the hell do I get out of here?" she shouted in frustration.

He put his shirt back on and followed her to the door. Just as she managed to flip the lock, he put his hand against the door to prevent her from opening it. "Please, wait," he said, no longer sounding as cocky and sure as he had a moment ago. "I'm going to go out on a limb here and guess that you're not the stripper Dave hired to entertain me for my birthday."

She was intensely aware of how close he was standing. "I don't know anyone named Dave," she said as formally as she could. "And I am *not* a stripper."

He didn't look too happy. "I see. Well, this is embarrassing. I'm afraid there's been a misunderstanding. It's really pretty funny." He started to chuckle, but immediately sobered when she gave him a raised eyebrow look. "Well, you probably wouldn't think so. Please. I'm very sorry.

Can we start over? I'll leave the door open." With a gesture, he invited her to sit down in the chair facing his desk.

Only because she felt like what he could tell her might help her with her hallucinations did she agree to take a seat. By the time he walked back to his desk, he'd buttoned his shirt, though left it untucked. As he sat at his desk, Mai cast a quick glance back to make sure the door was open. It was—and that made her feel safer, but did nothing to dampen her anger.

He held out his hand to her over the desk and said in a very businesslike tone, "Nick Blackhawk. It's very nice to meet you . . . Ms. Groves, was it?"

Mai hesitated before accepting his offer. His hand was so large, it swallowed hers. His skin was warm and rough, like a true outdoorsman's, and the rasp of it against her skin was arousing on a primal level. "Yes," she said in a voice that sounded a little breathless. "Mai Groves. I'm a reporter."

"A reporter? Mai Groves. Mai Groves." He tested the sound of her name. "I don't think I've heard of you."

"Probably not," she replied with a saccharine-sweet smile. "My stories don't normally appear in *Penthouse*." The words were out before she could stop them.

To her surprise, he laughed. "I deserved that. I'm sorry I assumed you were—"

"A stripper?" she finished for him.

"I can explain—"

"This should be good."

"You see, every year for my birthday, my friend Dave sends me a stripper. Sometimes, it's obvious who they are, but sometimes they come posing as something else. One year, it was a policewoman. Anyway, today is my birthday and, well, I thought you were this year's birthday treat. It was an honest mistake and I'd be lying if I said I wasn't a little disappointed to find out you're not."

Mai remained quiet, unable to sympathize with his dilemma.

"In my defense," he continued, "your outfit is a bit . . . misleading. Most women dressed like that are sending a message."

"Well, in my case, that message is that I just moved into a new apartment and everything—I mean everything—is still in boxes. So when I got a call from your receptionist telling me to come in ASAP or I'd miss this chance to talk to you, I grabbed the first thing I could find. So it was either come dressed like this—or not come."

He gave her that rakish smile again. "Then I'm very glad you made the decision you did." She wasn't sure exactly what he meant by that. Fortunately, it turned out he didn't expect her to say anything. "You came to interview me—what do you want to know?"

Mai pulled her notebook and pen from her purse. "I read an article about a case you helped the police with involving the disappearance of the . . ." Mai consulted her notes. "The Rollins children."

He looked thoughtful. "Yes. I remember that case. We were lucky to find the children still alive."

"The article said you went into the spirit realm?"

"Yes."

"My article has to do with spirit walking and how it relates to dreams and nightmares—I was hoping you could tell me more about it."

He seemed surprised by her question. "All right. Well, as you may know, spirit walking is the ability to transport one's spirit outside one's corporeal form into the spiritual plane. My people are known as Los Paseantes de Espíritu, the Spirit Walkers. We are born with the ability to enter the spiritual plane and have been trained from birth on how to use that ability."

Mai conjured an image of hippies tripping on LSD and

talking about out-of-body experiences. "What's that like—having your spirit float around outside your body? Can you see your body?"

He smiled. "In a way. Think of time and space in our universe as being like the human body. We have the corporeal form—the body as a whole and then all the sublayers, like organs, blood, muscle and tissue. But we also have the mind with all its various levels of thought—conscious and subconscious. Most people know that other dimensions exist. Some have even traveled to or through them."

Mai thought of Lexi and Darius living in the Immortal realm of Ravenscroft and nodded.

"The spiritual plane is more like the dimensions of the mind. They are less tangible, and when we go there, we don't take our corporeal form."

"I had no idea there were that many dimensions out there. So to find the missing teens, you went to the spiritual plane and what? Searched for their thoughts?"

"Their residual energy, actually." She must have looked confused because he went on. "Okay, think of it like this. When you touch something, you leave behind fingerprints. Most of the time, you can't see those fingerprints, but that doesn't mean they're not there. Because the spiritual planes are interwoven with the physical ones, we're all moving through them and leaving behind our prints, only these prints are made of residual energy. When I'm in the spiritual plane, I see people's residual energies as patterns of light. Even after someone has come and gone, they leave behind an energy trail that slowly dissipates over time."

"And the teens last year left behind energy patterns?"

"Yes. We got lucky because I was able to get to the place of abduction within hours of the event. Violence and fear give off strong energy patterns—as do Thesas demons. I started searching at the spot where the teens were believed to have disappeared and was able to follow the energy patterns straight to the cemetery. The demons were preparing a spell to sacrifice the kids. Fortunately, we got there in time."

"What happened to the demons?"

"The death magic they had unleashed was contained, and they were destroyed."

Mai knew from having read the article that the incident had been a little more involved than that. "So this spirit walking—is that how you go into people's dreams to help them?" She hurried to explain her question because there was a confused expression now on his face. "I read another article that talked about how you also go into dreams to help them with their troubles, nightmares"—she shrugged—"hallucinations."

He shook his head. "Only the shaman of our tribe performs dream healing."

Mai stopped jotting down notes long enough to look up. "I thought *you* were the shaman."

"No, that would be my father. Nicolas Blackhawk, Sr."

She had the wrong Nick Blackhawk after all. "Thank you, Mr. Blackhawk, for taking the time to meet with me. I appreciate it," she said, putting her notebook back in her purse.

"Is that it? No more questions?"

"That's it." She stood. "I know you must be very busy and I don't want to keep you."

"Anytime, Ms. Groves." He opened a drawer and removed a business card. "Please feel free to call me. My direct number is on the front." He turned it over and jotted another number on the back. "And this is my cell phone number—just in case you have any more questions."

She never intended to use it, but tucked the card into her purse anyway. He got up from his desk when she rose and walked her to the door. There, he took her hand once more into his. "Again, I'm very sorry for the misunderstanding."

The contact of his skin against hers was just as deliciously disturbing now as it had been earlier, and mumbling something incoherent, Mai fled his office as soon as she could. His touch burned long after she left.

By the time she arrived home an hour later with a bag of groceries in her arms, she'd forgotten all about Nick Blackwell.

Not only had the trip to the bakery and meat market been necessary in order to have food in the house, but she'd hoped it would be calming. It had been, up until she'd gone to pay for the meat. That was when she'd looked into the face of the cashier and found herself staring at a demon.

No one else seemed alarmed and that's when she'd realized it was just another hallucination. She'd managed to pay the woman without causing a scene, but the episode had left her shaken. It was another indication that she wasn't over her post-traumatic stress.

She set her bags down on the dining table and was about to unpack them when a very definite clinking noise came from down the hallway toward her bedroom.

Someone was in her apartment.

She clutched the lightning bolt around her neck, ready to pull it free, and slowly backed toward her front door. What if this wasn't real, either? Frozen with indecision, she heard the noise get louder.

"Who's there?" she called, not sure whether she wanted to hear an answer or not.

"Mai? Is that you?" Will stepped into the hallway, using one of her towels to dry his hands. He smiled when he saw her. "I thought I heard the door open."

"What are you doing here?" Mai asked, irritation replacing her earlier fear.

He gestured into the bathroom. "I remembered that the bathroom faucet drips and I never got around to fixing it before you moved in. So I came up here to work on it."

Mai tried to remember whether she'd noticed the drip before. "I appreciate it, but I really wish you wouldn't do that when I'm not at home."

"Oh, sure. I understand."

It seemed almost too easy. "Are you done?"

"Just need to get my tools." Will couldn't stop the smile from touching his lips as he turned and headed back into the bathroom. He liked that she wanted to be with him while he worked. It would give him a chance to show off for her.

He tossed her towel into the hamper, picked up his toolbox and went out to talk to her. She was standing beside the table, pulling out the contents of her bags, her back to the mirror. From his vantage point, he could see her shapely butt reflected in the mirror. He liked the look of it, could imagine his hands grabbing it.

"Was there something else you wanted?" she asked him, pausing in the middle of reaching into a bag to look at him.

"There's always something I want," he replied smoothly. He smiled when he saw her eyes open wide. "What about you? You want me to fix . . . something?"

"What?" Her voice sounded a little sharp. "What I want is for you . . ."

Her words faded as Will's attention was drawn to the reflection in the mirror. He watched her bend forward to lift something out of the bag; saw the back of her skirt rise up her thighs until he knew, beyond any doubt, that she was wearing no panties.

The realization spiked through him, giving him an instant hard-on. The bulge in his pants was too obvious to hide and he didn't bother trying. He saw her gaze drop to it, saw her eyes widen and a blush stain her cheeks a delicate pink.

You're moving too fast for her, he thought to himself.

Picking up his toolbox, he started for the door. He didn't make it two steps before she moved to stop him, cupping his groin with her hand. Mesmerized by the way she touched him, he couldn't look away from their reflection in the mirror. Not even when she unzipped his pants and palmed his length could he look away.

The muscles of his legs trembled in anticipation as she knelt before him. When she took him into her mouth, he thought he might spill his seed there and then.

Fighting for control, he barely suppressed the groan rumbling deep in his chest. Part of him wanted to close his eyes so he could focus on the feel of her around him, but knew he didn't dare.

He placed his hand against the back of her head to hold her in place. "So good," he moaned.

"I beg your pardon?"

Her clipped tone tore his attention away from the mirror and the illusion the genie was showing him. Will tried to focus on the woman still standing beside the table and recall what she'd been saying during his lapse of attention. "You don't want me coming into your place when you're not home," he summarized. "Got it."

She nodded and Will, receiving no encouragement to stay, picked up his toolbox and headed for the door.

"I hope you have a great evening," he said, infusing his voice with warmth and seduction. "And don't forget to call me if there's . . . anything . . . I can do."

She gave him a weak smile, no doubt overcome with emotion, and closed the door as soon as he stepped out. He knew that she watched him through the peephole and decided to gift her with a show. Setting down the toolbox, he stretched his arms and back, flexing them the way he'd seen bodybuilders do on TV. Then, not wanting to overdo it, he picked up his toolbox and continued down the hall to the elevator.

He couldn't help thinking he'd made great progress with her. It wouldn't be long before there'd be no need for her to hide her interest.

As he walked past apartment 14-A, he remembered getting a call about the broken closet door. He glanced at his watch. Just after four. He'd go see what the problem was. Maybe the door was simply off its tracks, in which case it wouldn't take long to fix. He hoped the older sister wasn't home. Whenever he came over to fix anything while she was there, she stood around and glared at him. It made him uneasy.

He knocked on the door and waited. He was pleasantly surprised when Sarah answered.

"Hi, Sarah," he greeted her warmly, all the while trying to see past her into the room. "How are you?"

"Oh, hi. Did you get our message about the door?"

"Sure did. That's why I'm here."

"Oh, right. Well, Jenna's not home right now. Could you come back later?"

Will glanced at his watch and pretended to consider her request. "Might be a couple of days before I could." He tried to sound apologetic. "But if you don't mind waiting . . ."

He saw Sarah trying to decide whether Jenna would be more upset that she let him in while alone or about having to wait to get the door fixed.

Sarah stepped back, apparently having made her decision. "I guess it would be better if we didn't have to wait."

"Whose room?" he asked, stepping inside.

"Jenna's."

She led him through the main room, passing the table piled high with her college books. Having never been to college himself, he wondered if the rumors about college women were true. Was Sarah the fast and loose kind of woman who didn't care who she opened her legs for?

"Sometimes they get stuck open," she said, breaking

into his thoughts. It took him a second to realize she was talking about the closet doors and not her legs.

"I can fix that," he said—and he *was* referring to both.

Once inside the room, he walked over to the closet. The doors were closed, so he tried sliding them open. They caught in the carpet and refused to move.

He put a little muscle behind his next attempt and they grudgingly moved. He pulled out his flashlight and played the beam along the top tracks and saw that one of the runners was loose and the door was hanging at an odd angle. "I can fix it. I'll need to replace the runner," he told her. "But you're in luck—I've got a spare downstairs. Be right back."

"Oh, great. Thanks."

Will left his tools there and hurried down to the storeroom. Soon, he was back in 14-A, hard at work with Sarah looking on. He glanced at her sitting on the edge of the bed, leaning back on her arms, posing for him. He raked his gaze over her appreciatively. "What time does your sister get home?"

He almost laughed when she sat up and crossed her arms. "Any time now."

She was lying and they both knew it. Perhaps she was being coy. Maybe she wanted him to come to her, toss her on the bed and make love to her. He considered it. But what if he was wrong and she wanted to take things slowly? He didn't want to frighten her.

For now, he'd focus on fixing the doors. The rest would come later.

He'd barely started when she cleared her throat. "Um, you're okay here by yourself, right?" she said, standing. "I just remembered that I promised Mai I would take her . . . something."

She didn't even wait for his response before hurrying out of the room.

When he heard the front door open and close, Will laughed quietly to himself. He'd forgotten how young and naive Sarah was—thanks, no doubt, to her older sister's obsessive protectiveness. He'd obviously excited her—which had made her nervous.

He set about his work, thinking that he'd made the right decision to go slow with this one. He didn't want to frighten her off before he'd had a chance to enjoy her.

Mai was about to start dinner when there was a knock on her door. Her first thought was that it was her vampire friend Ricco coming to visit as he'd promised when she'd called him to tell him she moved. Then she remembered that he was still out of town at some vampire council meeting. She went to the door and peeked out to see Sarah standing there.

"Hi," Mai greeted her after opening the door.

"Hi." Sarah sounded relieved. "I hope I'm not disturbing you."

"No, of course not. Come in. Is everything all right?"

"Yeah. Everything's fine," Sarah hurried to assure her. She offered up an apologetic smile as Mai closed the door. "Actually, Will's over at my place fixing the closet door and I didn't want to be there alone with him."

Mai gave a soft laugh. "I know exactly what you mean. What is it with that guy? I came home and found him in my apartment."

"That happened to us once. Jenna went nuts. She really chewed him out for it, too."

"Well, I asked him not to come by when I'm not at home, but judging from the way he acted, I don't think he was paying too much attention."

"He's a dork."

They shared a laugh and Mai thought again how much she liked Sarah. "I was just fixing myself some dinner. Would you like to join me?"

"Thanks, I'd like that, but maybe I could take a rain check? As soon as Will's gone, I need to get back to studying. But please, if your food's ready, don't let me stop you from eating."

"Actually, I only just started it. Come talk to me while I work?"

"All right."

Sarah followed her into the kitchen and leaned against the counter while Mai cut up vegetables.

"So, how are things going?" Mai asked

"Great." Her tone didn't match the word.

"Everything all right?"

Sarah sighed. "I'm taking an extra class this semester, which has turned out to be harder than I expected. I'm burned out on school and just want the semester to be over."

"Will you have your degree then?"

"No. I still have another full year."

"So you'll get about a month off before classes start up again? That'll be nice. Or will you have to work that month?"

"I wish."

Mai paused in her chopping to look at Sarah. "You want to work?"

She smiled. "I know, call me crazy. The thing is, Jen's working two jobs just so I can go to college. I know she's tired, but she doesn't feel like she can afford to take time off. I've offered to help by getting a job of my own, but she refuses to let me. Says I need to focus on getting my degree."

"Wow." Mai was impressed. "It's great that your sister is willing to do that for you."

"Yeah. She's been terrific. I was thirteen when we lost our parents and Jenna, who was nineteen, dropped out of school and started working to support us both because she didn't want me to end up in foster care. When I graduated from high school, I thought I'd be able to help, but she insisted I go to college."

That was true devotion, Mai thought. "Your sister really loves you."

Sarah smiled. "Yeah. I know she does, but I feel bad—like she's throwing away her life for me."

Mai finished cutting her broccoli and set down her knife. "Maybe you should talk to her. Tell her how you feel."

Sarah sighed in frustration. "I've tried, but I never seem to say the right thing."

"I don't know if you're interested, but I have several books on negotiation. I bought them when I started writing freelance—for when I talk to editors to help me get the deals I want. I haven't read them yet, but maybe one of those would help you with your sister—if you're interested in reading it?"

Her eyes lit up. "Are you sure you don't mind?"

"Not at all. I think I left them in the bedroom. Let me see if I can find them."

Sarah nodded. She supposed anything was worth a try.

"I'll be right back." Mai wiped her hands on a towel and disappeared down the short hallway.

Left alone, Sarah slowly wandered about the living room while she waited. Several framed photographs and knickknacks were displayed on the bookcase. One picture in particular caught her eye. It was of a stunningly handsome couple with a newborn baby in their arms. She picked it up for a closer look and as she did, a flicker of movement off to the side caught her eye. Thinking that Mai had returned, she looked around—but found she was still alone.

There was another flicker of light. It looked like it was coming from the mirror. Curious, Sarah moved closer.

There was something odd about the mirror. Behind her reflection, a shadow moved across the glass. It was almost like it was *behind* the glass. It was odd and left her feeling uneasy.

"I found it," Mai hollered from the other room, causing Sarah to turn toward the sound.

She opened her mouth to ask Mai about the mirror, but at that moment, two arms reached out and grabbed her. She sucked in a breath to scream as her world tilted. There was a horrible sucking noise followed by a cold blast of air.

Then she was on the other side of the mirror, staring into Mai's living room.

CHAPTER SIX

"Here you go." Mai held up two books as she walked back into the living room. "Sarah?" She looked around, but Sarah wasn't there. Nor was she in the bathroom. A quick search showed Sarah wasn't anywhere in the apartment.

Maybe she'd gone back to her own place to study. Mai thought it was a little odd that she would disappear without saying good-bye, but then again, maybe Mai simply hadn't heard her. She considered going to Sarah's apartment to make sure that Sarah had really gone back and to double-check that Will was gone, but then she decided she was allowing her own paranoia to get the better of her. The last thing Sarah needed was another overprotective big-sister type.

Mai set the books on the counter so she'd remember to give them to Sarah later, then returned to the kitchen to finish cooking dinner. As her thoughts drifted back to the incident at the grocery store, she wondered if she'd been too hasty in canceling her therapy appointments.

Then she remembered that her therapist was dead. Murdered. She wondered who would have killed him and then answered her own question—anyone who'd been going to him for therapy, she imagined. Even she hadn't liked him that much, but she hadn't wanted him dead.

She forced herself to stop thinking about Dr. Barbour, but then her thoughts turned to Nick Blackhawk. Why he came to mind, she had no idea. He was the last person she wanted to think about. Sure, he was attractive in a rugged outdoorsy kind of way, and he had that arrogant cockiness that was both incredibly annoying and sexy.

She closed her eyes to clear her head and saw Nick's laughing brown eyes. Ugh. Maybe she should go to Ricco's tonight and let one of his vampires help her forget all her worries. Except that old routine no longer sounded appealing to her, either. She could have better sex in her dreams. How pathetic was that?

Even worse was that once the idea was planted, she actually became excited at the prospect of possibly having another erotic dream that night.

It was enough to make her go to bed early.

Mai wasn't conscious of dreaming, though she knew she must be. One instant she was caught in a never-ending loop of typing at her laptop only to discover that the words of her article were disappearing as fast as she could type them. The next instant, *he* was there.

It was her rescuer, the same man she'd dreamed of the night before.

"You came," she whispered, rising from her chair to cross the room to him.

She felt one of his hands settle at her waist as the other cupped the side of her face in a gentle caress. His gaze was filled with a barely suppressed hunger that, even in the dream, caused her breath to catch. "I can't stay away." He bent his head close so his lips could sample hers. Once. Twice. Brief, gentle kisses that left her craving more.

Wrapping her arms around his neck, she held him to

her, drinking deeply from his lips. His demanding response was exactly what she'd hoped for.

"This is crazy," she whispered when they stopped to catch their breath. "I don't even know your name." She peered into his face, but in her dreamlike haze, his features swam in and out of focus.

"What is in a name?" he whispered back, trailing kisses across her lips and throat. "A rose by any other name would smell as sweet."

"A man who knows Shakespeare. Be still my heart."

He chuckled and pulled her into a hug. "I've missed you."

Taking her by the hand, they started walking. Between one step and the next, they went from standing in her apartment to walking barefoot along a sandy beach. Mai thought she could feel the sun beating down on them as their feet squished in the cool, damp sand along the water's edge. The gulls' cries mingled with the rhythmic rush of waves cascading ashore. Once again, Mai was filled with that same sense of total contentment and peace that she'd found only once before and it was with this man.

The part of her that recognized she was dreaming warned her it wouldn't last, but she refused to listen. Not right now.

As the sun set over the horizon and the sky glowed in hues of red and orange, they stopped to sit. Mai put her head on his shoulder as he wrapped his arm around her.

"I wish we could stay here forever," she said.

He smiled down at her and with his free hand, brushed the hair from her face. "Me, too, love."

His endearment warmed her and she closed her eyes, savoring the moment. The loud clap of thunder that suddenly struck startled her. Opening her eyes, she saw that the clear night sky had been replaced by dark, angry, roiling clouds. A chill wind blew across where they still sat.

"What's going on?" Mai shouted, trying to be heard above the next clap of thunder. "Where did this storm come from?"

"You need to wake up," he shouted back.

"What?"

He stood and pulled her to her feet. Then he kissed her while the wind buffeted them from all directions. Finally, he lifted his head. "Wake up."

The command was so insistent, Mai opened her eyes, immediately wide-awake. The silence of her room was especially stark compared to the thunderous noise of her dream. She didn't understand what had awakened her and was thinking that if she fell back asleep right away, she might find *him* again when she heard someone pound on her front door.

Who would be knocking at this hour? She glanced at the clock beside her bed. Three in the morning. Scowling, she climbed out from under the covers and pulled a sweater on over her pajamas.

Tiptoeing to the door, she held her breath and leaned close enough to peer out the peephole. Jenna stood on the other side, looking upset. Mai turned the lock and opened the door.

"I'm sorry to wake you up, but is Sarah here?" Jenna asked.

"What? No." Mai struggled to make sense of the conversation. "What's going on?"

Jenna frowned. "She's not at home and I don't know where she is. She's never just gone off without telling me where she's going." It was obvious that Jenna didn't know whether to be irritated or scared.

"Why don't you come in? Let me get dressed and then I'll help you look for her." Mai knew she wouldn't be able to sleep until she, too, knew what had happened to Sarah.

Jenna looked uncertain. "Are you sure you don't mind?"

Mai shook her head. "Not at all."

After Jenna stepped into the apartment, Mai closed the door. "I saw Sarah earlier this evening. She said Will was fixing the closet at your place."

"Did she seem okay?" Jenna asked. "There wasn't anything bothering her?"

"No, she seemed fine. She didn't want to be alone with Will so decided to take a study break and come chat. That was all."

"Did she say anything that would make you think she was planning to run away?"

Did a twenty-year-old run away? Mai wondered. Or did she just get tired of being treated like a kid and move out?

"No," Mai said thoughtfully. "I didn't get the impression that she was thinking of leaving."

"Damn it!" Jenna exclaimed suddenly. "It's not like her to just disappear. If she's gone and gotten herself hurt . . ." Her voice cracked with emotion and she fell silent.

"Jenna, I don't mean to suggest anything here, but when you got home, you didn't notice anything . . . odd, did you?"

"Odd, how?"

"A broken lock on the door? Signs of a struggle inside the apartment?" *Blood on the walls or floor?* Jenna would have said something if that had been the case.

Jenna shook her head. "No. Nothing."

"Did you call the police?"

"Yes, and they said disappearing isn't against the law. They suggested I talk to Sarah's friends to see if they know anything and after that, if I still feel she's missing, then I should go down to the station to file a report. I don't know any of her school friends." She heaved a shuddering breath. "It's like she's vanished without a trace."

Mai's thoughts raced. According to Nick Blackhawk, it didn't matter if Sarah left on her own or someone abducted her, she would have left a residual energy trail behind. And Nick knew how to follow that trail. "Maybe not entirely without a trace," Mai suggested slowly.

"What do you mean?" Jenna asked.

Mai quickly explained her idea to Jenna. "It's no guarantee," she quickly added, "but it's something." Did she dare call Nick Blackhawk at this hour? It would be rude.

Absolutely. By her way of thinking, she owed him one for thinking she was a stripper.

Grabbing her purse, she searched through its contents until she found his card. Mai had no doubt he could help her. The question was, would he?

Nick rubbed his eyes and sat up in bed. He was exhausted despite getting plenty of sleep. For the last two nights, his dreams had been erotically charged and extremely realistic.

Normally, that wouldn't have bothered him in the slightest, but he'd been with the same woman in each dream—and that was unusual. Unless he'd been with his spirit mate, in which case that wasn't unusual—it was disturbing. Nick's life was planned and those plans didn't include a spirit mate.

At that moment, his cell phone rang and he picked it up off the nightstand, wondering who the hell thought it was okay to call him this early in the morning. "Hello?" he growled.

"Mr. Blackhawk?" a female voice asked. "This is Mai Groves—I spoke to you yesterday?"

Nick frowned, remembering the wood nymph. "Ms. Groves. It's a bit early in the day for an interview, don't you think?"

"I'm sorry that I woke you. I have a . . . situation and you're the only person who can help me."

He wasn't at all sure he should believe her. "I can understand why you're still pissed at me, but don't you think it's a bit childish to make crank calls?" He heard her heavy sigh.

"If this was a crank call, would I have told you my name?"

She had a point.

"What's the problem?"

"My friend has disappeared, possibly kidnapped. I was hoping you could come over and, you know, follow her energy trail."

"I don't do parlor tricks, Ms. Groves. I try to save my talent for legitimate emergencies. Just because a friend isn't answering your calls or isn't where you think she needs to be, doesn't make it an emergency."

"Mr. Blackhawk. Please believe me when I tell you that you are the last person on earth I would call for help, but this is important. A young woman is missing and her older sister swears that she would never go off without leaving word where she was going or when she'd be back. Her sister has looked everywhere for her. I can't shake the feeling that something bad has happened to her, but unfortunately, that's not enough for the police. I'd hoped it might be enough for you. And knowing that the residual energy trails dissipate over time, I thought it best to call you right away. I should have known you wouldn't help."

For reasons he couldn't explain, it bothered him that he had disappointed her. "Where was she last seen?"

"My apartment. She came over while I was fixing dinner, we talked and then while I was in the bedroom, she left. Presumably to go back to her place, but I didn't go check to be sure."

Nick rubbed his forehead. "Her apartment will be filled with her own spiritual tracings—it will be nearly impossible to pick out the most recent one and follow it—which is what you're asking me to do."

"I'll pay you," she offered.

He hesitated. "You really think you can afford me?"

"Please."

"My standard rate is a thousand the first hour and five hundred every hour after that." He paused, knowing he'd shocked her. "But I'll offer you a special discount."

"I'm not sleeping with you," she said sharply.

"My loss, I'm sure, but that wasn't what I had in mind."

"Oh."

He smiled. "I'll come over in exchange for you having dinner with me."

"You want to go out for dinner? With me?" She sounded wary.

"Yes, is that so hard to believe? But since I'm doing you a favor by coming over to help you look for a friend, dinner will be your treat and I leave it up to you whether you want to cook for me or we go out."

He heard her sigh. "Deal. How soon can you be here?"

"Hang on a second," he said, searching for pen and paper in the nightstand drawer. "Okay. Give me your address."

He wrote it down, realizing that she didn't live that far away. "I'm on my way. Try to keep people out of the apartment for now. It'll be less confusing for me."

"All right—and thank you."

Mai was on edge. She didn't know if it was because of the mysterious circumstances surrounding Sarah's disappearance or because she'd be seeing Nick Blackhawk again. Not that there was any reason she should look forward to that encounter. Her thoughts flashed back to the memory of him towering over her like a wall of sheer masculine strength. And the way he'd looked without his shirt, his tousled hair and knowing smirk giving him that rakish air.

Mai sighed. The last thing she needed was to romanticize Nick Blackhawk. No doubt, as soon as she saw him again, he'd open his mouth and say something totally irritating. Sarah was missing—Mai needed to stay focused on that.

She hurried out of her apartment and knocked on Jenna's door. Jenna answered with a look of expectant hope on her face. It died the instant she saw who was at the door.

"You haven't heard from Sarah?" Mai asked, though the answer was obvious.

"No. What about you—any luck?"

"Yes. He's on his way."

Jenna nodded, wrapping her arms about herself. "At this point, I'm willing to give anything a try."

Mai's heart went out to the woman. She might appear tough, but Jenna obviously loved her sister. Mai gave Jenna's arm a sympathetic squeeze. "I'm going to run downstairs and wait. Nick should be here shortly."

She turned to go, but Jenna's hand on her arm stopped her. "Thank you." Her voice broke over the words as she obviously struggled to control her emotions.

Mai wanted to tell her not to worry, that they would find Sarah; but she knew that might not be true—not in today's world. So instead she merely nodded and then hurried to the elevator.

When she reached the lobby, she saw Nick hadn't arrived yet. With nothing else to do, she decided to check her mail.

"Morning, Mai—how are you?"

Almost to the mailboxes, Mai nearly jumped out of her skin at the sound of Will's voice. She turned and saw him standing a short distance off and would have sworn he hadn't been there a second ago. "Will. You startled me. What are you doing up at this hour?"

"I could ask you the same thing," he countered, coming

toward her, his gaze traveling over her. It was a grossly obvious attempt at being seductive and would have been funny if it hadn't been so creepy.

"I'm waiting for someone," Mai explained, hoping it would discourage him. She should have known better.

Giving her a smile, he stepped closer. "You know, I only do the maintenance work as a hobby. I don't really need to work at all."

"Is that right?"

"Yes, it is." He straightened to make himself appear taller, inhaling deeply as he did. Mai's gaze flickered involuntarily to his chest, which was apparently what he'd intended because he gave her a knowing smile. "I was thinking that maybe we should go out sometime." He took another step forward.

Mai backed up, wanting to keep a comfortable distance between them. "I don't think so, Will, but thank you." She kept her tone polite but not too friendly, hoping he would back off. Of course he didn't.

"Let's stop pretending. You're single and lonely. I'm single. We could be good together, you and me."

He reached out like he wanted to touch her hair, but Mai leaned beyond his reach, leaving his arm hanging awkwardly in the air. It didn't seem to bother him nearly as much as it bothered her.

Her impulse was to tell him to leave her alone, but he had a key to her apartment. He could come and go as he pleased, no matter if it was against the law or not. She made a mental note to change the door locks.

It wasn't a question of turning him down as much as finding an excuse he would accept. "The thing is," she said, "I'm already seeing someone." *Not good enough*, a small voice in her head shouted when Will's expression didn't change. "It's serious," she hurried on. "*Very* serious."

"That's okay." He smiled. "I'm not the jealous type."

"But he is," a male voice growled from beside Mai, startling her because she hadn't heard anyone approach. "Hey, baby. Sorry I'm late."

She barely had time to register the amused sparkle in Nick Blackhawk's golden brown eyes before he pulled her firmly into his arms and took her lips in a breathtaking kiss.

CHAPTER SEVEN

Shock momentarily froze Mai as his warm, firm lips seduced hers. She'd been on a diet of no sex for so long that her libido roared to life. She lost all awareness of her surroundings; all sense of time and place. Her entire world centered on Nick. His strong arms holding her. His hard, muscled chest pressed against her body. His tongue running across the seam of her lips, coaxing them open so his tongue could tease hers.

When the kiss ended, she couldn't move.

What the hell had just happened? she wondered, trying to catch her breath. When she remembered to open her eyes it was to find Nick watching her with an amused smile on his face.

"Shall we go upstairs?" he suggested. "I think I'd prefer to continue this without an audience."

Mai was still trying to figure out why he kissed her when he turned to Will. "If you'll excuse us?"

Oh yeah. The lie about having a boyfriend. Now she remembered. "Where are my manners?" she said, fighting for composure. She needed to put some space between her and Nick so she could think, but his arm around her waist kept her pressed firmly to his side. "Will, this is Nick. Nick is . . ." She stopped, unable to bring herself to actually say the word.

"Her jealous boyfriend." Nick's smile was pleasant, though there was a definite edge to his voice.

"I haven't seen you before," Will observed, his comment sounding more like an accusation.

"Don't let it bother you," Nick said dismissively. "Now, if you'll excuse us."

Mai let Nick maneuver her over to the elevator. As they waited for it to arrive, Mai thought she felt Will's gaze boring a hole into her back and was actually grateful for the reassuring weight of Nick's arm across her shoulders.

Finally, the elevator doors opened and they stepped inside. Will was still staring after them like he couldn't quite make up his mind what to think. Then he started forward at a determined pace. Mai found his expression unnerving. He stared at her with such focused intensity, she automatically moved even closer to Nick.

The doors started to close just as Will reached out a hand to stop them. "I almost forgot that faucet in your bathroom. It needs repairing. I know it's early, but since you're awake, I could come up and fix it."

"I don't think so, Will," Nick said pleasantly enough, stepping forward to block the opening. "We're going to be busy."

The doors closed and as soon as the car started rising, Mai finally collected her wits. "That might have been a bit over-the-top, but thank you, I suppose."

"You suppose?"

She shrugged. "I had the situation under control."

Now he laughed. "Sweetheart, that guy was about five seconds from being all over you. Face it, I saved you."

"You didn't save me—you kissed me."

"I didn't hear you complaining."

"That's because you had your tongue halfway down my throat."

"Please, now you're embarrassing me. My tongue's not that long."

His comment shocked her to silence for several seconds and then she giggled. "You're unbelievable," she finally muttered.

"So I've been told." He sighed. "Look, I did you a favor back there. There's something not right with that guy."

Nick knew he needed to be careful. He wasn't sure why, but walking into her building and seeing the maintenance man hitting on her had raised a sudden, fierce need to rip out the other man's throat. He'd opted for staking his claim with the kiss instead. Something quick and indisputable. The minute his lips had touched Mai's, though, all his best intentions had flown out the door. Now it was all he could do to keep from pushing her up against the elevator wall for a repeat performance.

"Anyone tell you that you're impossibly arrogant?" she asked as the elevator stopped on the fourteenth floor and the doors opened.

"What can I say? Old habits die hard. Mai, wait up." He grabbed her arm and pulled her to a stop. "All kidding aside, I don't like that guy—there's something about him. I don't know what it is, but be careful around him, okay?"

She searched his face as if she wasn't sure if he was really serious, but then she nodded. "Okay."

He released her and let his hand drop to his side. God, he wanted to keep touching her. He took a step back and gestured down the hall. "Following you."

She continued to the first door, bearing a sign that identified it as 14-A. Mai knocked.

They didn't have to wait long before it was opened by a woman who appeared to be about Mai's age. She was taller than Mai with long, dark hair. Her eyes were red and swollen from crying.

"Has she called?" Mai asked without preamble.

The woman shook her head. "Nothing." She looked past Mai to Nick.

"This is Nick Blackhawk," Mai introduced him. "He's the man I was telling you about. Nick, this is Jenna Renfield, Sarah's sister."

"Please come in," Jenna invited, taking a step back so they could enter.

Nick walked into the room. There was nothing particularly special about the apartment: open textbooks on the dining table beside a spiral notebook and a pen, dirty dishes on the kitchen counter, a folded afghan on the couch.

"How does this work?" Mai asked, bringing his attention back to the reason he was there.

"First, I'd like to walk around and make a cursory search. Then I'll enter the spiritual plane to see what I can detect."

At Jenna's nod of permission, he made a complete circuit of the room, getting a feel for the place. He saw nothing to suggest the missing girl had been abducted. "The bedrooms?" he asked.

Jenna pointed down the hall. "You're welcome to look. Sarah's is the first one."

A quick survey of each room gave no indication that anyone had left in a hurry—either by choice or by force.

He went back to join the women in the front room. "I'm going to enter the spiritual plane now and see what I can discover. It's important that you understand that searching for residual energy patterns isn't an exact science. It doesn't come with guarantees." Both women nodded that they understood, so he went to the couch and sat.

"What do you need us to do?" Mai asked, walking over to him.

"It would be best if you both sat still until I return to my body. It'll make it easier to read the patterns while I'm out."

Mai gestured to the spot beside him on the couch. "Will it bother you if I sit here?"

Having you near makes me crazy, he wanted to tell her. "No."

There was no reason to put this off any longer and every reason to hurry. Making himself relax, he freed his spirit from its corporeal form. If one thought of the various spiritual planes in a linear hierarchy, the plane where the residual energy patterns were visible was located several levels below the dream realm. Of course, that was just an analogy since the realms were more interwoven than linear.

As his spirit moved into the spiritual plane, his brain automatically translated the contours of the energy fields into visual images.

He immediately found the residual energies coming from Mai and Jenna, shining like twin beacons of light—a rich forest green for Mai and deep purple for Jenna.

Mai's energy, especially, resonated along his senses, beckoning him closer. Unable to resist, he allowed his spirit to brush against it and received a pleasant jolt. If he'd been corporeal, he would have smiled.

Continuing around the room, he picked up a third energy pattern. This one appeared as a pale blue and Nick assumed it belonged to Sarah. To be certain, he moved down the hallway to the bedroom that had been hers. As expected, pale blue light was present here as well.

He left the bedroom and continued down the hall to Jenna's room. Here, he found more of the purple energy—some patches shining brighter, stronger than others. No doubt, these traces of energy were fresher, perhaps from earlier that day.

It wasn't the only energy pattern he found in the room, however. There were two others. The first was Sarah's pale blue trail lingering beside the closet. The second pattern, a darker orange light, gave off a strange but familiar vibe and it took him a minute to recognize it. The maintenance man. He'd been in that room recently.

Sarah's pattern seemed thicker here as if it was one of the last places she'd been. Concentrating on it, Nick followed the trail out of the room. Others had passed through this space, causing the pattern to dissipate. It made the trail harder to follow, but he thought it led to the front door.

In the spiritual plane, there were no doors to bar his path so he simply moved out into the hallway. The energy pattern continued down the hallway to the next apartment. Nick faded through the door and found himself surrounded by Mai's residual energy. This must be her apartment, he thought.

The blue energy of Sarah's lingered there as well. He traced it through the kitchen and then around the living room. The highest concentration of it, he found, was beside the dining table. There was something else there as well, but he couldn't tell exactly what it was. Even stranger was that this new energy pattern only existed in the one spot. There was no trail leading to or away from it. An anomaly?

He moved back out into the hall and paused. The pattern of Sarah's energy out here was older than the patterns he found inside, which was odd because he would have thought the residual energy of her leaving the apartment would be strongest.

He checked other floors, the elevator and the lobby but found nothing. Finally he returned to his body. When he opened his eyes, Mai and Jenna were watching him closely.

"I found her pattern," he told them. "The strongest traces start in the back bedroom and lead to the apartment next door. Yours, I presume?" he asked Mai, turning to her.

She nodded. "That's probably from when she came to see me. We talked for a while and then I went to get her a book. When I came back out, she was gone. I thought she'd come back here." She paused and her gaze fell. "I should have checked on her."

He could tell that Mai was getting upset. "You can't blame yourself. You had no reason to think she didn't return to her apartment." He turned to look at Jenna whose look of despair was heart-wrenching. "I picked up a pattern of energy that I think belongs to the maintenance man. Was he in your bedroom with Sarah?"

"Will?" Jenna quickly turned to Mai. "Didn't you say that Sarah told you he was at our place fixing the closet?"

"Yes," Mai said. "She didn't want to be alone with him."

"What time was this?" Nick asked.

"About six, I think."

Nick didn't tell them about Sarah's trail ending abruptly in Mai's apartment. He wasn't sure what it meant and saw no reason to worry them until he did. Instead, he stood. "Where does Will live? He and I are going to have a little chat."

Mai gasped. "You think he had something to do with her disappearance?" The expression on her face told him that she found the idea that Will had played some role in the girl's disappearance all too easy to believe.

"I don't know," Nick admitted. "Right now I just want to ask him what they might have talked about. Maybe Sarah said something that will give us a clue to where she is."

There was definitely something off about the guy, but Nick wasn't ready to accuse him of kidnapping—yet.

CHAPTER EIGHT

It had been several hours since Will had run into Mai and her boyfriend in the lobby. The encounter had left him furious. How dare that man steal away his woman?

A maintenance call to repair the toilet in 10-B came in around six o'clock and he was still fuming by the time he finished up an hour later and returned to his apartment, slamming the door shut behind him.

"Appear before me!" he demanded, going to stand before the mirror. He waited for the mist to come up behind the glass, but nothing happened.

Damn genie. Who the hell did he think was in control here? An ornately decorated wood box rested in the center of his dining table. He pulled it toward him and flipped open the lid.

Lying on a bed of crimson crushed velvet was his ceremonial dagger. With a handle of polished black onyx and a silver blade that glinted brightly beneath the lights, it was beautiful, though Will was too angry to notice. He grabbed it up and dragged the blade lightly across his scarred palm.

He didn't immediately feel the sting of his sliced flesh and watched, fascinated, as a thin red line appeared. Within moments, blood had pooled in his hand.

When there was enough of it, he pressed his palms together, coating them both before slapping them, open-faced, flat against the mirror frame. Pain shot through his hands and up his arms, fueling his anger.

"I call on Apep, the Great Destroyer, and Set, God of Evil, and Am-Heh, Devourer of Millions. I offer my blood as sacrifice and pray you grant me this boon. I call upon your powers of darkness to be my strength." He turned back to the mirror. "Genie—I summon thee."

This time, the mirror misted over, growing opaque. From within the depths of that cloud, a figure appeared. It moved closer until finally its features could be distinguished.

Will always thought the genie bore a strong resemblance to Hellboy at the end of the movie, when his horns had grown out and he wasn't chewing on a cigar. He was a large creature with skin the color of molten lava, which had always intrigued Will because the genie, to his knowledge, didn't have command of fire, nor did his dimension resemble the pits of Hell. Will figured the genie could assume any appearance he chose but chose to look like this just to intimidate Will. It worked, though Will would never admit it.

Will's first summoning of the genie had been a complete accident. It had been the night after his grandfather's funeral. Will, as the only living relative, had inherited everything—which hadn't been much. Just the old book of spells and his grandfather's ceremonial dagger.

The Johnson family was filled with generations of witches and wizards whose magical talent was more sham than genuine. Will had had no reason to believe his grandfather was any different than the rest of them. He'd been playing with the ritual dagger—running his thumb across the blade absently—while reading through the old man's spell book. A drop of blood, the wrong selection of words and a portal had opened.

"What do you want, oh wise and powerful Oz?" the genie mocked him now.

"I want to know why the tenant in 14-B isn't mine. I specifically *wished* that she notice me."

"She did notice you," the genie replied calmly.

"Then why was she out there kissing her boyfriend? If she noticed me, she shouldn't be interested in him at all."

"She *does* notice you—every time you're around." The genie smiled. "She just doesn't like what she sees."

"That's not what I meant when I made that wish and you know it."

"Then you should have been more specific," the genie said patronizingly.

Will gritted his teeth. The genie was nothing but trouble. It would serve him right if Will were to banish him into nothingness—that is, if Will knew the right spell. Since he didn't, he might as well make the most of the situation. "Okay—how's this for specific? I wish—"

The phone rang, interrupting his wish. Sighing, he went to answer it, careful not to get blood on the receiver.

"Will?" a familiar female voice asked over the phone. "This is Mai. In 14-B?"

Her voice was like a gentle caress. He loved hearing her speak. "Hello, Mai. This is a pleasant surprise." He was glad that despite the rapid beating of his heart, his voice sounded smooth and sexy.

"Are you going to be there for a few minutes? I wanted to come down and talk to you."

"Now?" His heart skipped a beat. His gaze raked the room. He'd have to put a few things away, but it was basically clean. He shot a look at his bedroom. The bed hadn't been made, but he supposed it was too much to hope she'd sleep with him this soon. Although . . .

"It's important," she urged.

"Okay. Come on down," he said into the phone, and hung up. Hurrying back to the mirror, he saw the genie still waiting for him.

"I wish her to—"

"Uh-uh," the genie interrupted. "Her? Which her are you talking about? Haven't I told you—be careful of your word choice."

Irritated, Will cast about in his mind for exactly the right phrasing. After all, he'd wished for her to notice him before and she had, but not in the way he'd expected. This time, he needed to be very precise. It would be nice if the wishes could involve formal names, but he'd tried that once and the genie had found someone else whose name happened to be the same to work the spell on.

He'd have to be creative, he thought. Mai was on her way down to see him, so perhaps he could play off that. "I wish that the next woman who comes through my front door wants to jump my bones."

The genie rolled his eyes and waved his hand. "Wish granted." Then he disappeared in a whirl of mist.

Soon there was a knock at the door.

"Just a minute," Will shouted, rushing to the kitchen sink to wash the blood from his hands. He dried them, tossed the towel aside and hurried to the door. He paused, his hand on the doorknob, and took a deep breath to calm his nerves. Then he opened the door.

At the sight of Mai standing in the hall with her boyfriend and Jenna Renfield, Will's good mood vanished. "What's going on?"

"Jenna's sister has disappeared," the boyfriend said, putting himself a little in front of the women. All three pairs of eyes bored into him, making him uneasy.

"What do you mean, Sarah's disappeared? I just saw her last night." They didn't look surprised at the news, and it occurred to him that they already knew he'd seen her.

"Wait a minute. You don't think I had something to do with her disappearance, do you?"

"No one's accusing you of anything—yet," the boyfriend said. "Right now all we know is that Sarah is gone and no one has heard from or seen her since last evening. We thought she might have said something to you that might help us find her."

"No. We didn't talk much. I had just started on the closet door when she decided to go next door. I finished before she came back, so I left."

The boyfriend gestured to Will's apartment. "Do you think we could finish this conversation inside?"

Will didn't have to look behind him to know the bloodied dagger still sat on the table and there was blood on the picture frame. Would they believe it wasn't Sarah's blood? Not likely. "I'm afraid my apartment's a mess."

"This won't take a second," the boyfriend said.

"Why? You think I have her tied up in back? She's not here." The boyfriend was really pissing him off. It was bad enough they had to compete for the same woman, but now the boyfriend was trying to accuse him of kidnapping Sarah? Ridiculous.

For a full minute, the boyfriend stood glaring, trying to intimidate him. Well, it wasn't working. Will had seen much scarier things than this guy.

Finally, when Will thought the silence had gone on for an absurdly long time, the boyfriend took a step back.

"Call us if you hear anything."

"Obviously." Will rolled his eyes. He watched them move back down the hallway and only when they'd stepped into the elevator did he finally go back into his apartment and close the door.

"Bastard," he swore out loud as he returned to the mirror. He hated that guy with all that was in him. "Genie— I know you're still here. What happened to Sarah?"

"How should I know?" the genie said in a bored tone.

"Give me a break. You know everything that happens in this building."

A slow smile spread across the genie's face, annoying Will further.

"Do I have to force you to tell me?" Will threatened. "Did you do something?"

Before the genie could respond, there was another knock on the door. Hoping that Mai had come back to apologize for her boyfriend's behavior, Will went to open it—and found the tenant from 10-A. "Oh, hello, Tiffany."

"Hi, Will." She greeted him with a tentative smile. She was about his age and had probably been a very attractive woman, two hundred pounds ago. "My sink's clogged again. Would you mind fixing it?"

"Sure," he sighed. "Let me get my tools." He closed the door almost all the way, leaving it standing ajar so as not to be rude. He kept his tools in the second bedroom and hurried back there to get them.

Knowing Tiffany, she'd purposely clogged the sink just so she'd have an excuse for company. She tended to be a bit of a recluse—not that Will held that against her. They all needed their privacy. "You should have just called me," he shouted to her as he strapped on his belt. "Could have saved you a trip downstairs."

"Oh, I didn't mind." Her voice sounded from right behind him.

He turned around to find her standing in the bedroom doorway. She smiled suggestively. "Has anyone ever told you how good you look in a tool belt, Will? So strong and"—she gave what sounded like a breathless sigh—"so commanding." She came up to him and ran one plump hand down the front of his chest as her tongue darted out to moisten her lips.

From deep within the mirror, Will heard the distinct

sound of a chuckle and knew the genie was laughing at him. His wish had backfired again.

Will wondered how he might reverse the spell; wondered if it was even possible. On the other hand, seeing the willing look on Tiffany's face made him realize just how long it had been since he'd last had sex.

He let his gaze travel over her plus-sized figure and decided things could be worse. It could have been eighty-year-old Edna Lawrence in 5-B who came looking for him.

"You sure are looking good today, Tiffany. Why don't you and I go back to your place?" he said, ushering her out of his apartment. "I've got just the thing to unplug your pipes."

It was noon when Mai took a cab back to the apartment building with Jenna and Nick. They'd gone to Sarah's school and walked around campus. While Nick had checked for any lingering signs of Sarah's residual energy, Mai and Jenna had questioned as many of Sarah's classmates as Jenna could find. The only thing they'd discovered was that Sarah hadn't been seen around campus since her last class the day before.

"I'm sorry I couldn't be more help," Nick apologized.

"No, I appreciate everything you've done," Jenna said. "Both of you. I guess knowing where she isn't does help some."

"There was nothing in the spiritual plane of the apartment to suggest a struggle," Nick continued. "I didn't pick up her pattern in Will's apartment in that minute or so I took to scan it. The patterns on campus are days old. Everything points to Sarah leaving of her own volition. Maybe she just needed a little time to herself and will return home when she's ready."

"I hope so," Jenna said, clearly unconvinced.

"She seemed burned out on studying," Mai offered.

"Maybe she went to see a movie . . . ?" *and ran into trouble.* Mai sighed. "We could call the local hospitals again?"

They'd already called them once, earlier that morning, and left their name and number in case a woman matching Sarah's description was brought in.

Jenna didn't respond and the three rode the rest of the way lost in their own thoughts.

"I'll come by later—for dinner," Nick told Mai as she followed Jenna out of the cab. She'd forgotten that she'd promised him dinner, but apparently he hadn't. She tried to ignore the way her heart jumped at the prospect of seeing him again.

"Seven o'clock," she told him, wondering what in the world she'd cook. She watched the cab drive away and then followed Jenna inside. Fortunately, the lobby was empty, which was a big relief. The last thing Mai wanted to do was run into Will.

Neither woman spoke much on the elevator ride up to the fourteenth floor and a few minutes later, Mai was waiting anxiously as Jenna unlocked her door.

"Sarah? Are you here?" Jenna shouted, hurrying inside. Mai followed more slowly.

The apartment was utterly silent.

Mai waited in the front room while Jenna quickly searched each room. "I'm so sorry," Mai said when it was obvious Sarah wasn't there. "Maybe we should try calling the police again?"

Jenna only shook her head. "They said they'd call if there was any news." She pointed to the answering machine, which showed no new messages with a bright, flashing "0." "It's making me crazy to wait. I need something to take my mind off worrying about her all the time," Jenna said. "Maybe I should go to the office."

Mai understood. "Call me if you need anything."

She left and went back to her place, thinking that Jenna's

idea of staying busy was a good one. She still needed to track down Lenny if she wanted to finish her article. Getting a message to him wasn't going to be easy, though. She wasn't even sure if he was still in town.

For the next two hours, she made calls to every place she thought Lenny might be. Always in the back of her mind was the worry of how she was going to tell him she'd lost his information. He'd risked a lot to give it to her and she had either misplaced her notes during her worst hallucination yet, or the information had been stolen from her pocket by an invisible attacker after he'd beaten her nearly senseless with meaty fists that left no bruises.

Yeah—she was going to get a lot of understanding on this one.

By six that evening, she was tired, frustrated and more than a little concerned. After exhausting all possible leads on Lenny, she'd done a final search of her apartment for her notes—and come up empty-handed.

Wondering if Jenna had heard from Sarah, she went to check. When Jenna didn't answer her door, Mai assumed she was still at work.

Just then, Mai's stomach growled and, returning to her place, she wondered if Nick had been serious about coming back for dinner. If he had, he was going to be disappointed because a quick check in the pantry showed her ill prepared to entertain. Pulling open the refrigerator door, she speculated on her culinary ability to turn leftovers into a fancy meal. Not likely.

"Maaaiiii."

Mai cocked her head to one side and listened. Had she heard her name? Thinking someone was at the door, she went to check. There was no one there.

Strange, she thought.

"Maaaiiii."

Mai whirled around, her gaze darting about the room.

"Who's there?" She felt foolish talking to an empty room but there had definitely been a noise coming from inside her apartment.

"Maaiii."

Pulse racing, she clutched the lightning bolt Darius had given her. What was going on? Where was the voice coming from? Was this another hallucination?

She pressed her hands against her head in frustration. "There's no noise. It's not real."

"Maaaiiii."

"No!" she shouted, her voice sounding especially loud in the otherwise quiet of the room.

A flicker of light flashed across the mirror, catching her eye. She moved closer to get a better look and saw that the glass was turning cloudy, like a curtain of mist was falling behind it.

Every fiber in her tensed, but she couldn't look away. The swirling mist grew thicker, drawing her close enough to see that something lay just beyond the mist.

Pale and ghostly with dark vacuous eyes, a face appeared.

"Maaaiiii."

CHAPTER NINE

Mai's heart slammed against her chest as adrenaline shot through her. She stumbled back from the mirror, unable to take her eyes from it. The face was still there. She needed someone else to see it. The idea motivated her and she hurried to the door. Before it disappeared, she needed a witness to prove she wasn't losing her mind.

Pulling open the apartment door, she cast another nervous glance at the mirror, but she could only see the side of the frame from this angle. Darting down the hallway, she knocked on Jenna's door. There was still no answer.

She hurried to the elevator and punched the down button. She'd drag someone up from the lobby if she had to. She looked back at her apartment, not even wanting to think about what could be happening inside. When the elevator arrived, she didn't even wait for the doors to fully open before she rushed through them, slamming into a hard body. Hands grabbed her and she screamed.

"Hey, it's just me. Are you all right?"

The familiar voice slowly registered and she stopped struggling. "Will?"

The super smiled down at her. "You okay? You seem upset."

Will! He could be her witness. Clutching his arm, she pulled him out of the elevator, her personal dislike for him forgotten for the moment. "Hurry. There's something in my apartment—I need you to see it."

"It'd better not be a mouse or a roach. I just had the place exterminated."

"No, it was a face. Or a ghost. Or something."

She dragged him into her apartment and over to stand in front of the mirror and pointed.

"I don't see anything," he said.

"No. There was a face." She turned to stare at the mirror, which had returned to normal.

"Where?"

"In the mirror." She dropped her head and stared at the floor, feeling utterly dejected. Why was she even surprised?

"Oh, sure. I see it now."

"You do?" She hardly dared to hope.

"Sure. It's right there." He pointed to his own reflection and smiled, leaving Mai to feel even worse than she had a moment before

"It was there," she said, mostly to herself. "A face. And the mist. And the voice. It was . . ." She stopped talking because Will was staring at her like she was crazy. Maybe he was right.

She rubbed her temples hoping to ease the ache building in her head. "I know I saw something," she muttered under her breath.

"I believe you." He put an arm around her shoulder. "And I can see that it frightened you, but you're safe now." She wasn't exactly feeling reassured and he must have sensed it. "Maybe I should stay with you for a while."

Great, she thought. Let Will comfort her? Had hell frozen over? "Thanks, Will." She eased out from under his arm. "I think I'll be okay."

"Are you sure? Because I don't mind staying—all night if necessary."

"It won't be," a deep voice said from the doorway.

Mai turned at the sound and saw Nick standing there, so big and tall he practically filled the doorway. Her sense of relief at seeing him surprised her.

"What's going on?" he demanded, coming forward to stand beside her. She moved closer to him without even thinking about it. He was a tower of strength and she was selfish enough to want to lean on him because she had no one else. "Tell me what happened," he said softly. "Is it Sarah?"

"No, not that." She noticed the woodsy scent of his aftershave and breathed it in, immediately feeling better. "I thought I saw something in the mirror." It sounded absurd now.

"I'll take the mirror off the wall for you—store it downstairs," Will offered.

Mai gave the idea serious, if brief, consideration. She had to learn to control her hallucinations, and removing the mirror wasn't going to help her accomplish that. "No. That's okay." She took another breath and tried to commit Nick's scent to memory. "I'm all right. Thanks."

"Are you sure?" Nick asked, finding her expression so forlorn he had to fight the urge to pull her into his arms. But he wasn't really her boyfriend—he was just pretending to be. He wondered who believed the lie more at the moment—Will or himself. He was afraid he knew the answer.

He walked over to the mirror and examined it. "What exactly did you see?"

She hesitated, and he wasn't sure why. "It sort of got cloudy and then—I thought I saw a face."

She looked like she expected him to laugh, or tell her she was imagining things, but he'd seen stranger things than disembodied heads—though not recently. And he wasn't seeing any now, either. "Just to be clear, it's not there now, right?"

She glared at him. "No. It's not there now." Her frosty tone held a definite bite.

He held up his hands in a placating gesture. "I just wanted to be sure we're all on the same page." He went over to the mirror and searched it thoroughly, viewing it from all angles, tapping the surfaces front and back. "I'm sorry, Mai. It looks like a plain old mirror." He turned to Will. "Did you see the face, too?"

Will gave Mai an apologetic look. "No."

"I know what I saw, Nick, whether you believe me or not," Mai said.

"I believe you," he said sincerely. He held her gaze as she searched his, perhaps trying to decide if he was being straight with her. He was.

Aware of Will watching them, Nick started feeling that three was definitely a crowd. He turned to the man and held out his hand. "Thanks for being here. We won't keep you. I'm sure you have other things to do."

Will, apparently, wasn't leaving without making one last effort. "I can stick around if you want me to," he told Mai.

She shook her head. "Thanks, but I'll be fine now that Nick's here."

The primal beast inside Nick purred at her choice of words and he had to work hard not to gloat openly as he crossed to the open doorway and waited for Will to leave.

"Call if you need me," Will offered. "I can be here at a moment's notice—anytime, day or night." This last was said with a defiant glare at Nick, who might have shut the door a bit too quickly after Will stepped through.

When he turned back around, he found Mai watching him. He moved to her and lightly rubbed her upper arms with his hands, acutely aware that she didn't pull away. "There are any number of explanations for what you saw. It could have been a trick of the light, reflecting your face back to you. Or the TV."

"It wasn't on," she replied dryly.

"I don't suppose you have any sprites or pixies living in the building? It'd be just their kind of prank to make you think your mirror is haunted."

"I haven't met any of my neighbors other than Jenna and Sarah, but I suppose there could be sprites in the building. Pixies wouldn't come to the city."

"True." He waited a heartbeat before continuing. "There's another possibility," he ventured. "It could be legitimately haunted."

"The building's not that old."

"Doesn't matter. There are so many displaced spirits in the city looking to anchor themselves someplace. One of them might have anchored themselves to your mirror."

She studied the mirror, a frown on her face. "I suppose . . ."

"Tell you what. If you want, I'll have a friend of mine come over and do a sweep of the place. When he's done, he'll put wards on your apartment to keep the spirits out."

She sighed. "Thanks. I'll think about it."

"Whatever you want to do." He glanced at his watch. "What do you say we get out of here? I'll take you to dinner."

She frowned. "I thought I was supposed to treat you."

He looked at the bare table and then glanced into the kitchen, where there was obviously nothing cooking. When he turned back to her, she looked embarrassed— and tired. "If you'd rather, I could take a rain check?"

He saw the way her gaze flickered to the mirror and knew that despite the way she was acting, she was still on edge. Before she could respond, he countered with another suggestion. "Or we can order delivery and you can treat me to dinner some other time. Tonight will be my treat."

"Really?" The hopeful note in her voice made him glad he'd suggested it.

"Absolutely. I noticed an Anthony's on my way over here. I think they deliver."

Her eyes lit up. "That sounds good."

Smiling, he pulled out his cell phone and tapped in a number. Minutes later, he'd placed their order, charging it to his credit card. After he put his phone away, he noticed that Mai was frowning at the mirror.

"There's an explanation," he assured her. "We'll find it."

Her eyes were shadowed when she finally tore her gaze away long enough to look at him. "What if the explanation is that I'm losing my mind?"

"It's not."

"How can you be so sure?"

"Because I know people."

She gave a ladylike snort of disgust. "Please, you know people. At your office, you thought I was a stripper."

He smiled, remembering the encounter. "In my defense, you *were* dressed the part, what with the short skirt and tight blouse."

"You shouldn't judge a woman by the clothes she wears."

He smiled. "If you'll recall, I was perfectly willing to judge you without clothes."

A small smile touched her lips. "Thank you."

Now he was confused. "For what? Wanting to see you out of your clothes?"

She rolled her eyes. "No, for making me laugh and staying for dinner. And just for being here."

"You're welcome."

"If you don't mind, I think I'll go slip into something

less comfortable than these ugly sweats," she said. "And don't go reading anything into it, okay?"

"I promise. I won't even be thinking about you—stripping off your clothes, standing naked just a few feet away. No ma'am. No sexual thoughts here." He let his gaze travel over her body, marveling that even in her sweats, he found her appealing.

She gave him a mock scowl and hurried down the hall. When he heard the door close, Nick projected himself into the spiritual realm. Slowly, he moved about the room, picking up residual traces and identifying as many as he could. Mai's green energy field was the strongest, obviously, and Will's orange energy pattern was still present.

He continued around the room, stopping in front of the mirror for a long time. There was an energy pattern here that he didn't recognize and yet felt vaguely familiar. Like something he'd encountered before—if he could only remember when or where.

At that moment, the door buzzer sounded. Thinking it was the deliveryman with their food, Nick returned to his body and went to answer it.

"Yes?" he asked, speaking into the intercom.

"Delivery," came the curt response.

"Come on up. Number 14-B." He pressed the button that would unlock the building's main door.

"Food's here," Nick told Mai a few minutes later when she came out of her bedroom.

"Did you buzz him in?" She'd changed from the baggy, oversized sweats to leggings and an oversized tailored shirt. If he'd thought she looked good before, now she looked even more attractive. The outfit accentuated both her petite stature and her generous curves. Plus, she'd brushed her hair until it hung in twin silken curtains about her face.

"Buzzed in and on his way up," Nick replied, trying not to stare.

"Wait a minute." She stopped and put her hand on her hips. "How did you get in here today? I don't remember buzzing you in. And for that matter, how'd you get in that first morning?"

He'd wondered when she'd ask. "I have my ways." A knock sounded on the door and leaving her to wonder how he'd done it, he went to answer it.

Taking the bag of food from the deliveryman, he tipped him and then carried the bag to the kitchen counter. As Mai went to carry plates to the table, he reached into the bag to lift out the containers.

As he went to set the first one down, the lid came undone and the bottom fell open. He automatically leaned forward to block the container from falling to the floor and in the process, got hot tomato sauce splatter across his shirt and jeans. "Damn." It burned. When he jumped back in surprise, he saw that sauce had splattered over the counter and floor.

"You okay?" Mai asked, hurrying over to him.

"Small accident," he admitted, trying to keep the steaming hot fabric away from his body. "Mind if I use your bathroom?"

"Of course not." She pointed to a door down the hall. "You go wash up while I take care of this."

"Thanks."

As soon as he stepped into the bathroom, he stripped off his shirt and held the soiled section under the water, cleaning it as best he could. Then he wiped off his jeans and washed his stomach, chest and arms. When he finished, he looked around for something to dry himself with. Opening the bathroom door, he stuck out his head. "Do you have a towel I can use?"

"Oh, sorry. I just washed them. They're in the bedroom." Mai washed her hands to get rid of the sticky sauce and dried them with a paper towel. Then she hurried down the hall, images filling her head of Nick standing with soap in his eyes patiently waiting for her. When she reached the bathroom, however, the door stood open and Nick was gone. The hallway was too short for her to have missed him, which left only one other place he could be.

Moving toward her bedroom, she tried to remember if she'd picked her dirty clothes up off the carpet. "Did you find what you needed—oh."

Mai's breath caught in her throat and she couldn't take her gaze off him. He wasn't wearing a shirt and from where she stood, with his tanned bare chest and bulging biceps, he was male perfection. A little thrill of awareness shot through her.

"I found one," he said, looking up from the towel after wiping his face. He seemed amused at her discomfort and she thought he made an extra show of draping the towel around the back of his neck as he faced her. Her gaze wandered across the flat planes of his chest before following the washboard abs down to the waistband of his still-wet jeans.

She forced herself to focus on his hands. That was a mistake because she'd always had a thing for hands and his were large, strong, capable-looking hands; hands used to hard work. She found herself imagining how those rough palms would feel against her arms, her neck—her breasts. An invisible shudder ran through her.

She needed to get a grip. It wasn't like she'd never been with a man before. She'd even been with good-looking men before. Ricco, with his refined features, was possibly the most beautiful man she'd ever laid eyes on, but Nick was handsome in that primal, rugged way that had her thinking of cowboys and Western romance novels.

He came toward her and Mai became enthralled with

the way his body moved. When he stopped, he was standing close enough that she could have traced the outline of his muscles with her fingertip—or better yet, the tip of her tongue. Yes, she definitely wanted to explore the contours of his six-pack abs, run her fingers across the breadth of his wide shoulders, down his arms . . .

He'd let go of the towel and now tucked his thumbs into the belt loops of his jeans, where his fingers drew her attention to the straining fabric in front. This was a man who had something to offer a woman.

"Do you see how—hard—it is?"

She gasped, heat flooding her face as her gaze ricocheted up to his face. "I beg your pardon?"

"Not to think of sex when the person in front of you is half undressed."

"I don't . . . I mean, I'm not . . ." Words failed her; she couldn't think straight.

He seemed to know exactly what he was doing to her, because he bent his head until his lips were inches from her ear. When he spoke, his moist, warm breath brushed along the side of her neck. "Let's eat," he whispered slowly, uttering each word as if it was a caress.

Her eyelids fluttered closed as sensations swept over her. She became conscious of Nick's soft chuckle and had to force her eyes open again. She was alone. And mortified. The vow she'd made to give up casual sex had some definite downsides.

Then she remembered the last stranger she'd brought home for sex. It had been Tain, one of Darius' Immortal brothers, back when he was evil. The postcoital activities had involved hitting her with a blast of energy that sent her flying across her living room and almost killed her. The memory hit her like a cold shower.

She walked back into the kitchen with a practiced smile

on her face. Nick had his shirt on and was in the process of prying the lids off the food containers.

"What can I get you to drink?" she asked. "Water? Soda? Tea?" *Me? Stop it*, she thought.

"Water's great."

She filled the glasses with ice and water before carrying them to the table. Everything was ready, so they took their seats and began to eat. The lasagna they'd ordered was especially good and she suddenly realized how hungry she was. Every now and then as they ate, Mai cast a quick look at the mirror. It was not a good sign when the thought of having ghosts was almost reassuring. It was better than the alternative, which in this case would be that she was hallucinating—again.

She was about halfway through with her meal when she looked up to find Nick watching her. After a bit, she grew uncomfortable and tried to fill the silence. "Thank you again for coming over this morning to help us look for Sarah. That's more than the police were willing to do." She sighed. "It's just so frustrating, you know? It's like she's vanished into thin air. Of course, I only just met her, so maybe she does this a lot."

"If that's the case, it's likely we won't find her until she wants to be found."

"True," Mai agreed, trying to put it from her mind. It was the man in front of her who really interested her. "So, you run a survival training program in addition to the bodyguard work? That sounds interesting. Is it hard-core training for the military or do you teach team-building courses to overweight executives?"

He smiled at her. "A little of both."

"Is there a lot of demand for that kind of training?"

"Not when I first started the business. Back then, most of my clients were military."

"You train year-round?"

"For the military, we do. I'm afraid the corporate types wouldn't make it through a winter session, so we only offer spring and summer courses for them."

Mai got an instant image of men and women dressed in camo-pattern business suits hiking up a snow-covered hill. She shook her head to clear it. "So, what's the bodyguard work like?" Images of Kevin Costner and Whitney Houston sprang to mind. "Have you ever protected anyone famous?"

He laughed. "You mean like Brad Pitt or Jennifer Aniston?"

She felt a tingle of excitement at the thought that he might have been Brad Pitt's bodyguard.

"Sorry to disappoint you, but no. My clients tend to be politicians."

"Have you ever worked with Bill Preston?"

"The mayoral candidate?" He frowned. "No. Why do you ask?"

"No reason in particular," she said, being evasive.

He obviously wasn't going to let her off that easily. "Please don't tell me you're doing a story on Preston."

"No, of course not."

He scowled at her. "You're a bad liar. What kind of story?"

"I'd rather not say if you don't mind. I'm still working on it."

"Just the fact that you're not telling me lets me know this is some kind of exposé, am I right?" She refused to answer him, so he went on. "Be careful, Mai. Some of those politicians with skeletons in their closet are dangerous. You don't want to be part of the body count."

"Are you speaking figuratively?"

"Not necessarily."

"I'll be careful," Mai promised, not sure what else to say. Fortunately, the phone chose that moment to ring.

"Are you going to get that?" Nick asked.

"No. It's probably just a solicitor."

They fell into an awkward silence as they listened to the machine pick up the call. Mai listened to her own voice tell the caller she couldn't come to the phone, followed by the tone.

"Yeah, it's me," Lenny's voice said. "I'm not calling again. You want to talk? Meet me tonight at the Obelisk in Central Park. It's nine o'clock now. I'll be there for the next hour and then I'm leaving town—forever."

Mai glanced at her watch. With traffic, it would take her twenty minutes to get to Central Park if she took a cab. At least she knew exactly where in the park to go once she got there. Only one thing was keeping her from leaving. "I've got to go," she told Nick.

He stared at her, aghast, his food only half finished. "You're kidding? What about our dinner?"

"I'm done, but you can stay and finish. Just please lock the door when you leave."

"Please tell me that you're not planning to go to Central Park at night."

She rolled her eyes. "Of course I am."

He shook his head. "I'll go with you."

"No, thanks. I'm a big girl. I can take care of myself."

He sighed. "I'm not going to talk you out of this, am I?"

"No. This is too important."

"Okay." He set his fork on the edge of the plate and wiped his mouth. "I guess I'll leave so you can get out of here. I enjoyed dinner." He pushed away from the table and stood.

"Thanks for coming over," Mai said, feeling guilty to be

rushing him out the door after everything he'd done for her.

"Glad I could help." He gestured down her hallway. "Do you mind if I use your bathroom one last time?"

She waved him on. "Help yourself."

She followed him down the hall, turning into her room as he shut the bathroom door behind him. She shut her bedroom door and quickly changed clothes, wanting to wear something warmer and less likely to attract notice than what she currently had on. She was still trying to decide between two shirts when she heard the bathroom door open.

"I'm going now," Nick hollered to her. "Don't bother showing me out. I'll call you later—and be careful."

He was gone before she could even say good-bye. His abruptness struck her as odd, but she couldn't afford to think about it. Instead, she shoved money into her pocket, grabbed her credit card and keys and left.

In the end, she decided taking the subway would be quicker than a cab. On the ride to the park, she knew she should have been preparing her questions for Lenny, but she couldn't get thoughts of Nick out of her head. When the man wasn't irritating her, she actually liked him. And there was definitely a physical attraction between them. Anytime he was near, she felt her body come alive. That worried her because if he ever wanted to do more than steal a kiss here and there, she didn't think she'd put up much resistance. Then, when he got tired of her and moved on, she'd be a worse emotional wreck than she already was. Psychotic *and* heartbroken—what a great combination.

Mai was still in a bit of a daze as she climbed the steps out of the subway. The Upper East Side was always busy, so even though it was dark, she still felt perfectly safe. She slipped into a park entrance and began quickly making her way toward the secluded bower behind the Met that housed the Obelisk. The farther into the park she walked, the fewer people she encountered. And the looming museum ahead did nothing to calm her nerves. Just as she rounded the last curve, she stopped dead in her tracks.

The walkway sloped down and at the very bottom, Lenny lay on the ground, blood pooling beneath his body. Hovering over him, a figure searched Lenny's pockets.

A small gasp escaped Mai's lips and the figure looked up. Their gazes met over the distance and Mai found herself looking into her own shocked expression.

CHAPTER TEN

Time stood still as Mai stared at—herself? This couldn't be right? Was it another hallucination?

A ringing started in her ears and tiny tremors shook her body. What was wrong with her that she would have visions about killing a man? What kind of person was she?

An unstable one, she thought. One who could no longer tell the difference between reality and illusion. Unlike with the mirror, she couldn't blame this on ghosts.

A new sound penetrated the ringing in her ears. It was a sharp staccato accompanied by a bite at her ankles. The ground seemed so far away. With a sense of detachment, she watched a tiny chunk of sidewalk break away in a puff of dust inches from her foot.

A flash of movement in front of her caught her attention and she looked up to see the figure racing toward her, yelling something, though the words were incomprehensible. Mai didn't move, half expecting the image to vanish before it reached her and half hoping it wouldn't.

Between one breath and the next, everything returned to normal speed.

"Run!"

With her double almost to her, Mai heard the ping of

something hard hitting the sidewalk and finally realized what it was—a bullet. There was another burst of dust and when Mai looked down, more of the sidewalk was gouged out.

Someone was shooting at her!

Before she could react, her double caught up to her. Grabbing her arm with what felt like a real flesh-and-blood hand, her double spun her around and shoved. "Run."

Mai didn't need any encouragement. Maybe if she ran hard enough, fast enough, she could escape this nightmare.

The path curved and Mai raced around it, the other woman on her heels. Up ahead, the public restroom came into view. Mai's double steered her to the far side, where they stopped long enough to catch their breath.

"Are you all right?" her double asked, running her gaze over Mai like she was searching for injuries.

Don't answer, Mai cautioned herself. *Don't give in to the hallucination.* Images of padded cells and straitjackets flashed through her head and a wave of dizziness washed over her. She must have swayed a little on her feet because her double reached out and grabbed her by both arms, a look of alarm in her eyes. "Damn it, Mai. Answer me. Are you hurt?"

"I'm fine," Mai said between gritted teeth. "Most likely insane, but I'm not hurt."

The pressure on her arms eased as her double leaned back against the wall again. "Keep your voice down," she whispered. "And you're not crazy."

"No?" Mai hissed back. "Listen to me. I've taken talking to myself to a whole new level. I think that qualifies as crazy. At least my visions are getting better. Those bullets seemed almost real."

Mai's double winced. "The bullets *were* real, which is why we need to get you out of here."

The shadows in the areas of the park where the lights didn't reach were dark and ominous. Anyone could be hiding there. The last thing she wanted to do was step away from the protection of the building, out into the open. "I'm good right here, thanks," she whispered.

"No, we can't stay here."

"I can't believe I'm standing here arguing with myself."

"Quiet," her double cautioned her again, turning to place her finger over Mai's lips when her voice got louder. "You're not arguing with yourself, you're arguing with me."

Mai arched an eyebrow at the woman. "Then who the hell are you?" she whispered around the finger.

"Nick."

"Nick? *My* Nick?" The words were automatic and she saw the woman smile ever so slightly.

"Yeah. *Your* Nick."

Mai ignored the way he stressed the word "your." "Prove it."

"Mai, we don't have time for this."

Mai crossed her arms over her chest and continued to stare at her double, who quietly cursed under her breath.

"Fine. My name is Nick Blackhawk. I came over for dinner tonight, a dinner which, by the way, you were supposed to treat me to. Instead, I ordered Anthony's, which ended up all over my shirt."

"Anyone could have known that." It was his turn to arch an eyebrow and she capitulated. "Okay, fine. You're Nick. Why do you look like me? How is that even possible? And where'd you get those clothes?" He was wearing a T-shirt and pair of jeans that looked suspiciously familiar. The shoes, she finally noticed, were definitely his own.

"I stole them from your bathroom before I left, okay? As for why I look like you, I'll explain that later," she—he—promised.

Son of a . . . "That was my favorite outfit," she lamented.

"I'll buy you a new one, okay? But first, can we worry

about getting back to your place? After I take a look around."

Nick closed his—her—eyes and grew still. The air around him shimmered like waves of heat coming off the sidewalk in summer. Mai had seen this once before, back in Jenna's apartment when Nick's spirit had left his body. If Mai had had any lingering doubts that it was him, they were gone now.

A minute passed and then another. Mai cast a nervous glance around. How long did it take to search the area?

"Oh," she gasped, seeing her double's eyes pop open again. "You're back. Well?"

"All clear. Let's go."

Mai looked back in the direction of the Obelisk. "What about Lenny? Shouldn't we call an ambulance?"

"They can't help him now." He grabbed Mai's hand, but she pulled back, refusing to move. "Shouldn't you . . . you know?" She waved her hand to encompass his entire appearance. "Change back?"

"Can't. I'm bigger than you. If I change here, these clothes will rip and I'll be nude. Or rather, you'll be nude." He drew in a raspy breath. "In any event, we'll attract too much attention. And I'm not wasting energy assuming another appearance because this one bothers you." He pushed away from the wall, leaving two ugly red stains behind.

"Oh my God. You're hurt." Mai held him in place so she could look at his back, which of course looked like her own. The T-shirt he wore had two small holes and was soaked in blood. "Why didn't you tell me?"

"I'll be all right."

Fortunately no one followed them, and after leaving the park they were able to get a cab right away. Giving them only a curious look and a disinterested shrug, the driver ignored them while Mai helped Nick into the backseat.

They rode in silence, and after what seemed like forever, the cab finally stopped in front of her building.

"We're here," she told Nick. He opened his eyes and let her help him out. His face was pale and she worried that he might be on the verge of passing out. If he did, she wasn't sure how she'd get him back to her apartment.

Standing at the front of the building, holding on to Nick's arm, she took a second to close her eyes. If her magic would just work this once . . .

She went through the steps slowly, as she did when she had first learned to use her magic. Center herself and focus. First came the prickling of magic along her scalp, like the wind blowing through her hair. The smells of the forest came next, reminding her that no matter where she lived, she was a creature of the woods. Power coursed down her arms and legs, building to a peak, and then as it broke over her, she willed herself and Nick to her living room, fourteen stories above.

Cracking open her eyes, she saw the building's main door still in front of her. She'd been so sure it would work this time. That it hadn't left her feeling sick.

The weight of Nick's stare had her looking up into her own face, where she saw the concern reflected in his eyes.

"Everything okay?" he asked.

"Yeah," she muttered, quickly keying in her access code so they could go inside.

The trek to the elevators seemed to take an inordinately long time and pressing the call button, Mai prayed that the elevator arrived before they ran into anyone—specifically, Will.

They'd been lucky up to this point and she thought their luck might have run out when she heard Will's distinctive, off-key whistling coming from the stairwell. Seconds before the lobby door opened, the elevator arrived.

Mai hustled Nick inside and pushed the button for her floor hoping the doors would close quickly.

"Mai?"

She heard Will calling through the closing doors and willed them to close faster. She didn't breathe easier until the car was moving.

As she stepped out of the elevator minutes later, the distance down the hall to her apartment seemed impossibly long. "Hang in there, Nick."

"I'm fine."

She heard the pain in his voice.

When they reached her apartment, she propped him against the wall while she searched her purse for her keys. Soon, she had the door unlocked and was helping Nick across the threshold.

"We should see to those wounds now." She steered him toward the bathroom. "And you should probably get out of those clothes."

He nodded, but when he reached for the hem of the shirt, Mai saw him wince. "Better let me help," she said, reaching into the bathroom drawer to pull out a pair of hair shears. Starting at the bottom of the shirt, she cut it open, pulling it gently away from the skin as she worked.

It was disturbing to see herself looking so pale and bleeding from bullet wounds. It could have been her for real if Nick hadn't gotten there first—only she might not have been as lucky. She could be lying dead beside Lenny this very minute. That cold realization washed over her and the fear she hadn't felt earlier when she'd been numb with shock finally got a toehold on her.

Lenny was dead. And Nick had risked his life to save her. Because of her, because of her story.

"We really should go to the police," she said, feeling torn. It was the right thing to do, but if they did, then the police would want to know why Lenny was shot and soon her "big" story would be someone else's headline news. "I mean, someone killed Lenny and they tried to kill you."

"Actually, someone tried to kill *you*—they just didn't know they were shooting at me instead."

Now she felt really awful. "You took a bullet for me— I'm so sorry."

"Forget it," he said. "Hazards of the job—at least, lately."

"But I didn't hire you to be my bodyguard."

"Perks of dating someone in my line of business—the protection comes for free."

"I didn't know we were dating."

"Now you do."

She smiled. "I guess I do."

"Good, that's settled. Now, what do you say we get these bullets out? They're starting to hurt like a son of a bitch."

"Oh, sorry." She helped him pull off his shirt and tossed it aside. The two holes were glaring dark holes in his blood-covered back. "Are you sure we shouldn't take you to the hospital?" She found a clean washcloth and started wiping away the blood.

"If they'd hit anything important, I wouldn't be standing here now. I don't think the bullets are in too deep, so you shouldn't have any problems getting them out."

Her hand paused in midwipe. "What? No, I can't do that."

"Sure you can." He turned to face her and Mai found herself staring at a woman's bare breasts. Hers—more or less. He noticed her scrutiny and gestured to himself. "What do you think? Did I get it right?"

She cleared her throat, embarrassed. "It's not a perfect replica," she said. "But it's close enough."

"Well, I was working with limited data. Now, what were you saying about taking out the bullets?"

She swallowed and forced her gaze up to his. "I can't do it. I . . . faint at the sight of blood."

"Liar. If you did, you would have fainted back in the park. Now, could we get to work? Do you have any peroxide? Maybe some alcohol? Oh, and a pair of tweezers."

She found the tweezers in the drawer and set them on the counter. Then she searched through the cupboard under the sink and found the two bottles. "Here's peroxide." She held out the brown bottle. "And the rubbing alcohol." She held up the light plastic bottle.

He took the peroxide but gave her back the alcohol. "I was thinking more like Jim Beam, Jack Daniel's . . ."

She colored. "Oh. Right. To deaden the pain."

"Something like that."

"I'll be right back." She hurried into the kitchen and found a bottle of Jack Daniel's—a gift from Lexi before she moved to Ravenscroft. Taking a glass from the cabinet, she carried both back to the bathroom.

"Oh . . ." She came to a sudden halt at the sight of Nick, back in his normal form, looking very male and very naked standing in the center of her bathroom.

At her gasp, he reached out and grabbed a towel. "Sorry about that," he mumbled, wrapping it around his waist.

He didn't seem to notice the way she stared at him, and though she tried not to, she couldn't help it. There was just so much of him. The muscles of his chest and arm contracted and bulged as he took the bottle and glass from her.

She watched him pour the whiskey, enjoying the way he moved. In a single gulp, he drained the contents of his glass and then poured another. This time, he handed the glass to her. "Drink it," he ordered.

"Oh, no, thanks."

He pushed it toward her. "I insist." When she still refused to take it, he grabbed her hand and shoved the glass into it. Her hand was shaking so bad she would have dropped it if he hadn't cupped his hand around hers and held it steady. "Drink it, Mai," he said tenderly. "What you're feeling is natural after what you've just been through, but I really would like you to be as calm and relaxed as possible before you start digging around on my back."

Mai found it hard to resist this gentle side of him. She gazed into the eyes that regarded her so tenderly and for the first time in a very long while, she didn't feel so all alone. "You drink it. I'm fine." She held the glass out to him in hands that were now rock steady. It was a testament to how much pain he really was in when, instead of arguing, he took it from her and drank.

She watched the rise and fall of his Adam's apple with a fascination akin to a schoolgirl's crush and had to force herself to look away. "Is there a trick to this?" she asked, picking up the tweezers. "Other than dig around until I find the bullet and then extract it?"

"Less digging and more extraction would be good, but yeah. That's pretty much it."

The fatigue in his voice caused her to look at him without regard for his virility. This time, she noticed the pallor of his skin and when she placed her hand on his arm, his skin felt clammy. "Maybe you should lie down. You're not looking so good."

"I'll be fine as soon as we get this lead out of my body." He looked around. "There isn't enough room in here. How about we go into the kitchen? I can lie on the floor."

"Don't be ridiculous." She headed out of the bathroom and into her bedroom. He followed her, holding the towel around his waist. She went over to her bed and pulled off the comforter because she didn't want to get blood on it. The sheets she didn't care as much about.

"You'll be more comfortable here and neither of us will have to get down on the floor."

He smiled weakly. "Wish I'd known it was this easy to get into your bed. I'd have gotten shot days ago."

Mai ignored his teasing and waited for him to stretch out, facedown, on the bed.

"Looks like you did get shot not too long ago." She lightly touched the two irregular round scars where the skin was new and pink—one on his side and the other near his shoulder blade.

"Like I said, hazards of the job. I got those on my last case."

Mai angled the lamp beside the bed so it shone down on his back, giving her extra light to see by. "How long ago was that?"

"Last week."

Incredible. Wounds that new should have looked raw and angry. "How fast do you heal?"

"Fast enough that we don't want to leave those bullets in there much longer or you'll be cutting through new skin to reach them."

"Okay. Okay. I'm on it." She picked up the peroxide and poured it into the wounds. Immediately it bubbled and Nick sucked in a quick breath. "Sorry. Did that hurt?"

"Mai. No matter what you do from this point forward, it's going to hurt. So just get it over with."

"Okay. Here goes." Taking a deep breath, she inserted the tip of the tweezers into the first puckered wound and tried not to scrape the sides as she dug for the bullet.

"You know," Nick said, his voice slightly muffled by the pillow. "I was worried to tell you what I was because I thought it would upset you, but you seem to be handling it well."

"Oh, sure. I've known a few bodyguards in my time. It doesn't bother me."

"Cute."

She heard the smile in his voice. "Actually, my best

friend is a werewolf," she continued absently while she probed the wound for the bullet. "And I spent some time with a guy last year who could shift into a dragon, so . . . shape-shifters don't really bother me much."

"I'm not a shape-shifter."

"You're not?" She frowned, perplexed. "Then what are you?"

"I'm a chameleon."

"No way." Mai had heard of the beings, but had never met one before. "Being able to look like any living creature must come in handy."

"Guess it depends on the circumstances," he said dryly. "By the way, next time we're in a situation like that, you should leave."

"I thought that's what we were doing when we raced out of the park."

"I don't mean running. I mean teleporting."

Mai was glad his back was to her so he couldn't see how embarrassed she was. "I couldn't."

"Look, I appreciate you not wanting to leave me, but next time—"

"No. I mean I really couldn't—can't." She shrugged though he couldn't see her. "My magic's been a little off lately. It's a long story."

"I'm not going anywhere."

She debated what to tell him and in the end, opted for the truth. "About a year and a half ago, an ancient demon tried to destroy the world by killing off all the living magic. Do you remember hearing about it?"

"Sure. A group of witches discovered the problem and summoned the Immortals to deal with the demon. Everyone thought the Immortals were just a myth, so it was a big deal when they turned out to be real."

"Well, the Coven of Light witches and the Immortals didn't go up against the demon alone. There were a handful of others with them—vampires, shape-shifters, witches—and a wood nymph."

"You."

"Yeah. Me."

"Not exactly the normal company a wood nymph keeps."

"What's that supposed to mean?" Mai asked, not sure if she should be offended or not.

"Only that those other beings you listed are warriors and fighters by nature. Wood nymphs tend to be more fun-loving and carefree."

"Yeah. Well, I guess you're right because I'm the only one who came away from the experience with psychological problems. Except Tain, of course. He's one of the Immortal warriors. He was held by the ancient demon and tortured over the centuries until he didn't even really know which side he was on anymore.

"Of course, he seems to be better," she continued. "He's definitely fighting for the good guys now. In fact, I heard he recently got married."

"So the experience screwed up your magic?"

"Among other things." The tweezers hit something hard and Mai froze. "I think I found a bullet."

"Yeah," he groaned. "Felt like it."

"Sorry." She didn't like causing him more pain.

"It's about to hurt a hell of a lot worse. You have to get the bullet out and that's going to mean digging around until you can grab it." He sighed and she saw his hands grip the pillow and hold tight. "Might as well get it over with."

"Okay." She peered into the hole and wished the lighting was better. Looking around her room to see if she had a lamp she could angle over the bed, she spotted her mini book light.

It would do. Leaving it attached to the book, she laid the book on his back and angled the light so that it was shining directly into the wound. Then Mai leaned over it and looked into the hole.

To her immense relief, the bullet was visible and she set to work. It took several attempts before she succeeded and each one had Nick sucking in his breath.

Once she had the bullet out, she started on the second. This one was a little deeper than the first and a fresh wave of guilt hit her. It should have been her lying here, not him. He shouldn't even have been there.

"Can I ask you a question? Why'd you go to the park?"

Nick was silent for a second. "After I heard that phone call, I was afraid you might be headed into trouble. So I decided to go in first."

"When I first saw you, I thought you'd killed Lenny."

"And now?"

The image of that figure leaning over Lenny's body was still vivid in her mind.

"Damn it, Mai. Did you see a gun in my hand?"

"No, but you could have hidden it."

"True. I could have thrown it into the woods and then used telekinetics to fire the bullets at both of us as we were running. I think it was an especially brilliant move on my part to shoot myself in the back. But I couldn't fool you, could I? You were onto me the entire time. Damn, now I'm totally screwed."

"Fine," she grumbled. "You made your point."

"Did I? Good, then let me make one more. You need to be more careful. You could have been lying dead right there alongside what's his name."

"Lenny."

"Whatever. The point is, you've got to think before you walk into a situation like that."

"Do you think you could lecture me later? I mean, I'd hate for you to pass out from the pain when I stab you with these tweezers right in the middle of a good rant."

She knew her irritation was more with herself than him since she'd just had the same thought seconds before.

He fell silent and didn't say anything else until after she'd found and extracted the second bullet.

"They're both out," she announced when she was done. "I need to clean the wounds before I can bandage them."

"Do it," he grumbled into the pillow.

She poured the peroxide into each wound and watched it bubble up. She waited until the bubbles disappeared before repeating the process. Then she patted both wounds dry.

In her bathroom, she had antibiotic ointment and bandages. Returning her book light to the nightstand, she hurried to get them. Soon, she had the wounds clean, treated and bandaged. Feeling pleased with her work, she stopped to admire it and noticed how white the bandages appeared against Nick's smooth, tanned skin.

He still hadn't moved and she took a moment to appreciate how broad his shoulders were. The rest of his back was equally wide and muscled—and tapered to a waist that was lean but not too thin. Of course, she'd seen equally good-looking men at the vampire bars.

At that moment, Nick rolled onto his side and she took back her earlier thought about having seen equally good-looking men. She wasn't sure she'd ever seen anyone that looked this good to her.

She let her eyes linger on the planes of his chest. He was delectable and what she could do with—and to—that body!

"Take a picture, it'll last longer." The sound of Nick's tired voice had her gaze snapping up to see a lazy smile splashed across his face.

She hoped he couldn't see her blush. "I thought you were asleep."

"I am. I can tell because I only see such beautiful angels in my sleep." He smiled. "Thank you."

"I should be thanking you. You saved my life."

"My pleasure." He struggled to sit up.

"What are you doing?" Mai asked, hurrying to his side so she could push him back down. It didn't take much effort on her part. He was still weak.

"I should get out of here and leave you alone."

"I don't think so," she said more firmly, trying not to notice how the towel was slipping off. "Besides, you'll attract a lot of attention if you go now. You don't have any clothes to wear."

"Speaking of clothes," he said. "Check the pockets of those jeans I had on. That guy you were going to meet had something in his hand, a piece of paper. Right before you showed up, I grabbed it."

Maybe it was another copy of the information Lenny had given her before. If so, maybe she could make sure that Lenny's death counted for something.

"Thanks, I'll take a look. Can I get you anything?"

"No," he said, his voice fading. "I'll just rest here a minute."

Before the last word was out, he was sound asleep.

Mai left him there and went to the bathroom. The clothes he'd been wearing lay in a heap on the floor. She picked up the jeans and reached into each pocket until she found the paper Nick had mentioned. Dropping the jeans to the floor, she opened the note.

A sense of satisfaction filled her. Lenny had died trying to give her this list of dates and names. This time, she wouldn't let anything happen to it. She took it into the kitchen and laid it on the counter; then using her camera phone, she took several pictures of the names and dates. She checked the pictures to make sure she could see the writing well enough to read it and then e-mailed the photos to her e-mail box. Now it didn't matter what happened to the paper itself. She had several backup copies.

Refolding the paper, she put it and her phone back into her purse. Then, grabbing a garbage bag from under the sink, she returned to the bathroom. It didn't take her long to throw the clothes away and clean up the mess.

Then she went back into the bedroom to check on Nick. He seemed to be sleeping peacefully. Worried that he might get cold with no clothes on, she pulled her comforter over him, thinking how odd it was to have him in her bed.

Glancing at the clock, she saw that it was late. Tired and feeling grungy, she gave Nick another look to make sure he was sleeping peacefully and then went back into the bathroom to shower.

With all that was happening, it was hard not to think about the last time she'd gotten information from Lenny and she half worried that when she stepped out of the shower, there would be a message scrawled across the mirror.

She stood under the hot water until her skin started to wrinkle, then finished and got out. There were no words written on the mirror and Mai wasn't sure if Nick's being there had made a difference or not.

Drying quickly, she wrapped a towel around her body and went back into her bedroom for the clothes she'd forgotten to get earlier. She'd let him have her bed while she slept on the couch.

Nick had moved about on the bed and the comforter was now down around his waist. She debated pulling it back up, but decided against it. If he got cold, he could pull it up himself.

Bending over her dresser drawer, she dug through it for a nightgown that wasn't too suggestive. She thought about putting it on there. After all, Nick was completely out of it. It wasn't as if she were undressing in front of him. But no, she couldn't do it.

She was on her way out of the room when a groan from

the bed stopped her. Hurrying over to his side, she placed her hand lightly against his forehead. He felt warm, but she wouldn't have said he was feverish.

Eyes still closed, he mumbled something, but Mai couldn't make out the words. "Nick. Hush. Everything's all right."

"Mai?"

"I'm here, Nick." She sat on the edge of the bed and brushed the hair from his forehead, hoping to ease his troubles so he could sleep better.

His breathing grew steadier, but she didn't get up and leave. He was as handsome in sleep as he was awake, though some of his rakish charm had been replaced by a boyish innocence.

It was crazy to think like that, she scolded herself. Despite what he'd said earlier, they weren't really dating. One partial meal together did not a date make.

Deciding it was time for her to leave, she pushed off the bed, only to have Nick's hand reach out and grab her.

"Don't go," he whispered, pulling her down to him.

"Are you feeling okay?" she asked, getting worried.

He grumbled something incoherent and Mai realized he was more asleep than awake. She tried to ease her wrist from his grip.

"No. Stay." Before she realized what he intended, he pulled her onto the bed beside him and held her there. Trapped, she lay nestled in his arms, wondering what in the hell she should do.

If she was honest, she'd admit that she liked being there, her back to his front, her head nestled between him and the pillow and his arm covering her like a favorite warm blanket. She could stay like this all night, she thought.

Almost immediately, guilt hit her. This was wrong. She felt like she was taking advantage of him, but he felt so good and some part of him must have found comfort in her being there, she argued.

All right. She'd stay for a few minutes—maybe to the count of one hundred. Then, when he was sleeping soundly, she'd slip out and go to the couch.

One . . . two . . . three . . . four . . . five . . .

Her eyelids grew heavy and she let them close, still counting.

Fourteen . . . fifteen . . . sixteen . . . seven . . .

CHAPTER ELEVEN

Sarah sat in the vast darkness of the void into which she'd been pulled. Not far away, the creature that had kidnapped her stood by a portal talking to Will. Who would have thought the idiot super could be involved with the magical creature holding her?

"Are you crazy?" Will hissed. "What makes you think you can kidnap a girl and not get caught?"

"Who says I don't want to get caught?" the creature asked.

"And what do you think I'll be able to do for you then? I can't protect you."

"I don't expect you to," the creature said. "I want them to know I'm here."

"No," Will snapped. "It's too dangerous."

"For whom?" the creature asked. "For you, maybe?"

"I'm not the one who kidnapped the girl." There was a moment of silence before Will spoke again. "What are you planning to do with her?"

"I haven't decided."

"I won't let you hurt her. I wish you to release her—now!"

"No."

"Genie, I command you," Will shouted, crazed with rage. "Release the girl."

The genie chuckled. "You have no idea how tired I am of your pathetic demands. Make me handsome," he mocked. "Make me rich. Make me . . . lovable."

The genie's laughter echoed through the darkened hallways as Sarah scooted away unobserved.

This dimension reminded her of being in an old, decrepit house with no electricity. The hallways stretched on endlessly and were lined by doors that led to who knew where. Yellow wisps of smoke floated below the ceiling like ghosts, their eerie glow providing just enough light to see by. These, she had learned, were the remnants of unfulfilled wishes. Somewhere her own wish for freedom mingled with the others.

She'd lost all perception of time. She could have been gone minutes or days.

She wondered how her sister was doing. Would Jenna think she'd run away? Surely not. She'd never given Jenna any reason to believe she'd do that. But would she suspect foul play? Her heart sank. Even if she did, she couldn't know about the genie.

Sarah had moved far enough away now that Will's and the genie's voices were faint. Thinking it safe to stand, she glanced behind her to make sure her absence hadn't been noticed and continued down the hall, moving as quietly as she could.

The hallway branched before her. With no idea of how to escape, she chose passages at random hoping that one would eventually lead to freedom.

She ran until her lungs labored for air and she could run no more. Tears of frustration sprang to her eyes as she looked around. The section of hallway she was in now looked the same as the section she had just left. She could even hear the faint hum of male voices off in the distance.

Her desperate race to escape had led her nowhere.

Unwilling to give up, she opened one of the many doors. A light shone at the end of the room. She moved closer to it and found herself standing in front of a window.

Peering through the glass, she was reminded of a funhouse mirror. If she moved too much one way or the other, the image distorted. But if she held just so . . .

She could just make out the shapes of a couch and chairs. Off to the side, colored lights flickered. This looked like someone's living room, and the lights were coming from a television. Was someone watching a show? If so, maybe she could get their attention?

She looked around and spotted a pair of legs sticking out from behind a chair. She followed them up until she saw a young boy sitting on the floor, leaning back against the couch. He looked to be about ten or eleven.

She rapped on the glass to get his attention. She had to do it twice more before he looked around.

Encouraged, she rapped louder. This time, the boy jumped to his feet, gazing wildly about the room.

"Help!" Sarah shouted. "Please, help me."

"Mom!" The boy ran screaming from the room. When he reappeared, he was standing behind a woman who held a bat in her hand. They approached the end of the hallway slowly, then stopped to look around.

After a few minutes, the woman's gaze fell on the television. "Are you sure it wasn't the TV you heard?" Sarah heard the woman ask.

"No, Mom. I'm positive. It was a ghost."

"Well, I don't hear anything." She glanced at her watch. "We're late. Are you ready to go?"

"Yes, ma'am."

"Okay. Grab your stuff."

"But, Mom, what about the ghost?"

The woman looked around the room. "If the ghost

knows what's good for it, it'll be gone before we get back."
Then she smiled and with her free hand, ruffled his hair.

Sarah watched them disappear into the back and debated trying again to get their attention, but she couldn't
shake the image of the woman beating her with the bat
before she had a chance to explain. Not that Sarah blamed
the woman. In this day and age, it paid to be cautious. A
lesson Sarah wished she'd not had to learn the hard way.

Sarah backed away from the mirror, left that room and
walked to another door. Behind it, she found another
room with a window. It was another living room, but this
time it was empty.

Sarah went to the next room and found the same thing.
There was something familiar about all of these rooms
and it took her a minute to figure out what it was. They all
looked like hers. Not the decorations or the color of the
carpet, but the layout. Could it be that each of these win-
dows was looking into an apartment in *her* building?

She went into the next room and stood at the window,
peering into another living room. Just below the window,
she could make out a dining table. Of course. These win-
dows were the mirrors hanging on the walls behind the
tables.

Sarah felt a surge of hope. If she was right, then behind
one of these doors was a window looking into *her* apartment. If she could find it—and then, if Jenna was
home . . .

The thought of escape spurred her to race out the door
and start checking each room. It seemed to take forever,
and the hallways in this place all looked the same. After a
while, she didn't know which hallways and rooms she'd
explored and which she hadn't. And time was running out.
The genie would eventually notice she was gone and come
looking for her.

She pulled off a shoe and whacked its heel against the door. To her delight, the hard sole left a small dent. It wasn't the best solution, but it was the only one she had.

Now as she checked the rooms, she left a small indentation on the door before moving on to the next.

She got so used to looking into rooms she didn't recognize that when she finally hit one she did, it didn't register right away. She moved closer to the glass and stared at a familiar photograph on the bookcase facing her. An attractive woman with long black hair stood beside a handsome man with tattoos covering his arms and chest. Between them, they held an infant. She'd seen this picture before. These were Mai's friends—which meant this was Mai's apartment!

Unfortunately, Mai was nowhere to be seen. Sarah banged on the window but after a few minutes gave up. She was so close. With renewed hope, she quickly moved into the hall to find her own apartment, marking doors as she went.

Three rooms down, she found the window looking into her apartment. Sarah hardly dared believe her luck when she saw Jenna sitting at the table. She looked horrible, like she hadn't slept in days, and her eyes were red from crying.

Sarah rapped her knuckles against the window. "Jenna," she shouted.

Jenna's head snapped up. She'd heard. Sarah pounded on the glass again. "Jenna. Help me. I'm behind the mirror."

Jenna's gaze shot around the room, coming to stop on the mirror. "Sarah?" Jenna stood to face the mirror, her eyes wide in shock. "How?"

A noise from somewhere deep in the labyrinth of hallways told Sarah the genie had finally noticed she was gone. "Hurry, Jenna. He's coming."

"Who?"

"It's a genie. He pulled me through and I can't get out."

Resolve hardened the features of her sister's face as she raced into the kitchen. Sarah saw her pull a knife from the cutlery block and bring it back to the mirror. Her lips were moving and Sarah knew she was casting a spell. Jenna, who'd been born a witch, hadn't practiced witchcraft since she was a teenager and Sarah prayed her sister still knew enough to help her.

Sarah watched—and listened to the noise from the hallway grow louder. "Hurry," she pleaded with her sister.

Jenna raised the knife and drew it across her open palm. As blood welled up, she slapped her palm against the mirror. The glass that had been there dissolved and suddenly, Sarah could reach through.

"Jenna."

Her sister's eyes had taken on the white light of her magical power and Sarah knew Jenna was seeing through her inner sight.

"Hurry," Jenna gasped, then continued with her chanting.

Sarah threw her leg over the edge of the mirror. Jenna dropped the knife and with her bloodied hand still applied against the mirror frame, grabbed Sarah with the other and pulled.

As soon as Sarah touched her sister's hand, she felt Jenna's magic envelop her.

"You will not leave," the genie bellowed, grabbing her from behind. "You are mine."

"Jenna!" Sarah tried desperately to fight off the genie, but he was too strong. She felt herself being pulled back into the mirror. "No. No!" she screamed. If she didn't get out now, she never would.

Sarah felt Jenna's power falter as her attention was diverted from her spell. Then she was chanting again, faster, louder.

The genie began uttering words under his breath and

Sarah felt caught between two magical forces. The surge of living magic and the burn of death magic.

Suddenly Sarah was lifted bodily and sent crashing back into the darkened room of her prison. She landed hard, hitting her head against the floor.

Her vision filled with little white lights and an incessant ringing started in her ears. She was dizzy and her vision began to tunnel and fade. The last thing she heard was Jenna's scream. "Sarah!"

Nick was dreaming of her again.

They were lying together and he was running his hand along the curve of her hip and waist, reveling in the feel of her soft, smooth skin. He found the shape of a woman's body—of *her* body—glorious. He could stay this way forever and be content merely touching her.

But he was greedy tonight and wanted more. She was lying with her back to him, so he leaned forward to kiss the side of her neck, just below her ear. She leaned back into him and he sensed, more than saw, the smile touch her lips. She raised her arm and ran her fingers through the hair at the back of his head, then slowly guided him down so his next kiss touched her lips.

Even prepared as he was for the resulting explosion of need and desire, it still amazed him. He couldn't remember ever wanting to be with a woman this much.

He rolled her fully onto her back so he could gather her into his arms and deepen the kiss. He heard the small sound she made—a delicate moan—and knew she was as aroused as he.

"I love—" He stopped, horrified even in his dream at what he'd almost said. She waited for him to finish and he quickly collected his thoughts. "I love being with you." He bent to kiss her, to distract her. It was the truth, he loved being with her, but that hadn't been what he'd started to say.

"I love being with you, too," she sighed between kisses. She arched her body into his and he felt his body tense in anticipation. He wanted this. He wanted her.

Lowering his mouth to her breast, he tongued her nipple to a tight, stiff peak before pulling it into his mouth. He heard her breath quicken and smiled before doing the same to the other breast.

Her hands gripped his shoulders, squeezing tighter each time he pulled on her nipple, then relaxing their grip when he laved it with his tongue.

His own body was rigid with need, but he ignored it. He wasn't done loving her yet and knew the moment he took her, it would be over for him.

Sliding his hand between her legs, he slipped his finger between her folds. Her hot, slick wetness was waiting. Encouraged, he probed a little deeper and felt her muscles squeeze his finger.

"Yes," she gasped as he slipped another finger into her. She was tight and the scent of her arousal filled his senses. His need was now more than he could endure, so he withdrew his hand and positioned himself between her legs. He fit himself to her opening and entered her slowly, though it nearly killed him.

They'd made love before, but this time felt better than anything that had passed between them before. He wasn't sure what was different, wasn't sure he cared. He withdrew only to fill her again. She shuddered beneath him as her nails raked his back. The small pain from the scratches only stoked the flames of desire burning inside him.

He couldn't silence the groan torn from deep inside him. He was so close, but he didn't want it to end. Not before she found her release.

Then she cried out as her inner muscles tightened around him like a hand, gripping him. It drove him over the brink. With a primal roar, he spilled himself into her—

—and woke from the dream to find himself lying between Mai's thighs, his cock still throbbing deep inside her womb.

CHAPTER TWELVE

A thousand thoughts filled his head only to vanish when Mai's eyes flew open.

"Oh God," she moaned in the voice of someone in shock. "I can't believe that just happened."

He frowned, not sure how to interpret her reaction. He'd expected surprise. Hell, *he* was surprised. But the sex—what he could remember of it—had been great. To think it hadn't been for her was a bit deflating—in every sense of the word.

Sensing his best course of action was to give her space, he eased himself out and rolled to the side. He needn't have worried about small talk. As soon as he was off her, she shot out of the bed and raced for the bathroom.

He gave her a few minutes while he used his discarded towel from the night before to clean up. He still had no clothes to wear, so pulled the sheet off the bed and wrapped it around his waist. Then he went to the bathroom door and knocked.

"Mai. Are you okay?" There was no answer. "Mai. Open the door. We need to talk."

Silence.

"I'm sorry. I didn't mean for that to happen. I mean, it

was great, but I'm sorry to have, you know, caught you—caught us both," he quickly corrected, "by surprise." He shut his mouth before he made matters worse, but damn! It was hard to regret something that mind-blowing.

The silence from the bathroom continued and a new, horrifying thought occurred to him. "Mai—oh God. Please tell me I didn't force you. I'm sorry." He wanted to tell her he'd never do it, but what if that's exactly what he'd done? Just because he'd been asleep, it was no excuse. He dragged a hand down his face as his mind imagined how horrible it must have been for her. He had no idea what to do to make it better.

He heard the sound of the doorknob turning and then Mai walked out, dressed in the same outfit she'd worn the day before.

"You didn't force me," she announced, pushing past him to go back into the bedroom.

"Oh." Relief flooded through him, quickly followed by another fear. He went to the bedroom doorway and stood there, watching her pull the remaining sheets off the bed. "You weren't a virgin, were you?" He thought about the question and quickly dismissed it. "Of course you weren't." She'd stopped tugging on the sheets long enough to scowl at him. "You weren't, were you?"

"No." She quickly rolled the sheet into a wad and threw it to the floor with some force, glaring at him as she did.

Still feeling guilty and, not knowing exactly why she was upset with him, he walked over to her as she pulled extra linens from the chest of drawers.

"Stop, please," he begged her, taking hold of her arms and forcing her to look up at him. "We should talk about this."

"Why?"

Why? Caught off guard, he took a minute to answer. "Well . . . what if you get pregnant?" It was the first thing he thought of and he realized with a start that the idea of her carrying his child wasn't as terrifying as he would have thought. He tried to imagine Mai, her belly round and swollen with his child. A surge of protectiveness welled up inside, catching him unawares.

"I'm on the pill, so don't worry."

Her apathy was unsettling. "I wasn't worried. It's just that neither of us expected this to happen." He smiled. "Prayed. Hoped and dreamed, sure."

Her expression softened marginally, and her lips twitched in an effort to hide a smile. She shook her head and there was a trace of laughter in her voice when she spoke next. "And to think I was worried that taking two bullets in the back might have slowed you down."

Relief washed over him to hear her joke. "I told you last night, I heal quickly. So, how about dinner tonight?"

She frowned. "Dinner?"

"Yeah. You know. That meal you eat at the end of the day? Preferably joined by someone you're dating." He smiled. "Someone you might have even slept with?"

She rolled her eyes. "Look. I'm not mad at you for what happened. It was as much my fault as yours, but that doesn't mean we should have a repeat performance."

He gave her his best shocked look. "I would never suggest a repeat performance." He sounded indignant.

"You wouldn't?" She sounded dubious.

"Of course not. What kind of man do you think I am?"

"The male kind," she mumbled.

"Well, for the record, the next time we have sex, we'll be awake for the entire thing. Now, if you'll excuse me." Checking that the sheet was securely wrapped around his waist, he headed for the front door.

"Where are you going?"

"To the Dumpster out back where I was forced to hide my other clothes."

She cocked an eyebrow. "Dressed like that?"

He rubbed a hand across his bare chest, gratified to see her gaze follow the movement. "I'm sort of out of options, in terms of clothing."

"Wait here a second."

He ignored her order and followed her to the bedroom, where he found her rummaging in the corner of the closet. When she stood up, Nick was surprised to see her holding men's sweatpants and a T-shirt. "These might be a little snug, but maybe you can, you know, adjust your size. I think your shoes are still in the bathroom where you left them last night."

He held the pants up to his waist. They looked like they might actually fit, though they'd be a bit on the short side. The shirt was definitely too tight and he wasn't about to make himself look thin and scrawny just to make it work. "Whose are these?"

"They belong to a guy I used to date. He must have left them at my place the last time he stayed over, and, well, they got packed up with everything else when I moved. I found them when I unpacked."

"What guy?" Nick realized, too late, that he sounded like a jealous boyfriend.

"Ricco. He's a vampire."

"You used to date a vampire?" He wasn't sure what he'd expected her to say, but it sure as hell hadn't been that.

"Not just any vampire. The First Fang of the largest gang in town—and we're still close, so you might want to think twice before you make any snide comments."

He frowned. "I don't know if I approve of you dating a vampire." He hadn't realized he'd said it aloud until she replied.

"I don't know that I care what you think."

Knowing he'd deserved that, he kept quiet as he took the clothes into the bathroom and put on the pants and shoes. He found the hair shears in the same drawer they'd been in last night and cut away the sleeves and neckband of the T-shirt, turning it into a looser muscle shirt.

He found Mai in the kitchen and when she saw what he'd done, her eyes opened wide. "You destroyed the shirt."

"Yeah, but now it fits. If your boyfriend has a problem with it, tell him to come see me."

"You don't want to mess with a vampire."

The irritation he'd tried to keep at bay bubbled up. "If you're so worried about him, tell him to come see me at night, then. I wouldn't want your boyfriend to burn up trying to get payback for his damn shirt."

Mai rolled her eyes. "You're impossible. And for the record, he's not my boyfriend." She didn't know why she was giving Nick such a hard time over the shirt. Well, that wasn't true. She did know. She was mad at herself. How could she have sex with him? She wasn't even sure she liked him. Her inner self threw up her arms and screamed in frustration. Her vow to wait until she was in a serious relationship before having sex—tossed out the window at the first contact with a hot male. His declaration that they were dating didn't count.

He was watching her and she knew she had to get her act together. He'd saved her life last night. She owed him.

"I'm sorry," she said, turning back to him. "You're right. It's just a shirt—and it's not even one of Ricco's favorites. Which is probably why he left it here. Yours now."

"Truce?"

She smiled. "Truce."

"Excellent." He glanced around her kitchen. "I don't suppose you have anything here to eat?"

At the mention of food, she realized how hungry she was. "I have a little. Eggs and bread, I think."

"Works for me unless you'd rather eat out? My treat?"

The offer was tempting and probably much safer than

sharing a cozy breakfast for two in her apartment. "Let's eat here," she heard herself saying.

He smiled. "Sounds good—especially if you have coffee? I'll even make it if you tell me where you keep it."

"The pantry," she told him, pointing. "How would you like your eggs cooked?"

"Fried hard." He set about making the coffee while she got the skillet out of the cabinet. While she cooked, she sneaked a peek at Nick standing beside her and couldn't help feeling a little breathless. He looked so damn good in that cut-up T-shirt. Yummy.

"Tell me about yourself," she said in an effort to distract herself. "Where do you live? How did you get into security work? Tell me about your family—parents? Brothers? Sisters?"

With the coffee starting to brew, he turned around and leaned against the counter, looking at her with a gleam in his eye. "You really are a reporter, aren't you? By the way, do you mind if I make toast?" He was already flipping open the lid on her bread box.

"No, please do." She blushed. She hadn't even thought about what she sounded like. He intrigued her despite her best efforts not to let him. If he wanted to think she was asking out of a reporter's sense of curiosity, then she'd let him. "Guilty as charged," she said. "I didn't mean to pry."

The smile he gave her seemed so intimate it warmed her. "I don't mind. As you know, I'm a chameleon and a spirit walker. It's the way of Los Paseantes de Espíritu."

"I can't believe I've never heard of your people before."

"We've gone to great lengths to fly under the radar. Besides, it's pretty easy for us to go unnoticed. Blending in is what we do. If the government knew there was a tribe of chameleons living nearby, they'd find some use for us—spying, testing. So there's a reason we keep to ourselves."

Mai understood the need to blend in and be treated like

everyone else. Finished cooking the eggs, she transferred them to plates. Nick poured out two cups of coffee, then placed the carafe back on the warming plate so it could stay warm.

"I have two younger brothers—twins," Nick continued as he set the two cups on the table and went back for the toast as it popped up from the toaster. He carried it over to the table and they sat at the table to eat. "My father is the tribe's shaman and has been for as long as I can remember. And my mother . . . well, she's human."

"You say that like it's a bad thing." She offered him a tentative smile because she'd detected an uneasiness about him when he talked about his mother. "Is it unusual for your people to marry humans?" She took a drink of her coffee so he might not notice just how important it was for her to know the answer.

"No. It doesn't happen often, but it's not unusual. What is unusual is that they're spirit mates."

"Spirit mates? I'm not familiar with that term. Is it like soul mates?"

"Something like that. The spiritual realms are complex, but it's not impossible for two halves of a single spirit to find each other. When they do, they forge a special bond."

"How do you know when you've found your spirit mate?"

He smiled. "Easy. If you have to ask, then you haven't found yours. It's complicated finding a spirit mate in the spiritual realm, but it's a hundred times harder finding your spirit mate in the physical realm—because dreams don't really give any details about where they are or what they really look like."

"So you could be in the same room with your spirit mate and not even know it." Their gazes met and for an instant, time seemed frozen.

"I'd know her if I met her." He sounded like he was

trying to convince himself more than her, but Mai, being a reporter, was more focused on what he hadn't said.

"So you've found your spirit mate in the spiritual realm?"

"No," he replied a little too emphatically. "I don't believe in the fairy tale of two souls united in love, living out their lives in eternal bliss."

"Why not?"

"Because spirit mates don't walk out on you, taking half the family when they leave."

Though shocked by the confession, Mai was also sensitive to the hurt in Nick's voice. "I'm sorry," she said. "I didn't know that you'd been . . . mated? Is that the term? Or that you have children."

"What? No, not me. My parents. They were spirit mates and I know they loved each other, yet my mother left my father almost twenty years ago. Even took my younger brothers with her. I haven't seen them since." His face took on a closed expression. "Yeah, I'm not sure I believe in the fairy tale."

"Why would she do such a thing?" Mai asked, not understanding.

"I asked myself that same question for years. My mother's reason, according to the note she left, was because she was afraid for my brothers, because they were born nulls."

"Nulls?"

"Without the ability to change or walk in the spirit world. Some of the more superstitious members of our tribe thought they were cursed and wanted them cast out. Others said mating with a human was tainting the tribe."

"How horrible."

"Yeah. It was hard on my folks. My father wanted to take his family and leave, but he was the shaman. There was no one else who could take his place. He is very dedicated to his faith and believes that his purpose in life is to help others. He just didn't understand how much his own family needed him.

"The position of shaman is handed down from father to son, so he started taking me with him at an early age to visit the people who needed him. One day we had a particularly tough visit scheduled. We knew it would take all day, so we left early." He sighed. "I should have known something was wrong when my mother tried to talk me into staying home with her. But I was enjoying the work and didn't want to get stuck babysitting my younger brothers. Before my father and I left, she held me a little longer than usual and told me that she loved me.

"My father and I were gone all day and didn't finish until well after the sun went down. We came home to a dark and empty house, with only a note from my mother telling us she had taken the twins to live in an environment where they wouldn't be judged or ostracized simply because they had no magical abilities."

Mai was stunned. Her heart ached at Nick's pain. She could well imagine how abandoned and hurt he must have felt.

"It couldn't have been an easy thing for your mother to do," she said as kindly as she could. "It must have broken her heart to leave you behind." Mai reached out to touch Nick's arm. She wondered what she would have done under a similar situation. "Did you ever see her again?"

"No. She never came back and I never looked for her."

"Why not?" The idea was inconceivable to Mai.

"If she wanted me in her life, she wouldn't have left."

"Oh no. That can't be the case," Mai said. "No mother would willingly leave behind a child."

"And yet that's precisely what my mother did."

"She must have felt she had a good reason to leave when she did."

"I guess we'll never know," he said shortly. He took a

bite of food and chewed carefully before swallowing. "Tell me about you. What's your family like?"

She shrugged and buttered a piece of toast. "I guess they are like you'd expect for wood nymphs. I grew up with my extended family all around me. The Don Groves family. He was my great-great-grandfather. All of his kids, their kids, their kids' kids and so on down the line."

"That sounds nice," he said.

Mai looked at him, shocked. "Are you kidding? Imagine five generations living in an assortment of RVs and traveling together from city to city. I never had any privacy. And there was always a ton of chores to be done. And when we weren't setting up camp or tearing it down, we were entertaining the townspeople. If there's one thing wood nymphs excel at, it's having a good time. I could hardly wait to get away to the big city where I would finally have a life of my own."

"Do you still see your family?"

"It's been a while," she admitted. "When I first arrived in New York City, I didn't want to see them. Then I got busy and—well—there just hasn't been time."

"There's always time," Nick told her softly. "If it's important, you find a way."

She understood. From his perspective, family was important. His family had walked out, leaving him alone with a father who obviously hadn't cared enough for his own wife and sons to fight for them.

But just because Nick had lost some of his family didn't mean that she should feel bad for wanting some distance from hers. It was just one of those differences between them that couldn't be resolved. She didn't try.

Instead, she finished eating her breakfast. "Would you like more coffee?" She hoped he would refuse because now that she was finished eating, the embarrassment of waking up naked—ugh! It was too much to think about.

"No, thanks," he said to her immense relief. "I should probably go. I've got some work to do."

"Okay." Then she thought of something. "Do you need money for a cab?"

"Nope. Not taking a cab."

He didn't elaborate and so Mai didn't ask. "All right. I guess I'll see you later."

He smiled. "Yes, you will."

She walked him to the door. "Thanks for—you know, everything."

He cocked an eyebrow. "You're welcome."

She felt awkward. "'Thank you' seems so inadequate for saving my life."

"Oh, that. Yes, well, you're welcome."

Now she was confused. "What did you think I was thanking you for?"

He smiled.

"Right. I don't think so," she told him, stepping out into the hall after him.

"Are you walking me to the elevator?" he asked with a grin.

"No. Sorry to dash your hopes. I wanted to see if Jenna's heard from Sarah."

"I'll go with you."

"Sure." They walked the short distance to the next apartment in silence. When they reached Jenna's door, Mai knocked. After a minute, she knocked again, louder. "Maybe she's still asleep," she said.

There was no sound from inside the apartment. Mai knocked once more. "She works two jobs," she said. "So maybe she's at work. I'll check back later."

There was an awkward moment as she turned to Nick to say good-bye again. He was looking down at her with a grin on his face. "Thanks for everything—and I'm *not* talking about just breakfast and the medical treatment."

She cringed. She didn't want any further reminders of that morning. She was already afraid she'd be reliving it in her daydreams—and enjoying every memory.

He turned and started walking toward the elevator. Watching him leave, she felt like a young child watching her parent leave after being dropped off at day care. She didn't want him to go. She was pathetic. She forced herself to turn around and head back to her apartment.

"Mai, wait."

His voice came from right behind her and she spun around, startled. "What's the matter?"

He was standing in front of her, having covered the distance between them without her noticing. "I forgot something."

"What?"

"This." He snaked an arm around her waist and pulled her to him, throwing her off balance so she clutched him for balance. His lips came down on hers, warm, firm, masterful. He kissed her until she was breathless, until her head was spinning and her ears were ringing.

And ringing.

It suddenly stopped and a disembodied male voice asked, "Hello? Jenna? Are you there?"

Nick lifted his head and as if on cue, they both turned to face Jenna's door.

"Jenna, pick up if you're there. Damn it. You were supposed to be here an hour ago. Walters is going crazy." There was a deep sigh. "Okay, look. Call me as soon as you get this. Bye."

Nick slowly released Mai and they took a step back. Any embarrassment she might have felt was now replaced with worry over Jenna.

"Do you think something's happened to her?" Mai asked Nick, nodding to the door.

"I don't know. How well do you know her? Is she the kind to not show up to work without calling first?"

"I don't know her well, but my impression is that she's not." Mai knocked on the door again. "Jenna? Are you in there?" She grabbed the knob and turned. Locked.

"I'll be right back."

As Mai watched, Nick closed his eyes and grew very still. As it did the night before, the air around him shimmered as he projected himself into the spiritual plane.

She waited beside him, wondering where he was, what he was seeing and when he'd be back.

She was so deep into her speculation, she didn't notice his return until his eyes opened.

"She's in there, but her energy pattern is faint. I picked up other patterns as well, but nothing I recognized." He paused. "We need to get in there."

"Maybe you could change yourself into a roach or something and crawl under the door," she suggested.

He stared at her as if she'd sprouted a horn from the center of her forehead. "There are limits to what I can do, thank God. About as small as I go is a hawk. Now, if you want larger, like a bear, to break down the door—that I can do."

"Maybe we should just see if Will has a key." She started back to her apartment, Nick following on her heels.

She went into the kitchen and found Will's phone number taped to her refrigerator door. She picked up the phone and punched in his number.

It rang several times and Mai was afraid she was about to get his machine when he answered. "I told you, baby, I need a few minutes to recharge."

"Will?"

There was an obvious pause on the other end. "Who is this?"

"It's Mai, in 14-B."

"Oh, Mai. Sorry. I thought you were someone else. Not that I'm not happy you called. I am. I'm thrilled. I—"

"Will, I need your help," Mai interrupted. "I think Jenna Renfield in 14-A might be in trouble. I'm pretty sure she's in her apartment, but she's not answering her door."

"Maybe she's upset and doesn't want to talk to anyone."

"Maybe. But what if she's so upset about Sarah's disappearance that she's gone and done something horrible and now needs emergency medical care? You're the only one with a key."

She heard him swear beneath his breath.

"I'm on my way up."

"Thank you." Mai disconnected the phone and turned to Nick. "Well, he's coming, but he's not happy about it."

"As long as he's on his way."

They went back to Jenna's door to wait for Will. Nightmare visions raced through Mai's mind and she prayed they found Jenna asleep or drunk.

A loud dinging announced the arrival of the elevator and when the doors opened, Will stepped off. He was looking a bit haggard, but not so tired he couldn't shoot a dark look at Nick when he saw him standing beside Mai.

He knocked loudly on Jenna's door and then put his ear to the door, listening. After knocking a second time, he pulled his ring of keys from his pocket and within seconds had the door unlocked.

"Ms. Renfield," he called as he pushed the door slowly open. "It's Will Johnson. Are you here? Ms. Renf—fuck!"

Alarm shot through Mai. She shoved past Will to see what had caught his attention. The large wall mirror had shattered into a billion pieces and lying amid the broken glass on the floor was Jenna.

CHAPTER THIRTEEN

"Oh no." Mai rushed over to Jenna, whose body lay below the shattered mirror and had hundreds of tiny shards of glass stuck in it. She was covered in blood, but none of the wounds seemed bad enough to explain why she wasn't responding.

Mai gingerly felt for a pulse at the woman's neck and almost collapsed with relief when she felt a beat. "She's alive. We need to call an ambulance."

Nick hurried to Jenna's phone and made the call while Mai lightly held her hand. "It's okay, Jenna. You're going to be all right." Mai had no idea whether it was true, but knew if Jenna could hear her, it was important that she believe it.

"Ambulance is on its way," Nick said a moment later, coming over to squat next to Mai.

"What the hell is going on here?" Will was staring at what was left of the mirror, looking shocked and distressed. Mai ignored him and watched Nick as he walked around the apartment.

"No signs of an intruder," he said, returning to her side.

He placed a comforting hand on her shoulder and gave it a squeeze. Then he turned to Will. "Why don't you go down and wait for the ambulance so you can show them up?"

Will turned as if in a daze to look at Nick and then slowly nodded. He cast one last worried glance at the mirror and then left.

"What do you think happened?" Mai asked Nick as soon as Will was out of hearing distance.

"I don't know. We'll have to wait until she wakes up and can tell us."

To Mai, it felt as if the ambulance took forever to arrive, but then the next couple of hours passed in a rapid blur. She and Nick followed the ambulance to the hospital and answered as many questions as they could. Then they spent another hour in the waiting room before having a chance to talk to the doctor. It had been a short conversation.

"We don't know what's wrong with her," the doctor had said. "She has cuts that are obviously from the mirror, but otherwise she's fine physically. No evidence of head trauma or anything else. No reason why she shouldn't be awake— and yet she's not. We'll run tests and see what we find. I realize you're not family, but if there's anything more you can tell me about her, that would help—is she a shapeshifter? Wood nymph? Witch? Is there any reason to believe her condition is the result of a magic spell?"

Mai exchanged looks with Nick before shaking her head. "I don't know."

He nodded. "That's okay. I'll have a magic specialist take a look at her just to be safe. Based on what you've told me about her sister, though, I wouldn't be surprised if the problem is psychological. Unable to deal with the loss, she may have simply retreated into herself. We'll do everything we can for her. In the meantime, you might as well go home. I can call you if there's a change in her condition. Just leave your names and numbers at the desk."

Mai and Nick opted to stay in the waiting room a little longer, on the chance that Jenna woke. By late afternoon, however, they conceded there was really nothing they could do.

"Hey, you okay?" Nick asked moments later as they rode in the cab.

"I feel so bad for them. First Sarah and now Jenna."

She was frustrated. She couldn't solve her own problems. How was she supposed to help someone else?

"I know," Nick agreed as the cab turned a corner. Mai looked out the window and saw that they weren't returning to her apartment.

"Where are we going?"

"My place. And before you jump to the wrong conclusion, we're going there because I'd like to change into my own clothes."

When the cab finally stopped, they paid the driver and got out. Mai did a double take as she looked up at the building in front of her. "You live here?"

The building was definitely upper-end living.

"You sound surprised."

"I am." At his raised eyebrows, she realized how her comment might have sounded. "What I mean is that it's just not what I expected."

He took her hand and again she felt that warm sizzle of awareness. Inside, Mai looked around the lavish lobby area. The floors looked to be made of marble, not tile. The walls were painted in a textured pattern, unlike the drab plain walls of her own building.

There were two elevators instead of one and Mai watched Nick enter a code into the keypad of one, realizing that this must be a private elevator.

Mai had always considered herself to be more worldly than her upbringing, but the more she saw of how Nick lived, the more she felt like the country bumpkin.

They rode the elevator to the top and when the doors opened, Mai found herself looking at the large, well-decorated open living area of his apartment. The living room alone had to be larger than her entire apartment.

Mai checked to make sure her mouth wasn't hanging open as she stepped into the place and looked around.

"This is really nice," she said. "Big. You live here alone?"

"No. I have a roommate."

As if on cue, one of the bedroom doors opened and an attractive, slightly rumpled-looking woman stepped out wearing only a T-shirt. She gave Mai a quick look before turning all of her attention to Nick. "Hiya, Nick."

"Hey, Pamela. How are you?" He gestured to Mai. "Mai, this is Pamela. Pamela, this is Mai."

"Hi," Pamela said, but made no move to shake hands.

Mai was too stunned to make the gesture. This was Nick's roommate? What exactly was the nature of their living arrangement? And why did she care? Just because she'd had sex with the guy this morning didn't mean they were dating or anything. Okay, he'd said they were dating, but still. It had been one dinner, she reminded herself. One dinner and sex, she amended. If anyone should be upset, it was Pamela. Her roommate had come home with another woman in tow.

Feeling Nick's gaze on her, Mai looked at him, doing her best to keep her expression neutral. She must have failed because he furrowed his brow in surprise. She thought she caught the faintest hint of a smile touch his lips.

He turned back to Pamela before she could be certain. "Is Dave here?" he asked.

Pamela had padded into the kitchen to grab a bottled water. She took a swallow and gestured to the bedroom. "Yeah. He's still in bed."

Nick walked over to the closed door and gave it a sharp rap. "Dave. Come out here. I want you to meet someone."

Nick walked back to Mai, gesturing to the door. "That's my roommate. Pamela is a . . . friend . . . of his."

From the way he said it, he'd meant "friend with benefits." Mai cast a glance at Pamela. She'd obviously caught the innuendo and gave Mai a wink before raising the water bottle to take another long drink.

Just then the door to the same bedroom opened again and a man stepped out wearing only a pair of boxer shorts. He was as tall as Nick with similar, if longer, brown hair and the same muscled physique. He looked at Mai and a slow smile came to his lips, instantly transforming him into one of the most handsome men she had ever seen. He had a compelling smile that invited one to smile back.

He came toward her, holding out his hand. "Well, hello. This is indeed a pleasure. How do you and Nick know each other?"

Nick stepped forward and extracted her hand from Dave's when he held on to it a little too long. Dave's smile only grew larger.

"Mai's a reporter and she came to see me the other day about a story she's doing. We've been seeing each other since," Nick replied.

"Really?" Dave asked with a devilish smile, which he aimed at Nick, who grumbled something under his breath.

Mai thought she should say something to break the tension. "So, you two work together?"

"Work together and play together, so to speak," Dave said. "We've been best friends ever since fifth grade when Nick kept Leo Greywolf from beating the crap out of me for kissing his girlfriend."

"Only because I liked your mom's cooking. Dave's mom is the best cook in the village and she always invited me over for dinner," Nick told Mai. "If I let something happen to Dave, she'd stop inviting me over."

Dave gave a shout of genuine laughter. "My mother loves

you and you know it. The only thing she would have done to you if something happened to me is ask you to move into my room. You're like a son to her."

Nick grinned. "I'm the son she never had."

"No, you're the daughter she never had."

"Watch it," Nick warned.

Dave looked him up and down. "Know how I know you're gay?" he asked, stealing the line from the movie *40-Year-Old Virgin*. "Where'd you get that outfit?"

Reminded of what he was wearing, Nick grimaced. "Long story."

At that moment, Pamela finished her bottle of water and placed it on the counter. "I'm going back to bed," she announced, walking across the room. "You coming?" she asked Dave when she reached his door.

"Be right there," he said without bothering to turn around. His attention was focused solidly on Mai and only Nick noticed the small pout that touched Pamela's lips.

Nick decided he'd had enough. "If you'll excuse us," he said, leading Mai toward the door to his room.

Dave shot him a knowing smile. "Not at all. Mai, it was nice meeting you."

As they entered his room, Nick thanked the gods housekeeping service had come in. His bed was made and the room was clean.

"Have a seat anywhere," he said, going to his dresser to find boxers, undershirt and socks. He carried them to the attached bathroom and laid them on the counter.

As he searched through his closet for pants and a shirt, he noticed Mai taking in the room, checking out everything.

He carried his clothes into the bathroom and closed the door.

"How does your back feel?" Mai asked through the door. "We should have had the doctor look at your wounds while we were at the hospital."

"No need. Everything's mostly healed already."

"But last night it looked so bad."

"I told you, I heal fast." He pulled on his jeans but hadn't zipped them yet because he didn't like the way the waistband cut across his stomach when he bent to put on his socks.

"I wish Jenna could heal that fast," Mai said. "What if the doctor is right and the reason she's not waking up is psychological?"

"Okay." He wondered where she was going with this.

"Wouldn't that make it something you could help with? I mean, your father is a shaman and you said he was training you—so you must know how to do . . . whatever it is you do."

Her statement caught him so off guard that he opened the door to stare at her, forgetting about his pants.

"You want me to do what?"

Only once did she allow her gaze to drop to his open zipper before resolutely keeping it trained on his face. "I want you to . . . do that thing you do."

"You want me to go into her subconscious?"

Her expression brightened. "Yes."

"No." He didn't give her a chance to respond before stepping back into the bathroom and shutting the door. He was in the process of pulling on his shirt when he heard the door open behind him.

"Why not?"

He pulled the shirt down and turned to stare at her. "I'm not a shaman. I don't do that stuff."

"But you know how." Her expression was hard as she stared at him. "Don't you." It wasn't a question.

"Yeah, I know how. But I haven't done it in a while."

"Nick. Jenna needs our help. She needs your help."

"What makes you think I could help her? I couldn't even find where her sister went."

"I know you can do it." She looked at him with such confidence, as if he could save the world. He didn't want her seeing him that way. He didn't need the pressure. The people in his village had looked at his father with the same expression, the same hope in their eyes. And his father had done everything in his power not to disappoint them, even going so far as to allow his wife and sons to leave.

He sighed, dragging his hand down his face. "You don't know what you're asking," he warned her. "I just don't want you to get your hopes up that I'll accomplish anything."

"Then you'll try?"

He knew he would even as he'd tried to get out of it, so he slowly nodded. "Yeah. But I'll need to go back to the hospital to do it because it helps to be physically close."

"So how does it work?"

He walked over to the bed and sat on the edge. "You remember I told you that there's a spiritual plane that overlies the physical plane?"

She nodded.

"Well, it's a little more complicated than that. There is more than one spiritual plane. Think of it like a metaphysical onion, with the physical realm being at the center. The first layer out is the spiritual plane I enter when I'm looking for residual energy patterns. They're there because they're closest to the physical realm. Out from that are the layers representing the different levels of consciousness: dreams, wishes, subconscious thoughts, deep psychosis. Are you following me so far?"

She nodded.

"Okay, now imagine this onion as Picasso might have painted it—distorted, with the layers sometimes bleeding into each other. If Jenna has retreated into herself, then I have to peel through the layers to find where in the spiritual realm her consciousness is hiding and then I have to figure out what's keeping it there. How I help her will depend on what I find, but I can tell you this—whatever she's afraid to face is going to be unpleasant."

Mai nodded, looking very serious. "I understand."

"Good, because you're going with me."

CHAPTER FOURTEEN

"What?"

"I thought you wanted to help."

"I do, but I don't know how to spirit-walk."

"But you know how to dream," he said. "It's a lot like that."

She didn't look entirely comfortable with the idea. "Okay."

"For this first time," he went on to explain, "it'll be easier for me to lead you through the dream realm if you're already asleep, so let's get something to eat and then we can take a walk or go to a movie."

"What?" She narrowed her eyes at him. "That sounds more like a date than a trip into the spirit realm."

"Will it make you feel better to know that dinner, a walk and a movie are all intended to make you tired so when it's time to dream-walk, you can fall asleep easier?"

"I guess that makes sense," she admitted. "Okay."

He eyed her carefully. "You have any questions? Or concerns you want to talk about before we do this?"

"No worries," she said in a voice that was almost convincing. "I'm not afraid of the bogeyman."

"You should be."

She started to laugh at the joke and then saw he wasn't smiling. "There's no such thing . . . is there?"

"So they say. It's supposed to live in the dream realm, preying on the insecurities and fears of dreamers. Don't worry, though. I won't let anything hurt you. Just stay close."

She nodded. "You don't make this sound too promising."

She'd hoped he'd offer up words of reassurance, but he only checked the clock beside the bed. "We should get going. The sooner we do this, the better we'll both feel."

They left his apartment and found a nice Italian restaurant. Nick, Mai was learning, had a penchant for Italian food. He made sure she ate a good portion of her lasagna and drank at least two glasses of wine. She knew he was trying to make her sleepy and damn if it didn't work. The movie he took her to was nice but not too action packed and the walk afterward in the cool night breeze was relaxing. By the time they reached the hospital hours later, Mai found she was actually tired.

According to the nurse on duty, there'd been no change in Jenna's condition, which meant their foray into the dream realm was still on. Even though she was the one who had pushed Nick into doing this, she was starting to have doubts. What if they encountered some of her own psychological demons in the dream realm? She shuddered at the thought.

"Let's go find an empty room," Nick said, holding her hand as they walked down the hall. Every room they passed was occupied, so they caught the elevator and took it to the next floor. There were no empty rooms here, either, and Mai wondered what they'd do if they couldn't find one.

On the fourth floor, their luck changed. One wing was being renovated and while the work was nearly complete, the wing had not yet been opened for use.

They walked to the end of the hall and, with a quick glance around to make sure no one saw them, slipped into the last room. The room was dark, but from the illumination spilling in through the doorway, Mai saw that it was furnished.

"This will do," Nick said.

"If we're caught in here, we're going to have some explaining to do."

"Let me worry about that. Besides, anyone who sees you will know exactly why I wanted to get you alone." He winked at her and at that moment, she found his confidence and strength almost irresistible. That small, frightened, insecure part of her that suffered nightmares and hallucinations wished he would always be around.

Afraid he might see how she felt, she turned her back on him and walked over to the bed. Testing the mattress with her hand, she noticed how high off the floor it was. It came nearly to her waist.

"Need help up?" He didn't wait for her answer but turned her around so she faced him, then grasped her about the waist and lifted her as if she weighed nothing. A thrill raced through her.

"Thanks," she said breathlessly, staring into the dark depths of his eyes as he stood between her legs. The temptation to lean forward and kiss him was almost more than she could resist.

"Anytime." The way he said it made her think he wasn't talking about helping her onto a hospital bed. She smiled and waited to see what would happen next.

She didn't realize how much she'd wanted his kiss until she didn't get it. Instead, he walked across the room and shut the door.

The room was suddenly plunged into darkness. Mai couldn't even see her hand in front of her face. Scooting to the other side of the bed, she waited for Nick to join her.

He moved so silently that her only clue that he had was when she felt the bed give under his weight.

"Are you comfortable?" His voice sounded loud in the darkness.

"Yes."

"You're a bad liar. Roll onto your side."

She did as he asked, knowing it was the only way they'd both fit on the bed. It might have been a mistake because he immediately closed the distance between them and spooned her.

"Lift your head," he told her, stretching out his lower arm so she could use it as a pillow.

The slight chill in the air disappeared. With the front of Nick's body pressed against her back and his arm draped over her, she was more than toasty. She was hot and bothered.

There is no way I'm ever going to relax enough to fall asleep, she thought.

Her internal monologue turned into a lecture about doing this for Jenna and Sarah—not for herself. If Nick tried anything—if he tried fondling her or kissing her—she'd simply have to . . . let him. She silenced a groan, knowing that if Nick tried to make a move, she wouldn't do a damn thing to stop him. Making love to him this morning had been fantastic and if she had any regrets, it was that she hadn't been awake for more of it.

She sighed. Yes, sleeping with Nick Blackhawk was definitely something she could get used to.

"Mai?"

"Hmmm?" she murmured, feeling more relaxed than she would have thought possible.

"We're there."

Mai opened her eyes and was surprised to find she was standing in an open area, completely surrounded by a white light. It was almost like she was standing in the middle of a big white fluffy cloud. She would have been frightened except that Nick was there beside her. "Where?"

"We're at the threshold of the dream realm."

Mai looked around. It certainly wasn't what she expected. She turned back to Nick about to ask him about all the light when she noticed something else. "Why can't I see your face? I know it's you."

"You're seeing me with your mind's eye, not your body's eye. The physical senses only exist in this dimension as a means to interpret the things we encounter here."

"How will we find Jenna, then?"

"We'll find her." He held out his hand. "Shall we?"

Mai placed her hand in his and together they started walking though Mai had no idea how he knew what direction to take.

She thought she should be afraid, but being here with Nick felt familiar, safe.

As they walked, the white mist around them thinned. Mai heard shouts and laughter coming from up ahead and as they drew closer, she saw a child riding on a pony. The child was clearly enjoying himself as his smiling parents watched from nearby.

Mai wondered where they'd come from and turned to Nick, the question forming on her lips. "Someone's dream," he told her before she could ask. "We're seeing what the dreamer sees."

He kept walking and Mai was content to let him lead her, too busy studying the other dreams they passed.

At one point, Nick paused and cocked his head to the side as if he was listening. Then he reached out and grabbed a handful of air. At least, Mai thought it was air. When he pulled back his hand, it looked as if he was pulling back a curtain of light. Darkness lay beyond. A cold breeze crept out of the opening, sending chills along Mai's arms. There was a foreboding about this place, but

Nick was not deterred. He walked through the opening, with Mai right behind him.

Ahead of them, in the distance, Mai noticed a light. It shone like a spotlight on a lonely figure sitting with head down and knees drawn tightly to its chest. Mai felt a rush of excitement that they might have found Jenna and hurried forward. Nick held out his arm to prevent her from getting too close. When they reached the figure, it looked up. Mai stared in shock at the man's face. Crimson lines of blood ran in parallel paths from his forehead, across his eyes and cheeks, down to his jaw. Mai had a sinking feeling she knew what had caused the damage.

"Why?" he asked them, sounding desperate. "Why?"

Mai looked at Nick, who shook his head. At their silence, the man grew agitated. "Why?" he demanded angrily. When they still didn't answer, he dragged his nails down his face, in the exact same path of the other scratches. He hardly seemed aware of what he was doing.

Taking Mai by the hand, Nick led her away. "I think we found where the subconscious minds of the deeply troubled reside. Come on, let's see if we can find Jenna."

They walked farther and then, between one step and the next, they left the dark and stepped into someone's kitchen. Leaning against the counter was a teenage girl. Her arms were folded as she stared rebelliously at a middle-aged man and woman facing her from the other side of the center island.

"What do you think you were doing last night, young lady?" the man demanded.

"I went out with friends. I don't see what the big deal is."

"The big deal is that you didn't tell us where you were going or what you were doing."

"I'm eighteen," the young woman pointed out heatedly. "You can't tell me what to do anymore."

"As long as you're in this house, Jenna, you'll follow our

rules," the woman said. "And we don't want you practicing all that nonsense anymore. It's time you started acting responsibly—if not for yourself, at least for Sarah. She looks up to you. It's important that you set a good example."

Jenna? Mai took a closer look at the girl's face and saw that it was a younger version of the Jenna she knew. So they had found her, but was this a dream? She looked up at Nick, but he put a finger to his lips to warn her to silence.

"It's not nonsense!" Jenna shouted. "It's magic. And I know what I'm doing. You're just jealous because you're a null."

"Jenna, honey. We're not saying that magic is wrong, but it must be used wisely. And so far, you've not demonstrated to us that you know how to use it. Poor Mrs. Howard thinks her dog ran off. Can you even bring it back?"

The young Jenna hung her head.

"Exactly. Irresponsible," her mother concluded.

"Instead of playing around with something you don't know anything about, you should be focusing on getting into a good college," her father added.

Jenna threw her arms down in frustration. "I've told you a thousand times. I don't need to go to college to figure out what I'm going to do with my life. I'm a witch. That's what I am and what I want to do."

Her parents exchanged frustrated looks. "Jenna, you can't make a living being a witch. You need to get a solid education—and for that you'll need college." Mai could tell that Jenna's father was struggling to keep his patience.

"You're jealous that I have power and you don't," Jenna cried.

"That's ridiculous," Jenna's mother said. "We only want what's best for you, and since you don't seem to be able to make that decision on your own, I'm afraid we'll have to make it for you."

"I don't want you making my decisions. Can't you get that through your heads?"

Mai felt the prickle of magic on her skin and knew it was coming from Jenna. She hadn't known Jenna was a witch. Neither she nor Sarah had mentioned it.

"I don't need you telling me what to do," Jenna shouted.

"Jenna—"

"No!" Jenna screamed, eyes closed and hands fisted at either side of her head. "Why can't you go away and leave me alone?"

There was a flash of blinding light, a prickle of power like static electricity—and then a puff of smoke. When the scene cleared, Jenna was standing alone in her kitchen.

"Mom? Dad?" Jenna whispered, clearly in shock. "Where are you?" Eyes wide, she looked all around. Her parents weren't there. Jenna began to wring her hands. "No. No. I didn't mean it."

Nick and Mai followed as Jenna searched the house, calling for her parents. She hurried back to her room and opened a chest, pulling out candles and incense, which she set about the room. Then she took out an old book. Leafing through the pages, she stopped when she found the one she wanted. Immediately, she began chanting under her breath, tears streaming down her cheeks.

Mai got a sense of time passing in which Jenna cast spell after spell trying to bring back her parents. Had this really happened? she wondered. She couldn't even begin to imagine the guilt Jenna must have felt, but maybe it explained her dedication to providing a future for her sister.

The click of the front door opening echoed around them.

"I'm home," a young girl shouted. "Where is everyone?"

"Sarah," Jenna whispered. A look of deep regret and resignation was etched across her face.

At that moment, a young Sarah burst into the room.

"Hi, Jenna." On Sarah's seeing her sister's face, the smile on her own froze and slowly faded. "What's the matter?"

"Mom and Dad are gone."

"When will they be back?" Sarah asked, not yet understanding.

"There was an accident. I don't think they'll be coming back." Jenna clearly struggled to find the right words.

"What kind of accident?"

"It's my fault," Jenna said. "It's all my fault. I should have listened to them."

"What happened?" Sarah cried. "Where are they?"

"Don't worry, Sarah." Jenna hurried over and put her arm around her sister. "I'll take care of you."

Just then, everything around Mai blurred. Only the feel of Nick's hand felt real. When the image cleared, Mai and Nick were standing in a familiar room.

With a start, Mai recognized Jenna and Sarah's living room. Jenna, older now, was sitting at the kitchen table, which was still covered with Sarah's school books.

"Jenna! Help me."

At the faint cry, Mai and Nick turned toward the mirror, as Jenna did. An image appeared in the reflection, a familiar face.

"Sarah?" Jenna gasped, running over to the mirror. She laid her hand against the glass, trying to touch her sister's palm through the glass. "Oh my God. How . . . ?"

"Hurry, Jenna. He's coming."

Jenna ran into the kitchen and pulled out a drawer. Utensils went flying across the room and when she turned around, she held a knife in her hand. Hurrying across the room, she dragged the knife across her palm uttering a litany of words. A spell, Mai thought.

When she reached the mirror, she slapped her palm against the glass. It vanished and Jenna reached through to grab Sarah's hand.

"Jenna!" Sarah shouted.

As Jenna pulled on Sarah's arm, she chanted faster and faster. Mai saw the power gathering from the shimmer in the air. Then Jenna flung out her arms.

The instant the power hit the mirror, the glass shattered into thousands of pieces. Jenna caught the brunt of the blast and was thrown back. Mai didn't think she noticed the cuts across her arms and face because she was staring at the broken mirror with a look of horror.

"Sarah!" she screamed, but her sister was gone. "Sarah." She sank to her knees before the broken mirror. "Sarah."

The scene faded and when it cleared again, Jenna was sitting on the floor before Mai and Nick, arms wrapped around bent knees. With head bowed, she rocked back and forth muttering, "My fault. My fault. My fault."

Nick touched Mai's arm. "She might be able to hear us now that the memories are over," he told her softly.

At his encouragement, Mai knelt down beside her neighbor. "Jenna. It's Mai."

Jenna continued rocking back and forth, so Mai tried again, laying a hand on the woman's shoulder to get her attention. "It's not your fault, Jenna. Whatever happened to Sarah wasn't your fault."

"She's dead," Jenna said. "I killed her."

Mai turned to Nick. "How accurate is the memory?"

"It's hard to say," he said, crouching on the other side. "What we saw is what she remembers."

"And all that about Sarah being in the mirror?"

He shook his head. "I don't know. There's a lot of symbolism in dreams. Sarah being in the mirror could be a reflection of Jenna's younger self, trapped behind the demands her parents made on her."

"Yeah, but the mirror shattering—that was real. Maybe the rest of it is, too." Mai paused, remembering everything they'd witnessed. "When Sarah told me they'd lost their parents, I'd assumed they'd been killed. But now." She glanced over at Nick. "Do you think what we saw is what really happened? Could Jenna have accidentally made her parents disappear?"

"I don't know. She certainly is carrying around a lot of guilt."

Mai rubbed Jenna's back. "What can we do to help her?"

Nick scooped Jenna up in his arms and when he stood, they were suddenly standing in a sunny bedroom with a warm breeze drifting in through the curtains. Nick carried her to the bed and gently lowered her.

He sat beside her and began a low chanting. Mai couldn't make out the words, but they sounded peaceful and soothing.

Still chanting, he began rubbing the palms of his hands together quickly. In just a few seconds, the air around them began to glow with a yellow light until an orb the size of a soccer ball had formed.

Holding the light in his cupped hands, he positioned it over Jenna's head and released it. The orb floated downward until it touched her and was slowly absorbed. By the time the ball had completely disappeared, Jenna was sleeping peacefully.

"Sleep now," Nick said softly, laying his hand on her head. "Sleep and know that you did everything you could to save your sister and whatever happens—this wasn't your fault. Sleep and forgive yourself. Sleep and grow stronger so that you may meet the coming challenges. Sleep and when you are ready, you must wake."

Mai watched in fascination as Nick worked. When Jenna was resting peacefully, Nick gestured for her to stand. She walked around the bed and took the hand he held out to her.

"Are you ready to return?"

"Yes."

"Turn around." When she did as he asked, he moved up against her until they were pressed together. Mai realized that they were now standing in much the same position as they were in lying on the hospital bed. "Close your eyes and concentrate on the sound of my voice. We're going to leave now. When you open your eyes again, we'll be back in the hospital room. Okay. Open your eyes."

Slowly, she became aware that they were lying on the bed. It left her feeling unsettled because there wasn't a defining moment when she transitioned from the dream realm to the waking state.

"You okay?" Nick asked.

She opened her eyes and put a hand to her head. "Wow. This is all a little too much like *A Nightmare on Elm Street*. Some parts of that dream seemed so real."

He helped her off the bed and stood beside her, his hand steadying her, for which she was grateful. She still felt a little dazed.

"Think you can walk?" he asked after a minute.

When she nodded, he led her to the door and poked his head out. "All clear."

A wave of tenderness for Mai washed over Nick as he stood beside her in the elevator. He'd forgotten what it was like to enter the dream realm for the first time. It had to be unsettling for her. He gave her hand another reassuring squeeze and was glad she didn't pull away. When the elevator doors opened, they walked hand in hand to Jenna's room.

They found her sleeping quietly in bed, curled on her side, much as she'd been when they'd left her in the dream realm.

"We can come back tomorrow and check on her," Nick whispered.

"Do you think she'll be okay?"

"I don't know." Judging from what they'd seen, Jenna was carrying a large burden of guilt on her shoulders. How much of it had been symbolic and how much had been real, he could only begin to guess.

He waited by Mai's side for several minutes while she gazed at the sleeping woman. There was nothing more they could do for her at the moment. "Ready?"

She nodded and they left.

Mai was unusually quiet during the trip back to her apartment and Nick worried that taking her into the dream realm might have been a mistake.

"How are you feeling?" he finally asked her once they were at her place.

"I'm fine. It's just that it seemed so—real."

He understood. "It can at times, depending on whose dream it is and how much detail they've put into it."

"Would it be possible for someone to be taken to the dream realm without their knowing it?"

He thought about it. "I suppose it could be done—theoretically."

"Could you do it?"

"No. It would take more power than I have."

"Who *could* do it?"

"A Keltok demon, I suppose," Nick said.

"A Keltok demon?"

"Yeah. You know—the bogeyman." Nick paused, noticing the ashen color of her face. "Mai, is something wrong?"

Mai bit her lower lip and was quiet for a long time before she spoke.

"Something happened to . . . a friend of mine not long ago," she finally said. "She came home to her apartment and thought she was alone. Only she wasn't. A man dressed in black and wearing a ski mask attacked her, beat her up pretty good. Busted lip, broken nose, swollen eyes. She thought he was going to kill her. Maybe he would have, except that another man happened by. She thought he was one of her neighbors, but she thinks maybe now he wasn't. He chased off her attacker. When she would have thanked him, he disappeared. She thought she was going to have to call an ambulance, but she passed out before she could."

She paused. "When she came to, her injuries were gone. The blood was gone, her eyes weren't swollen and there were no bruises. My friend thought she was going crazy. That she had imagined the entire episode. I just wondered if a bogeyman could have been responsible."

Nick felt as if he'd been hit with a two-by-four. Mai had just described the dream he'd had when he'd been wounded and out of his head. He'd been so positive it had been a dream.

No, he hadn't, a small voice interjected. The woman he'd been seeing in his dreams—making love to in his dreams—was the same one he'd saved that day.

His spirit mate.

A lifetime of fulfillment and happiness, eternal bliss— his for the taking.

Thoughts of his father sprang to mind. His father had found his spirit mate in Nick's mother, but it hadn't stopped her from leaving.

Nick could even understand why spirit mates might not stay together. Shit happened; that was life. What he couldn't accept was the emotional devastation that came along with the split and knowing that he could never find that same level of happiness with any other woman. If that was eternal bliss, Nick wanted no part of it.

And yet all his careful avoidance had been for nothing. Despite his best efforts, he'd found his spirit mate; had even made love to her in his dreams. But while he'd been seeing her in his dreams, he'd been seeing someone else in the physical world. Not just anyone, it turned out. His spirit mate's friend.

A horrible sinking feeling overcame him. He'd cheated on his spirit mate by sleeping with her friend. And no matter how tempting he found Mai, he'd never be able to make love to her again.

CHAPTER FIFTEEN

"Nick?"

He felt Mai's eyes on him as she waited for his reaction to her story. "You say this happened to a friend of yours?"

She nodded.

He took a deep breath. "I'd like to talk to her—would that be possible?"

"I promised her I wouldn't tell anyone about the incident," Mai explained.

He wanted to keep pushing, but he'd been around Mai enough to recognize the stubborn set of her jaw. He'd try again later. Until he'd had a chance to meet the other woman and verify that she was the one in his dreams, he'd have to make absolutely certain that nothing more happened between him and Mai—no matter how much the wood nymph turned him on.

An awkwardness settled over them, so Nick backed up to the door. "I guess I should leave. We could both use some sleep."

Mai followed after him. "You could stay here," she suggested, her voice husky and full of invitation.

The last thing he wanted to do was leave her, but he knew he couldn't stay. The temptation would be too great.

"No. I've got some . . . work I need to do." It sounded lame even to his ears. "Some of my friends are NYPD homicide. I thought I might drop by and see them. There was nothing in the paper about finding a body in Central Park. I thought I'd see if they're keeping it out of the media on purpose—or maybe they never found the body."

She followed him to the door, standing close enough that he could smell the faint scent of her perfume. She watched him with eyes full of worry and longing. They pulled him like a tractor beam and he found himself bending toward her before he'd made the conscious decision to do so.

She raised her face to his, her tongue darting out to moisten her lips. His gut clenched. There was nothing he wanted more than to taste those lips.

A memory of being with his spirit mate wedged its way into his thoughts and effectively killed his desire. At the last second, he dodged her kiss and gave her a brotherly peck on the cheek. "I'll call you," he promised. And then he left—as fast as he could.

Mai stood staring at the closed door, one hand against her cheek. What was going on? He'd made love to her that morning and told her they were dating the night before. But tonight he was kissing her on the cheek?

It had been the story about her "friend." *Damn it.* He'd seen right through her lame attempt to hide the truth and knew she was the one who'd imagined a bogeyman beating her up. She rested her forehead against the door and only just resisted the urge to beat her head against it. Now he thought she was a lunatic *and* a liar. Great. Obviously, he was having second thoughts about getting involved with her—not that she could blame him.

Feeling very much alone, Mai went to bed. That night, her dreams were troubled and when she woke the next morning, she was beyond tired.

After fixing herself a quick breakfast, she called the hospital to check on Jenna. According to the nurse, Jenna seemed to be resting more peacefully, but still had not awakened.

Hanging up the phone, Mai considered calling Nick, but didn't want to appear to be chasing him. Instead, what she needed was something to take her mind off him.

She still had a story waiting to be written and now that she had Lenny's notes, it was time to finish it.

Two days later, nothing had changed. There'd been no mention in the news of Lenny's body being found, no sign of Sarah, no change in Jenna's condition, no erotic dreams—and no phone calls from Nick. The only good news was that Mai had finished her article.

Standing now in her kitchen, drinking coffee, she waited for the caffeine to chase away the mental fuzz that lingered from staying up too late the night before. She couldn't help daydreaming about the stir her article would create when it hit the stands.

Soon, Bill Preston was going to be very busy defending himself.

Filled with excitement and anticipation, Mai hurried through her morning routine. A short while later, she was putting the flash drive on which her story was saved into her purse and locking the apartment door behind her.

There was no sign of Will in the lobby and she went outside to stand under the bright sun shining down, warming an otherwise cool breeze. *It's a good day to be alive*, Mai mused, careful not to let any thoughts of Nick slip past her defenses and spoil her mood.

Fifteen minutes later, she was striding into the office of the *New York Voice*, making a beeline for Tom's office.

"Here it is," she said, holding out the flash drive.

"What's this?" Tom asked from behind his desk. He took the drive, but looked at it like he'd never seen it before.

"That is the biggest story of the year," she said, unable to hide the excitement in her voice. "Mayoral candidate Bill Preston has been funding his campaign with donations made by a shadow corporation owned by the Mafia. And that's not all. This guy has a closet full of corpses, people who used to work for or with him over the years and were about to go public with something they knew but who mysteriously vanished or died before they could say anything. Shall I go on?"

Tom's eyes opened wide. "You have facts to back all this up?"

She smiled. "Yep. It's all there on that flash drive—names, dates, times, scanned copies of incriminating documents as well as my article."

He eyed the flash drive with interest, then gestured to the chair in front of his desk. "Have a seat while I see what you've got here."

Mai watched as he plugged the flash drive into his computer. She knew the story was good and yet still found herself waiting with bated breath as he read. A lot rested on this. She'd been out of the journalistic game for long enough. She wanted to prove she was back—as a serious player.

She cast another nervous glance at Tom, whose expression hadn't changed since he started reading. What was he thinking?

Her cell phone beeped, telling her she'd gotten a text message. Tom didn't even acknowledge the sound. Checking her phone, she saw that Nick had written her to see how she was doing. Tom was still reading, so she typed back a quick response. Almost immediately, she received another message from Nick asking if she was free for dinner. She smiled. Maybe she'd misread the situation the other night.

She wrote that she would call him as soon as she could, and put away her phone. With any luck, she'd have something to celebrate and who better to celebrate with than Nick?

"Damn, girl," Tom said, pulling off his glasses and staring at her over the top of his monitor.

"Well?" It was hard to tell from his expression if he was impressed.

He laid his glasses on top of the desk. "I don't even want to know how you got half this stuff. It's all true?"

"Every single bit of it."

"Okay." He leaned back in his chair and rubbed his chin thoughtfully.

"Come on, Tom. Give me something. I'm dying here."

"It's good, Mai. Damn good." Tom leaned forward, suddenly all business. "I want to buy it."

She was back in the game. Mai smiled and held out her hand. "Thanks, Tom. I appreciate this."

"Just like that? You're going to let me have it without even shopping it around?"

"No. I'm going to let you have it for top dollar. And I'm not shopping it around because I owe you for the firefighters' training facility disaster."

He stood and came around the desk, giving her shoulder a familiar pat. "It's a good story, Mai. Come by next week so we can talk about putting you back on the staff—if you're interested."

When Mai left, her spirits were soaring. Everything was starting to come together. First the story, then a steady job if she wanted it and now—maybe—Nick?

She decided she'd better not count the proverbial chickens

just yet. Pulling out her cell phone, she glanced at the time. Not even 3:15 P.M. Dinner seemed like a long way away.

Deciding to enjoy the weather, she started walking in the general direction of her apartment while punching in Nick's phone number.

"Hey there," he answered, his tone warm and familiar.

"Hey there, yourself," she countered.

"How have you been?"

"Good, I guess. You?"

"Busy. I meant to call you yesterday, but . . . something came up. I didn't want to go another day without talking to you, so I thought maybe we could get together for dinner—if you're interested, that is."

She smiled. "Sounds good. You can help me celebrate."

"Oh yeah? What're we celebrating?"

"I finished that story I was working on and just sold it to *NYV*." She could barely get the words out she was so excited.

"This is the story on Preston?" Nick sounded like he wasn't sharing her enthusiasm.

"Yes. Soon the world will know what a bastard he really is."

"I thought you were going to keep a low profile for a while—at least until Lenny's killer is found."

She was a little irritated that he was lecturing her now of all times. "I finished the story last night and decided to go ahead and sell it. I have bills to pay, you know."

Her good mood evaporating, Mai raised her hand to flag a cab.

"Mai," Nick was saying. "I only want you to be prepared in case this thing turns sideways on you."

"I know," she sighed as a taxi pulled up in front of her. She climbed into the back and closed the door.

"Hang on a minute," she told Nick. Leaning forward, she gave the driver her address, then sat back to finish her conversation. "You worry too much," she said, trying to maintain a positive tone. "Everything will be—hey. What are you doing?" she asked the driver when he suddenly pulled over and stopped. Before she even knew what was happening, two men jumped into the backseat, one on each side of her.

"What's going on?" Nick asked.

"Get out of my cab, now," she demanded of the men, though they didn't even acknowledge her.

"Mai, what's going on?" Nick's voice blasted from the phone, drawing both men's attention. The one sitting to her right reached out and took the phone before she could stop him.

"Nick!" she screamed. "Help."

A fist connected with her jaw and Mai felt pain radiate through her body. For a second, she thought she would pass out, but she didn't. The man holding the phone closed it, cutting off her only connection with anyone who might have helped her.

"What do you want?" she managed to ask.

The men sat in stony silence as the cab drove along streets that were less familiar to her.

"Where are you taking me?" she asked, unable to stop the tremor in her voice.

"You'll see."

"Mai!" Nick clutched the phone to his ear trying to hear what was going on.

Ice-cold fear swept over him. He'd saved her once, back in Central Park, but he wasn't sure he could do it again.

The sound of flesh hitting flesh came across the phone, followed by Mai's cry of pain just before the connection was lost.

Anger warred with a feeling of desperation, but he shoved both aside. Right now he needed to remain calm.

He raced out of his office. "I've got an emergency," he told his secretary as he hurried past her.

She simply nodded. She'd worked with him a long time and this wasn't the first "emergency" he'd had. Down the hallway, he took the elevator to the top floor and, after that, the stairs to the roof.

There was no one else on the roof, no one to see him cross to the storage box and work the combination lock. No one to see him strip off his clothes and lay them inside the box or take out the foot-long pipe that held a tightly rolled pair of nylon pants and jacket before locking it again.

And no one to see him change into a large black hawk.

It took him a second to adjust to his new form, but then, grabbing the pipe with his claws, he flapped his wings and launched into the air.

The sense of freedom he always enjoyed in this form helped calm him. He flew across town to the office of the *New York Voice* and slowly began to make ever-widening circles. With his keen eyesight, he could make out the rats crawling in the trash bins far below. What he wanted, though, were the rodents who'd kidnapped Mai.

There were hundreds of cabs below, any of which could have Mai trapped inside. There was no way to follow them all. As he searched, he tried to put himself in Preston's position, because he felt certain the man was behind this. How would he get rid of a pesky reporter who knew too much?

There were plenty of things Preston could do to her alive that were too horrible to consider. No, Nick thought. Preston couldn't afford to leave her alive—but he also couldn't afford to have her body discovered.

So where did one dispose of a body one didn't want found?

The answer came to him instantly. It was a gamble and if he was wrong, it could cost Mai her life.

He flew along the East River. Since he wasn't sure if Mai's kidnappers would have kept the cab or disposed of it, he focused on finding a group of people standing near the water's edge.

From his soaring height above the city, it didn't take him long. In one of the more remote industrial spots, two thugs were dragging Mai toward the end of the wharf. She was kicking and fighting, making their job much more difficult, but her efforts only earned her a slap across the face.

Seeing her manhandled had Nick's blood boiling.

He did a quick visual sweep of the surrounding area to make sure there was no one else nearby. He needn't have worried. The goons holding Mai wanted no witnesses to their deed.

He considered landing behind the men, but they almost certainly had guns on them and he had nothing more than a lead pipe. The only other thing he had was the element of surprise.

Holding the pipe tightly in his claws, he dove for the ground. The men were too preoccupied with restraining Mai to notice him and he managed to crack one of them in the head with the pipe as he passed. The man automatically let go of Mai as he reached up to clutch his head.

Both men turned and at that moment, Nick dove at them again, shifting his form at the last second.

He crashed into one man as he landed, knocking him to the ground. Nick punched him in the jaw to make sure he stayed down.

No doubt startled at Nick's sudden appearance, the other man hesitated before pulling his gun. Nick turned just in time and struck the man's hand with the pipe before he could pull the trigger. Nick swung the pipe again and the man collapsed to the ground.

With both men lying unconscious, Nick turned to Mai

and held out his arms. She fell into them and Nick pulled her close. It felt so good to have her in his arms again. She felt so right there.

"I thought I'd lost you." His voice was hoarse with emotion.

He felt her tremble and held her tighter. "I was so afraid I wouldn't see you again." She rose on tiptoes and pressed her lips to his. He reacted instinctively, deepening the kiss until he eventually remembered why he shouldn't be kissing her at all.

A deep groan from behind them gave Nick an excuse to pull away. He set Mai to the side so he could check the two men on the ground. They were starting to wake up and Nick knew they'd be much harder to deal with once they did. He considered using his lead pipe to knock them out again, but another blow might kill them and he wasn't a murderer—unless he was given no choice.

Instead, he grabbed the first man by the hair and punched him in the face. It was hard enough that Nick felt the bones in his hand crack—but the man fell back unconscious. Nick did the same thing to the other man, only this time he actually broke a few bones.

Focusing on his hand and trying to ignore the pain, he knit the bones back together. Mai, who no doubt had heard the bones crack originally, grabbed his hand and examined it.

"Handy trick," she said. "I guess it makes up for all the damaged clothes."

He saw her gaze drop and remembered he was naked. He retrieved his lead pipe and pulled the clothes from its center.

"I don't suppose you still have your phone?" he asked as he dressed.

She pointed to the man lying closest to the edge of the wharf. "He took it."

Nick went back over to the thug and searched his pockets until he found Mai's phone. He grabbed the other phone he came across as well, but used Mai's to call 9-1-1.

Mai watched Nick take charge. Now that she was safe, the paralyzing fear that she'd managed to keep at bay hit her. As soon as he was off the phone, she slipped into his arms and rested her head against his chest, letting him be that column of strength she needed.

In what had to be record time, she heard the faint wail of sirens. Soon, the wharf was crawling with police. She told her story to the uniformed cops while Nick stood by her side. She was relieved when her kidnappers were cuffed and stuffed into the back of a patrol car.

The adrenaline rush was starting to wear off and Mai was wondering how much longer she'd have to be there when two plainclothes detectives came over to talk to her and Nick.

"Hey, Nick," the taller officer said. "What's going on here?"

"Ted. Paul," Nick greeted them. "This is Mai Groves. She's a reporter who's been working on a story about Bill Preston. My guess is he's the one behind the kidnapping. This is the second time this week he's tried to stop her. The first was two days ago when he shot at her in Central Park. Maybe you found that body?"

They eyed him quizzically. "If you know something about that shooting, you should tell us."

"I will, back at the station. You'll want us both to come down and give statements."

It took the better part of two hours before Nick and Mai were finally able to leave the station. "I don't suppose you still feel like eating?" Nick asked.

Mai smiled. "Actually, I'm pretty hungry."

He returned her smile. "Good. Tell you what—let me

get my clothes and wallet and then we'll go wherever you want."

Since she wasn't ready to be alone yet, Mai agreed. She had a brief moment of panic when Nick hailed a cab, but the cabbie turned out to be just a regular driver.

What surprised Mai was that he didn't take them to Nick's apartment, as she'd expected, but rather to his office.

"I was working when I got your call," he explained as they rode the elevator up. "I had to leave everything behind."

"Wasn't that your floor?" she asked as the elevator continued past it.

"Yeah. When I say I left everything here, I mean I left it on the roof—it's more private."

They reached the top floor and continued up the stairs to the roof. In all her years of living in New York City, Mai couldn't remember a time when she'd stood on the roof of a building. The sun had gone down while they were inside the police station, but this was the city that never slept. From up here, the lights along the skyline looked like one gigantic Christmas display. It was beautiful—provided she didn't get too close to the edge.

"You want to come over here with me?" Nick invited as he started across the roof.

"No, thanks. I'll just enjoy the view from here."

Nick came back to her. "You afraid of heights?"

"It's not so much a fear of heights as a fear of falling from a great height, but so long as I don't get close to the edge, I'll be fine."

"Why don't we go back inside? You can wait in my office while I come back and get my things."

"Don't be silly. We're already here." She waved his concern aside. "I'm fine, really. Go get your stuff."

After Nick walked off, Mai studied the view, becoming so absorbed with it that she hardly noticed the passage of time. It seemed he wasn't gone long at all before he came strolling back fully dressed in business attire, except for his tie, which peeked out from his pants pocket.

"Wow, you look different. Very nice," Mai complimented him.

"Thanks, but don't stand downwind. After all the changing, fighting and walking barefoot on the wharf, I'm in definite need of some soap and water."

"Let's go to your place, then, so you can shower."

He glanced at his watch. "It's almost eight. I really hate to put off dinner too much longer. I don't know about you, but I'm starved."

Mai had to admit she was pretty hungry herself. She'd run out of the apartment without eating lunch, and the bagel she'd had for breakfast had worn off a long time ago. "I can wait," she offered.

Nick was staring at her like he wasn't sure if he should take her offer seriously when her stomach chose that moment to emit a rather large growl. He smiled. "Yeah, that's what I thought. Food first, shower later."

"Or we could compromise. Let's go to your place and order pizza. Better yet, let's order it now since you know it's going to take them a good forty-five minutes to deliver. You could be done with your shower by the time it gets there."

"Are you sure you're okay with that? I mean, I really wanted to take you out tonight—and we have your story to celebrate."

"Actually, a nice quiet evening enjoying pizza sounds good. But I'll take a rain check on the dinner."

He smiled. "You're an easy woman to be with, Mai Groves—when you aren't off getting yourself kidnapped or shot at." He pulled out his cell phone and placed the order. Mai took a final look around, trying to memorize the view from the roof, and then they left.

Forty-five minutes later, Mai was sitting beside Nick on top of his bed, a box of hot pepperoni pizza open between them and an action thriller playing on his big screen. She was feeling so relaxed and content that the kidnapping had already faded to a distant memory.

"Sorry about the accommodations," he apologized. "Dave's little parties can get pretty loud. I thought we'd have more privacy in here. If you'd feel more comfortable, we could still go out."

"Are you kidding? And waste all this great pizza?"

"It's just pizza."

"I beg to differ," she said with a smile. "This is New York–style pepperoni pizza—only the best around."

He chuckled as he reached over to grab a dangling thread of cheese off the slice she held in her hand.

She caught his wrist as he started to lift the thread to his mouth and redirected it to her own. Tilting her head back, she took the thread *and* the tips of his fingers into her mouth. She heard the way his breath caught as she gently sucked each finger before releasing his hand and a thrill went through her.

"Careful, now," he warned. "You're walking a very thin line."

She smiled. "Maybe I like living on the edge."

He lifted a piece of pizza to his mouth. "Maybe I wasn't talking to you," she thought she heard him say.

The action thriller picked up its pace and Nick seemed to become absorbed in the story, much to Mai's disappointment. They finished the pizza before the movie was over, so Nick put the empty box on the floor and they both settled back against the headboard to watch the rest of the show.

The minute she'd decided she wanted to make love to Nick again, Mai lost interest in the movie. What confused her was Nick's reaction. She knew he was interested, but he refused to pick up on any of the cues she dropped. It became a challenge to break down his resistance. A touch here. A look there. She'd played this game many times before but never with someone she truly cared this much about.

Just how much she cared scared her a bit, but she wasn't going to let that keep her from trying.

She got off the bed and straightened the covers. "I felt like I was sitting on ridges," she offered by way of explanation. When she climbed back up, she made sure that when she settled back against the headboard, she was sitting close enough to Nick that their arms were pressed together. Feeling his body heat and hard muscle against her skin was enough to make her breathless.

Nick seemed completely unaffected—at least to a casual observer. However, Mai noticed the slight rise in his temperature, the deeper rise and fall of his chest, the way he moved his hands to his lap to cover what might be stirring below.

Any minute now, she thought, he would make his move. She'd done everything she could to get his attention short of throwing herself into his arms—which she refused to do. She'd already taken off her cardigan, shoes and socks under the pretense of being hot. She had no more clothes to shed and stay decent. She couldn't hop off the bed and pretend to pick up something so he'd look at her butt because she'd just been off the bed to straighten the covers. She couldn't lean over him to check the time because the clock was on the nightstand beside her. Her next move would have to be bold. The poker equivalent to laying her cards on the table. Winner takes all. Loser goes home to empty house feeling lonely and humiliated.

Nick sat beside Mai completely oblivious of the movie. All his energy was focused on not allowing his body to react to her—and that was no small feat. God, he wanted her. Fighting the two men on the wharf had been easy compared to this.

It certainly didn't help that she was doing everything she could to draw his interest. Little did she know that if he could have, he'd have had her beneath him in that bed so fast . . .

But having a spirit mate was like being in a committed relationship. Of course, he hadn't seen his spirit mate these last several nights and he assumed that was his fault. He didn't like being bound to one woman when he had such strong feelings for another.

He supposed he should do something to change that. He supposed—

The bed dipped as Mai pushed herself onto her knees. Then, before he could anticipate what she was doing, she'd pulled her sweater shell over her head as she straddled his legs, facing him.

"You're a hard man to distract," she said, looping her hands behind his head.

The movement forced her breasts together and the twin mounds of flesh were a temptation that drew his eye and made his pulse race.

She wiggled her hips, and his cock, already hard from her earlier attempts to make him notice her, strained to be free.

"Mai," he begged, "we shouldn't." He reached for her, unable to stop himself, and pulled her to him. "I can't," he muttered right before he kissed her.

Her lips were soft and sweet, and when he ran his tongue along the seam, she opened her mouth to give him access. His breathing grew ragged and he kissed her over and over again, unable to control his hunger for her.

Kissing her wasn't going to be enough. He needed more. He reached around her back to undo the clasp of her bra. She leaned back so he could slip the straps from her shoulders and let the bra fall away. Nick stared at her firm, full breasts and knew he was a weak man. He took them in his hands, caressing and kneading their fullness in turn. Her dark nipples were hard and stiff and he was taking one into his mouth before he'd made the decision to do so.

As he suckled her, Mai held his head, running her fingers through his hair. She moaned when he fastened on one nipple with his mouth and pulled. His need for her was nearly painful and he knew it was a matter of seconds before he had her beneath him. He could only remember one time that he'd been this aroused. It had been in his dreams with . . .

His spirit mate.

The thought of her was like being doused with an ice-cold bucket of water. He closed his eyes and fought for control.

"Nick?" Mai's voice was throaty.

"I can't, Mai." He lifted her off him and set her to one side so he could escape off the other side of the bed.

"Oh." The word, which sounded hurt and angry, was followed by a flurry of activity. Nick imagined she was dressing and kept his back to her, wanting to give her some semblance of privacy. "My mistake. I guess I misread the signals. When you said we were dating, I assumed that meant you were interested." Now she sounded clinical, as if she were discussing a lab experiment.

"It's not like that," he told her, finally turning around. She was dressed and there were so many emotions playing across her face that he didn't know how to begin to explain.

"It's not?"

He sighed. "I mean, yes, I'm interested. God, Mai, I can't begin to tell you how much I want you, but . . ."

She was watching him like a hawk. "But?"

"I guess you could say there's someone else."

"What?" Surprise made her voice sharp and loud. "Are you telling me that you're already involved with someone? Oh my God. Then why the hell did you have sex with me the other day? And why did you ask me out to dinner tonight?"

He rubbed a hand across his jaw trying to figure out what to say. "The other day—I didn't mean for that to happen. It just . . . did." Her harrumph told him what she thought of that explanation. "As for asking you to dinner, I did that because I wanted to . . ." He realized too late there was no way this was going to sound good.

"Yes?" she encouraged.

"I was hoping you'd changed your mind about introducing me to your friend—the one who had the bizarre dream."

She stared at him in total disbelief. He could see it on her face. Anger made her eyes shine bright and her jaw took on that stubborn set. "No. And before you ask, it would be a waste of time. She tells me that she's seeing someone—so I doubt she'd be interested in you. And don't bother seeing me out."

With that, she turned and walked out his door. A minute later, he heard the front door slam and knew she was gone.

He couldn't leave things with her this way. He'd give her time to cool off and then he'd try to explain things.

It was another sleepless night. Mai had wasted good tears over what had happened, first crying over Nick's rejection and then crying over her own humiliation. Somewhere around 4:00 A.M., she'd finally fallen asleep.

Now, four hours later, she felt about as good as she looked—which was like crap, she thought, staring into the bathroom mirror. She hoped taking a shower would make her feel better.

She let the water run until it was nice and hot. As she stripped out of her clothes, she noticed the steam escaping into the room. It brought back frightening memories and, unable to resist, she cast a quick nervous glance at the mirror. Her worried expression was all she saw staring back at her.

You're being silly, she told herself as she stepped over the tub and pulled the shower curtain closed. That hallucination had been in the old apartment.

As the water worked to relax her muscles, the tight rein on her thoughts loosened. It had been a strange couple of weeks, starting with her therapist's death, then Lenny's. Followed by Sarah's disappearance, Jenna's collapse and then the kidnapping attempt. On top of that, there was Nick's hot-and-cold behavior, which she couldn't begin to figure out.

She put a stop to her train of thoughts, afraid that if she continued, she'd want to get out and slit her wrists. Okay, not literally, but she was really starting to depress herself. She forced herself to focus on nothing more than shampooing her hair.

When she finished, she shut off the water and reached out for a towel to dry off with. Pulling back the curtain, she glanced at the mirror—and sighed. It was steamed over, but there was nothing unusual there.

Feeling relieved, she stepped out onto the bath mat and wrapped the towel around her. She'd just tucked in the end when a squeaky noise made her jerk up her head.

The sound came from the mirror. As Mai watched, a streak appeared through the steam on the surface. It ran vertically for about two inches and then stopped. A second line formed beside it, much shorter than the first. Then another started at the bottom beside the first and rose to about half the height before looping down, up and down again.

Mai's pulse raced as she stood spellbound, watching as more streaks appeared. They were forming more quickly now, spelling out words.

When they finally stopped, Mai stared at the message in horror as a cold chill raced up her spine.

I'm watching you.

CHAPTER SIXTEEN

A sickening sense of déjà vu gripped Mai as she stared at the words in the mirror. After the face in the mirror and Sarah's disappearance, Mai was no longer convinced this was another hallucination. It might have been better if it had been. At least, then, she'd know what she was up against.

This was something she didn't know how to fight and it scared her to death.

For half a second, she debated whether it was better to race from the apartment or to move slowly, making no sudden moves.

To hell with it.

Yanking open the bathroom door, she ran down the hallway. She'd almost reached the front door when suddenly a creature appeared, blocking it. Standing on two large hind legs, it was tall with scaly gray skin, four clawed arms and flashing green eyes. When it opened its mouth and roared, Mai saw rows of deadly sharp teeth.

She stumbled back, narrowly escaping the claw that sliced through the air where she'd just been. Dashing through the kitchen, she grabbed a knife from the cutlery block and held it in front of her, ready to defend herself. But the creature vanished.

Mai stopped and looked around, her every sense alert and wary. Where had it gone? She turned, afraid it might suddenly appear behind her, but it was gone.

Not about to be lulled into believing she was now safe, Mai made another dash for the front door. This time, she reached it and flipped open the lock. Grabbing the handle, she tugged on the door—but it wouldn't open. Thinking that in her confusion, she'd locked the door instead of unlocking it, she flipped the lock the other way. Still the door wouldn't open. She banged on it as the truth hit her. It wasn't stuck. Magic was keeping it closed. The same magic that had a monster stalking her in her own apartment.

When the creature suddenly appeared behind her, she turned and drove her knife into it—and hit thin air as it vanished yet again.

She looked around, anger replacing some of her earlier fear. When she felt the hairs on the back of her neck prickle, she whirled around. The creature was there, all four claws swiping the air. She dropped to the floor as it reached for her, and scrambled out of its path. She didn't move fast enough and a claw sliced the lower part of her leg. The pain she felt was real enough, as was the blood running down her leg.

She managed to put some distance between them, enough to let her get to her feet.

"Maaaiiii. Geeetttt oouuuttt."

Mai jumped at the sound of the wailing and saw the creature closing in. Frustrated, she raced through the kitchen, thinking if she could reach her bedroom, she could put a locked door between her and the monster. She hadn't taken more than a couple of steps when the creature suddenly appeared down the hallway, blocking her path.

Mai ran back to the living room, straight toward the picture window. She stopped short of opening it. Was she prepared to jump to her death to avoid the creature? What if it wasn't even real?

The cut on her leg said otherwise, but she didn't open the window. Instead, she climbed onto the chair in the corner, where she had the strategic advantage of being able to see the entire room. If she was going to die, then she would die fighting for her life.

Of course, she would have had better odds if she still had the knife.

She looked around for the creature, but it had disappeared again.

"Maaaiiii. Geeetttt oouuuttt."

The voice came from the mirror and wasn't helping her nerves any. No clothes, no weapons, and no help—

The cordless phone was mounted on its base on the kitchen counter. Maybe she could race across the room and grab it.

Mai waited, calculating her move, and then jumped from her spot. As soon as her hand fell on the phone, a man appeared, dressed all in black. It was the man who'd attacked her in her old apartment.

"I tried to warn you," he said sadly. "But you wouldn't listen." He was gone before Mai could think to pull off the necklace. She looked around the room trying to guess where he'd disappeared to.

The wailing from the mirror grew louder, less human in sound, raising the hairs along her arm and the back of her neck. The lights in the apartment started flickering on and off like in a cheap horror movie.

"Is that all you've got?" Mai screamed, sounding braver than she felt.

Then her apartment vanished around her and she was suddenly standing in Central Park before the Obelisk. Hearing footsteps along the path, she turned toward the sound. A woman with long straight black hair was walking toward her. As she drew closer, Mai recognized herself.

"You're late." The words came out of her mouth, but it was Lenny's voice she heard speaking. With the same kind of detachment one feels in dreams, she raised her hands before her and saw they weren't hers. These hands belonged to a man.

It didn't take her long to realize what was happening. The Keltok demon orchestrating this nightmare had cast her in Lenny's role and given how bad the gash in her leg hurt, compliments of the last nightmare, the bullet about to rip through Lenny's head would feel just as real. Only it wouldn't be Lenny's head this time. It'd be hers.

Mai tried to run, but her body wouldn't budge. She looked around for help and saw only the image of herself on the path, drawing nearer. Her heart leaped with excitement because maybe help was already here.

"Nick, is that you? We've got to get out of here." She heard the words in her head, but that's not what came out. "Try to hang on to it this time." She reached into her pocket and felt the folded piece of paper. She had just pulled it out when pain ripped through her head.

She fell to the ground, unwilling to accept that this was the end for her. It wasn't real, no matter how it might feel. It was like the first hallucination. She told herself that over and over, until the pain finally subsided.

When she opened her eyes, she was back in her living room, lying on the floor. The cordless phone she'd been holding in her hand lay beside her, now only a mangled piece of plastic and metal.

It was a stark reminder that not everything happening here was an illusion.

Taking stock of her surroundings, Mai shot up off the floor and raced for the door. A blast of power hit her with such force she was thrown onto her back half a room away. She lay there, stunned, trying to catch her breath.

Heat licked her ankle, scorching it. She looked down to see the cause and found her floor was on fire. She jerked her knees to her chest and looked around. The fire was spreading and already, bits and pieces of the floor, consumed by the flames, were disintegrating. Smoke formed a cloud just below the ceiling that grew larger every passing second.

Mai scooted back toward the chair since the floor behind her was more solid than the floor between her and the door. When her hands touched the edge of the chair, she levered herself into it right as the floor where she'd just been fell away. Beneath it loomed a seemingly endless well at the bottom of which ran a river of molten lava. Hell.

Even as she tried to figure out what to do, the rest of the floor gave way, crumbling in chunks until only the floor beneath the chair remained.

Burning heat emanated from the lava and Mai wrapped her arms around her bent legs to keep her feet from slipping off the chair; to keep her balance; to keep from falling.

She closed her eyes and kept telling herself it was just another dream.

She considered summoning Darius, but didn't want to waste her one shot. When she threw that lightning bolt, she wanted the demon to be on the receiving end of it. So she watched and waited, determined that in this battle of wills, she would be the winner.

Mai had no idea how long she sat there. The molten lava illusion continued to play, keeping her rooted to her spot. She became aware of a new danger after several hours as fatigue set in. Her eyes grew heavy and, more than once, she found herself jerking awake.

Mai realized that the creature—or bogeyman—wanted her to fall asleep. If she did, then she'd be easy prey. She needed to stay awake.

The day wore on. Outside, the setting sun made everything seem so calm and peaceful. Completely at odds with the hellish conditions inside.

The wailing in the mirror had continued at such an ear-splitting pitch that Mai had wondered why none of the tenants on the other floors had complained—unless, as she surmised, it was just another part of the illusion.

When the pounding on the door sounded, she didn't at first notice it. Thinking it was just the demon's next trick, she pulled the lightning bolt off the chain and held it in her hand. It would be like the demon to trick her into doing something foolish, like rush to the door thinking she'd found help only to find his creature waiting there for her.

The pounding on the door grew insistent and then there was a loud splintering crash as it burst open.

Mai threw the bolt of lightning.

Time froze for Nick. When Mai hadn't answered his phone calls, he'd been worried enough to go see her in person. When she hadn't answered the door, he'd gone into the spirit realm to check on her. He'd known right away there were problems. The energy patterns inside the apartment were all wrong. That's when he made the decision to kick in the door.

In the seconds that followed, he'd registered Mai perched on the chair, her arm outstretched toward him. The expression on her face was that of a fierce warrior. The instant she saw him, though, her expression changed to one of surprise and horror. He knew then that the brilliant flash of light sailing toward him hadn't been meant for him—and it wasn't going to be good when it hit.

If he'd been human, he might not have been able to get

out of the way in time. As it was, he narrowly dodged the light before it struck the wall.

There was a flash followed by two loud claps of thunder. The accompanying blast of power knocked him to the floor and left him dazed.

When his vision cleared, there was a savage-looking man in tattoos and a black duster holding a sword to his throat. By his side, a gray wolf snarled and bared its teeth.

A lesser man would have conceded defeat, but Nick was not such a man.

Tapping his own magic, he lurched to his feet, shifting to the form of a grizzly bear, knocking the sword aside with a powerful sweep of his paw. He'd made the transformation in the blink of an eye, but his opponents seemed unfazed.

Moving with lightning speed, the man was on him. Nick barely avoided the sword the second time it came at him and it cut a gash in his upper arm.

The wolf, perhaps sensing it didn't stand a chance against a bear, had shifted into a beautiful dark-haired woman who promptly hurled a ball of fire at his head.

Nick dodged the fireball, but knew that in a battle of strength, he'd not defeat these two. His only hope of surviving—and protecting Mai—lay in the element of surprise.

As the warrior closed in on him, his sword readied, Nick shifted again. The warrior hesitated. As Nick had hoped, the warrior had some affection for the female with him and when faced with her nude image, he'd known a moment of doubt. It wouldn't last, but a moment was all Nick needed. He started shifting forms at random and in such rapid succession, he appeared little more than a shadow as he slipped past the warrior to reach Mai. Such use of magic taxed his energy and left him drained so that when he finally reached Mai, he had only enough energy to assume his natural form.

Upon seeing him, Mai jumped from the chair. "Nick."

"Get behind me, Mai," Nick growled, pushing her behind him so he could face their attackers. Once again, the warrior held a sword to his throat and Nick wasn't sure how he was going to fight him, but he would find the strength somehow. Mai's life depended on it.

"Friend or foe, Mai?" the warrior growled.

"Friend," Mai said from behind Nick.

The shape-shifting woman took a step closer, holding another ball of flame in her hand and clearly not happy with Mai's answer. "Then why did you try to kill him with the lightning bolt?"

"I'd kind of like to know the answer to that myself," Nick said, not taking his eyes off the couple before him but talking to Mai. "If it's about last night . . ."

"It's not," Mai said quickly, but not before the other two cocked their eyebrows in curiosity.

"Last night?" the woman asked.

"Oh, for goddess' sake, everybody please relax." Mai tried to push her way past Nick, but he refused to let her into harm's way.

Behind him, he heard her huff.

"Nick, meet my good friends Lexi and Darius, an Immortal. Lexi and Darius, this is . . . Nick. We've sort of been working together on a missing person's case."

Just because Mai had made the introductions didn't mean that everyone immediately relaxed their stance. It happened in stages until finally the three were standing, staring at each other awkwardly. At least the warrior had lowered his sword even if he hadn't yet put it away.

"Do you think the three of you could not kill each other for a few minutes while I go into the bedroom?" Mai said. "I'll be right back."

"I'll go with you," Lexi said, giving Nick a final look before following Mai out of the room.

Nick didn't like letting Mai out of his sight, but she didn't seem concerned. Nick watched her leave and then turned back to find the Immortal eying him closely.

Mai couldn't think of a more embarrassing situation as she hurried into her room to find another pair of Ricco's sweatpants. She didn't even think Nick was aware that his clothes had been shredded when he turned into the bear. That had been an impressive sight seeing him standing there, so tall and powerful. Of course, having him standing buck naked in her living room was also an impressive sight and likely one to tease her awake at night, leaving her hot and bothered.

"Where did you find that hunka-hunka burning love?" Lexi asked, trailing her into the bedroom.

"It's not like that. We're just working together—unofficially." Mai let the towel she was wearing drop to the floor and quickly pulled on jeans and a top. Then she dug through the box of Ricco's clothes in her closet.

"So, you're telling me you've never slept with him?"

Mai's hand froze in the process of reaching for a pair of pants. It was a fair question to have asked the old Mai, but the new Mai didn't make a habit of sleeping around anymore. Not that Lexi had been around much to know that and not that it made the answer to her question any different. It had been an accident, but that didn't change the facts. "It's not like that," she said again as she pulled out a pair of pants. "He's not interested in me that way."

She didn't succeed in keeping the bitterness out of her tone and Lexi, of course, picked up on it right away. The teasing light left her eyes to be replaced by a look of sympathy. "I'm sorry."

"Why?"

"Because I can see you like him."

Mai had a feeling the conversation was about to get too deep for her to swim out of easily, so she pasted a smile on her face and let a little of the old Mai shine through as she shrugged. "Win some, lose some. It's no big deal."

She didn't wait to see whether Lexi believed her, but turned and left the bedroom.

Nick and Darius were still standing in the same spot. There seemed to be a battle of wills taking place between them.

"Better put these on," Mai said, pushing the pants at Nick. He took them without taking his eyes off Darius and pulled them on.

Mai noticed everything in the room had returned to normal. The burning floor and river of molten lava were gone. The wailing from the mirror had stopped. Everything was—normal.

She wanted to cry. She knew what they'd all think of her if she told them the truth. They'd think she was crazy. And she had no idea how to prove she wasn't.

CHAPTER SEVENTEEN

"Well, it was sure great to see everyone again," Mai said in her most upbeat voice, grabbing Lexi's hand and leading her over to Darius. "I wish you both could stay longer, but I know you have to get back home." She gave them each a hug they didn't return and then took a step back. "Bye."

Three pairs of eyes stared at her.

"If I didn't know better, I'd think you were trying to get rid of us," Darius said. "Unfortunately for you, I'm not Kalen, so I can't just teleport us out of here. The lightning bolt is part of me and that's why I was able to come when you threw it. As for Lexi, well, she hitched a ride when she realized what was happening."

Mai looked from him to Lexi and back. "So how long are you staying?"

"Until my mother decides to bring us back."

Knowing how unreliable Sekhmet could be, who knew when she'd summon them?

"While we wait," Darius continued, "let's talk about why you're in a hurry for us to go when you just got through summoning us. Something must have frightened you pretty badly to convince you to use the lightning bolt in the first place."

Nick crossed his arms and stared at her, looking almost as intimidating as Darius. "I'm with them—I want to know what's going on. When I opened that door, you looked scared to death. What happened?"

Mai realized she wasn't going to be able to satisfy them with anything but the truth. She sighed. "All right."

They listened quietly as she explained. After she finished, she saw Lexi and Darius exchange meaningful looks. "You told us you weren't having any more hallucinations," Lexi said.

"This wasn't a hallucination. It's something else. Something real." She was almost positive now.

"The therapist said that post-traumatic stress hallucinations can seem extremely realistic," Lexi reminded her sympathetically. "I can't even imagine how difficult it must be to deal with this, but you have to try to recognize when you're having one." She looked at the remains of the wall after the lightning bolt had struck it, then glanced significantly at Nick. "This could have been a real tragedy, Mai." Lexi put an arm around Mai's shoulders. "Maybe you should come to Ravenscroft with us. I don't think it's safe for you to stay here by yourself."

Mai shook off her friend's arm, stunned at the suggestion. "I'm not someone's crazy aunt to be shuttled from home to home where relatives can keep an eye on her. What happened here was real."

Lexi and Darius looked around the room. Mai knew they were making a point. If what she'd described had been real, then where was the damage? "Do you know how much magic it would have taken to create that kind of illusion? It would have to be a very powerful witch," Darius said gently.

"Or a bogeyman," she said, eager to share her revelation. "Who came to this dimension and pulled me into the dream realm without my knowing it."

Instead of sharing her excitement, they each looked at her with pity in their eyes—as if she were not only crazy, but crazy beyond help.

"You're talking about a Keltok demon," Darius finally said. "No one's seen a Keltok in centuries. I'm not even sure the species still exists."

"Of course they exist," she scoffed. "Tell him, Nick."

"It's true that one hasn't been sighted in a very long time," Nick said thoughtfully. "But what you're describing is within the bogeyman's capabilities."

"If one existed," Darius added, shooting Nick a scowl.

Mai looked at Nick and saw that he was frowning. He didn't believe she'd seen a bogeyman any more than Darius did. She turned away from them, not sure she could hide the sharp disappointment and frustration that cut through her.

At that moment, a shaft of bright light appeared in the middle of Mai's living room. At first, Mai thought this was the start of another hallucination, but then Darius said, "Looks like Mother's ready for us."

Lexi gave Mai a hug. "Are you sure you won't come back with us? We could have loads of fun and you wouldn't have to worry about working ever again."

"Thanks for the offer, but no." She stepped away and Darius held up the necklace with the lightning bolt once again dangling from it. He smiled as he placed the necklace around her head.

"It doesn't matter what the circumstances, if you need us, throw it and we'll come. Okay?" He kissed her forehead and took a step back.

"It's nice to have met you both," Nick said, shaking hands first with Darius and then Lexi.

"Keep an eye on our girl," Darius told him.

Nick nodded, but Mai noticed that he didn't say anything.

Darius took Lexi's hand in his. Mai had just enough time to think what a nice-looking couple they made before they stepped into the shaft of light and disappeared.

If Mai thought the situation was awkward before, that was nothing compared to how it felt now that she and Nick were alone.

"So now you know my secret," she said, unable to keep the bitterness out of her tone.

"The post-traumatic stress?"

"And the hallucinations."

"And there never was a friend, was there?" It was a statement, not a question.

"No." She gave a wry laugh. "Just me and my twisted nightmare."

He smiled, which she thought was an odd reaction.

"I wish you would've told me sooner," he said.

"What? And have you think I'm crazy, too? Or worse, feel sorry for me?" She shook her head. "I'm getting enough of that already, thanks. Look, I appreciate you coming to check on me and I'm sorry my friends tried to kill you."

Noticing his torn clothing on the floor, she busied herself with picking up the things that had spilled out of his pocket. He stooped to help.

Their fingers brushed when they both reached for his wallet at the same time. She was acutely aware of the contact and, looking up to see if he'd noticed, found herself drowning in his gaze.

Time stopped—and so did her breathing as she looked deep into his eyes.

"Mai, we need to talk." His tone was suddenly very serious and Mai had been in enough relationships to recognize the opening line of the It's-time-we-went-our-own-way speech.

She was afraid that if he rejected her right then and

there, it would be more than she could handle at the moment. Especially when all she desperately wanted was for him to hold her so she'd feel safe and protected. "Not tonight, please. I . . . I just want to go to bed. It's been a long day." She didn't have to fake the weariness in her voice. She was exhausted.

He looked torn but then he nodded. "All right. But first thing tomorrow, I'm coming over." He let her walk him to the door, which now hung off its hinges at an angle. "I'll call someone tonight to have that fixed. Maybe I should stay until it's finished?"

"No. You go on. I'll be okay."

He looked around the apartment. "You're sure?"

She bristled. "I think I can manage to not have another *hallucination* tonight." She wasn't sure how much longer she could keep it together.

"All right. I'll call you tomorrow," he promised.

"Sure, that'd be great." She didn't really expect him to call her ever again, but if he wanted to pretend, that was fine with her.

She didn't stand in the doorway like a lovesick fool watching him walk down the hall. Even she wasn't that pathetic. Instead, she pushed the door closed as best she could and considered calling Will to see if there was something he could do. He was the last person she wanted to see, though, so she changed her mind. Instead, she grabbed a knife from the kitchen and went to sit in the same chair she'd been in all day. At the moment, it was the only place she felt safe. Curling her legs beneath her and ignoring how the horrible gash in her leg had mysteriously vanished, she turned on the TV so it would mask the sound of her crying.

Nick rode the elevator up to the top floor. From there, he found the stairs to the roof. Sometimes, it was necessary to get away from people to think, and if ever he needed time to think and reflect, now was it. He breathed deeply as he took in the view of the city around him.

Next, he placed a call to have Mai's door fixed, agreeing to pay a premium price if they fixed it within the hour. Then he stripped out of the pants Mai had loaned him and stuffed one leg into the other. After placing his cell phone and wallet inside the pants leg, he tied off both ends to make a small bundle.

Then he focused his thoughts on soaring through the open sky, shivering once, twice as the wind brushed over his naked body. He blinked, adjusting to the change in vision.

When the transition to hawk was complete, Nick stretched his wings. Already, he felt free of human worries and emotions.

Remembering his clothing, he clutched the roll with his claws and then, with a few downward strokes of his powerful wings, he rose into the sky, making large, lazy circles.

It was good to be free, he thought. No worries. No responsibilities. Up here, all alone.

Far below, he saw a rat scurry along the wall of a building. It had been hours since he'd eaten and in this form, the rat was tempting. It would be so easy to swoop down and take it.

The part of him that was man decided he could wait to eat. For the moment, he needed air and exercise. And time to think.

There were two truths he needed to come to terms with. First, Mai wasn't crazy—which meant that as impossible as it was to believe, a Keltok demon had broken free of the dream realm and was harassing her. Nick knew this to be true because he'd fought the demon himself—though at the time he'd not realized it for what it was.

The second truth—and the one that was much more important—was that Mai was his spirit mate.

As the realization sank in, he felt its enormous impact settle around him. The woman he'd slept with in the dream realm and the woman he'd made love to in the physical world were one and the same. For someone who had dedicated considerable time and effort toward avoiding entanglement with his spirit mate, he couldn't have become any more entangled with her.

And the amazing thing was that now that it'd happened, he wasn't upset. In fact, the thought of spending the rest of his life with Mai was very appealing.

The struggle to accept the inevitable was over before it began. Nick felt an enormous weight lift and if he'd had lips in this form, he would have smiled.

Now all he had to do was convince Mai that he was the man of her dreams—in every way. That was certainly not something he was going to accomplish as a hawk.

He headed for his apartment, thinking he would pack a bag of clothes to take over with him when he went back to Mai's place, because once he got there, he wasn't leaving until they'd reached an understanding. From this point forward, the only men's clothing in her closet would be his.

In her apartment, Mai finally gathered the nerve to leave the security of her chair and move cautiously about the place. Despite what Nick and Darius had told her, she knew a Keltok demon was tormenting her—she just didn't know how to fight it.

After a thorough search of her apartment—without incident—she concluded that she truly was alone. The bogeyman, it seemed, was gone—for now.

Looking back over the day spent perched on the chair too frightened to move, it all seemed unreal.

She fixed herself something to eat and drink. Then she sat in front of the TV while she ate. The men Nick had hired to fix the door came and left. At that point, she could have gone to bed. She was exhausted, but too wired to sleep and so she sat on the couch and watched TV.

Four hours later, Mai woke up. So deeply asleep moments before, she felt confused and disoriented. It took a full minute before she realized she was still on the couch. Now she wondered what might have awakened her.

For several seconds, she sat perfectly still and listened, but only heard the sound of her own breathing.

Hoping a cup of hot tea might relax her, she headed into the kitchen. While she waited for the microwave to heat her water, she leaned against the counter, staring at the mirror above the table without really seeing it.

Lost in thought, she didn't at first notice the glass clouding over. When she did, it was as if she were watching it in a dream because she stared at it from across the room, feeling no alarm, no curiosity.

The cloudy spot grew larger and a streak appeared on the glass. Then another. Only this time, instead of letters written in steam, these were written in a bright red liquid. *Blood.*

Instantly, Mai was fully awake—and too afraid to move. She watched in fascinated horror as the letters slowly spelled out their message. *Help me.*

CHAPTER EIGHTEEN

Small tremors coursed through her as she stared at the message. Part of her wanted to scream. Another part wanted to cry. Was this another hallucination? Or had the Keltok returned?

Then another possibility occurred to her. Perhaps this was nothing more than a bad dream.

She knew of only one way to find out. Grabbing a knife, she held it above her open palm. "It won't hurt if I'm asleep," she told herself.

At the last second, she changed her mind about slicing her palm and instead, pressed the tip of the knife against her thumb. No pain.

She pressed a little harder.

"Motherfuck—" She dropped the knife as she clutched her bleeding thumb. So she wasn't asleep. That was good, except that meant everything else was real.

Emboldened by the thought, she moved closer to the mirror. The message stared back at her. She reached out and touched the cold, hard surface of the glass. Standing that close, Mai noticed her reflection disappearing, to be replaced by a white, swirling mist—and something hidden in its depths.

A face.

Frighteningly familiar. "Sarah?" Mai peered closer and saw Sarah mouthing her name.

"Mmmmaaaiii. Heeelllppp meee."

It was just like she'd seen in Jenna's memory—Sarah trapped on the other side of the mirror.

Heedless of her bleeding thumb, Mai pressed both hands against the mirror frame as Jenna had done. But unlike Jenna, Mai wasn't a witch. She couldn't cast a spell to get Sarah out.

"How do I get you out?" she hollered.

Sarah looked at her with pleading eyes, her mouth working, but the words indistinguishable.

"Think. Think," Mai ordered herself, still staring into the mirror. A darker shadow loomed in the background and she knew instinctively that if that shadow reached Sarah, it would be bad.

"Damn it." She looked around for something heavy to smash the mirror. She lifted one of the dining table chairs and tested its weight. If she struck the chair against the glass hard enough, it should shatter.

She raised it, ready to strike, but a motion from Sarah stayed her hand.

"Okay, got it. Can't break the glass," she muttered, setting the chair back down and belatedly remembering what had happened in Jenna's dream.

She pulled the mirror away from the wall and looked behind it. There was no opening on this side. If Mai had had any lingering doubts that the mirror was some magical portal, they were gone now.

Behind Sarah, the shadowy form drew closer. "I wish it were as simple as reaching in and pulling you out," she muttered, fighting her rising panic.

No sooner had she uttered the last word than the glass

vanished and Mai was looking directly into Sarah's frightened face.

"Jump, Sarah," she shouted, reaching for the girl's hand. With a mighty tug, she pulled the woman through the opening and they fell back against the dining room table. Sarah scrambled to her feet.

"He's right behind me," she cried, pointing into the mirror. "Throw your necklace."

Mai grabbed the lightning bolt, but hesitated. The words she'd uttered before the glass vanished along with bits of Jenna's memory and the blood on her thumb formed a clear picture of what she needed to do. Touching her bloodied thumb against the mirror's frame, she said, "I wish the mirror to seal."

Instantly, the glass reformed across the opening. Through it, Mai saw the dark shape lumbering forward. When it hit the glass, however, it fell back.

"Can it escape?" she asked.

"Not if we destroy its only way out," Sarah said. "Stand back." She grabbed the nearest chair and slammed it against the mirror.

Mai threw up her arms to protect her face as shards of glass flew everywhere. After a second, she lowered her arms and looked around. The only thing left of the mirror was the frame and the million tiny pieces of glass stuck in the carpet.

Still reeling in shock, Mai turned to get a good look at the girl. "Is it really you?"

Sarah's lips trembled as she fell into Mai's embrace.

"It's okay," Mai soothed her. "You're safe now."

"It was horrible," Sarah cried.

"What happened?"

"I was standing here, waiting for you to bring me that book, when a hand came out of the mirror and pulled me in."

"What grabbed you? What was that thing?"

Sarah's eyes were closed against the memory. "It was a genie."

Mai wasn't sure she'd heard correctly. "Like Aladdin's magic lamp genie?"

Sarah scowled at her. "This one is not some childish cartoon. He is ancient—and powerful."

Mai thought he'd have to be to have kidnapped Sarah and kept her trapped in a mirror all this time. "Did he hurt you?" she asked.

"I'm fine." A slow smile spread across Sarah's face as she looked around. "I can't believe I'm finally out."

Mai took Sarah by the arm and pulled her farther into the living room, away from the mess on the floor. "We were worried about you." They sat on the couch and Mai stared at her hands, hating to dampen the girl's high spirits, but the sooner Sarah knew about Jenna, the better.

"I'm afraid I have bad news for you," Mai began. "It's about Jenna."

Sarah's smile vanished as she bowed her head. "I know. She saw me in the mirror and tried to save me with her magic, but the genie came and they fought." She paused, taking a shuddering breath. "He killed her."

"No, she's not dead."

Sarah's head snapped up. "She's not?" She looked around the room. "Where . . . ?"

"She's in the hospital. She's . . ." Mai hesitated, not sure what to say. The last thing she wanted to do was weigh Sarah down with more worry and stress, not after what she'd just been through. There'd be time enough tomorrow to deal with it. With any luck, whatever it was that Nick had done to help Jenna while they were in the dream realm had worked and Mai wouldn't have to tell Sarah her sister was in a catatonic state. "She'll be glad to see you," she said instead. "Maybe tomorrow we can go—"

A knock at the door made both women jump. Taking a deep breath, Mai rose from the couch to look out the peephole. Immediately, she relaxed.

"It's Nick." She unlocked the door and opened it. "What are you doing here?"

"I know it's late, but what I have to tell you can't wait until tomorrow."

Mai wasn't listening. "I'm glad you came back," she said a little breathlessly. "Something wonderful has happened."

"What?" He followed her into the apartment, stopping when he noticed Sarah. "I'm sorry. I didn't know you had company."

"Nick," Mai said a little breathlessly. "This is Sarah Renfield."

Nick looked surprised, but quickly moved forward to shake hands. "You had us worried. Everything all right? Does Jenna know?"

"When you disappeared, Nick helped us look for you," Mai explained to Sarah. Turning back to Nick, she saw his gaze fall on the broken mirror. At his silent question, she nodded. "Sarah's story is—bizarre. Wait till you hear it."

As Mai told the story, she couldn't help thinking that if this part of Jenna's dream had been true—the part about Sarah being trapped behind the mirror—then the rest of it must be true as well. Which meant that Jenna had used magic to make her parents disappear. Mai felt sorry for the woman. It was tragic—but now wasn't the time to deal with it.

When she finished the story, Nick shook his head. "A genie? I didn't know they existed outside of folktales." At Mai's look, he went on. "You remember I told you that one of the spiritual dimensions is the wish dimension?" She nodded, so he continued. "When we were kids, our parents would tell us about an evil genie who lurks in the wish dimension, waiting for unsuspecting children to enter so he can take them prisoner. The stories were scary enough to keep us out of the wish dimension, but I never thought they were real." He turned to Sarah. "This genie—he didn't . . . hurt you . . . did he?"

She shook her head. "No."

"I wonder how long he's been haunting the mirror?"

Mai had been wondering the same thing. Maybe she was right in thinking there was another explanation for her hallucinations besides being crazy. Instead of a Keltok demon, though, it was a genie. Now all she needed to do was figure out how to stop him.

"We need to make sure he doesn't cause any more harm," Nick said, echoing her thoughts. "We need a way to stop him—or control him."

"I could call my friend Heather," Mai offered. "She's a witch. And if she doesn't know what to do, I'm sure someone in the Coven knows. Plus, now with the Immortals back, we have other resources."

Nick slowly nodded, deep in thought.

"Or we could go see Will," Sarah suggested, drawing curious looks from Mai and Nick. "He's the one who summoned the genie in the first place."

Mai and Nick exchanged glances. A visit to the super was definitely in order.

They considered waiting until morning to approach Will, but the more Nick thought about what Sarah had gone through—what they'd all gone through—the madder he got. According to Sarah, the genie had only done what Will had told it to do. And Will had told it to kidnap Mai. Nick felt the slow burn of simmering rage. The man had threatened Nick's spirit mate. In Nick's book, the offense was unforgivable. Just the thought of someone hurting Mai made him crazy.

He'd wanted to go see Will alone, but Mai and Sarah had refused to stay behind, so now the three of them stood at Will's door waiting for him to answer Nick's knock. After a minute, Nick knocked again, this time a little louder. Finally, they heard the sound of shuffling feet on the other side of the door, followed by the click of the dead bolt being thrown back.

"What the hell?" Will demanded, opening the door and running a hand through hair that needed brushing. Despite wearing jeans and a T-shirt, he looked like he'd just crawled out of bed. "Do you know what time it is?"

"Yeah, but this is important. We need to talk," Nick said.

"Can't this wait until morning?" Will eyed them suspiciously, but when his gaze fell on Sarah, he seemed genuinely surprised—and a little relieved. "Sarah! How . . . You're back!"

"Now, there's an interesting story," Nick said, sarcastically. "I'm sure you'll appreciate hearing it." Without waiting to be invited, he pushed his way past the super and into the apartment.

The place was furnished with expensive but mismatched pieces thrown together without regard to color or style. Hanging on the walls was a collection of expensive reproductions. In one corner, a large flat-screen television dwarfed the room. Beside it stood a state-of-the-art stereo system. In the opposite corner, a Bowflex home gym looked unused.

Material wealth seemed to be the common decorating theme and Nick wondered how Will could afford it all on a super's salary. He gestured around the place. "The genie help you get all this?"

"What are you talking about?" Will asked.

"Don't bother with the games," Nick continued. "Sarah heard you talking to the genie." Nick gestured to the mirror on the wall and started moving toward it. "This what you use to communicate with it?"

Will glared at them. "What is it you want? More money? A new car?" He turned to Mai. "Nice new jewelry, maybe? To graduate without having to take any more classes?" This last was directed to Sarah. "Fine. I'll make sure you get those things."

"No," Nick protested. "What we want is for you to seal the portal so the genie can't get out again."

Will waved them aside. "He already can't get out."

"What do you mean?" Mai asked.

"He's bound to the dimension by the laws of magic. He can't get out."

"Then how did he manage to kidnap Sarah?" Nick growled.

Will shrugged. "I didn't say he hadn't found a way to stretch his tether, but he's not getting out."

"How can you be so sure?" Sarah asked, sounding nervous.

"Don't worry," Will said with confidence. "He's not that strong—or that smart."

"That's where you're wrong," Sarah said softly. "I think he could have escaped at any time."

"Then why hasn't he?" Will demanded.

"Because if he left the wish dimension without a genie—then not only does the wish dimension collapse, but all those touching it collapse." She seemed to realize they were all staring at her. "That's what he told me."

"Are you telling us that the genie purposely hasn't escaped from his dimension because he cares about the safety of the world?" Nick's tone was heavy with sarcasm.

"You don't think a genie is capable of such a noble gesture?" Sarah demanded.

Will openly scoffed, drawing Sarah's anger.

"Well, he is," she snapped. "Or at least he was at one time." Some of the heat in her look subsided. "He told me how he used to be like you and me—free to move about in the physical plane. Then he was lured by the creature that was the genie at the time. The genie switched places with him—bound him to that dimension—and then escaped. That was over a hundred years ago."

Nick shot Sarah a glance. "After what he did to you, I'm not exactly shedding a tear here for him. Sorry." He turned back to Will. "Do you control the genie or not?" Nick asked, getting back to the point.

"Of course I do," he said, sounding smug. "I summoned him."

"How? And don't lie to us," Nick added.

Will scowled. "If you must know, I found a spell in *Kingsley's Book of Magic*. My grandfather left it to me when he passed," he explained. "After his funeral, I was leafing through it and found the spell. It was simple, really. All I needed was a mirror and some blood."

He stopped speaking, but Nick knew there was more to the story. "Go on."

"I didn't expect it to work. None of my other spells ever did." He looked at each of them, staring longest at Sarah. "But then the genie appeared in the mirror and told me that he'd grant my wish." He shrugged. "So I asked for a big-screen TV and"—he waved to the television in the corner—"it appeared."

"So you made another wish," Mai said. "And then another. Before you knew it, you had all this stuff—"

"And one out-of-control genie," Nick finished.

For the first time since they'd arrived, Will looked slightly unsure of himself. "I had things under control."

"Sure you did," Nick said without sympathy. "That's why Sarah was kidnapped. But we're going to change all that right now."

"How?" Will eyed him suspiciously.

"You're going to get rid of him."

"No." Will crossed his hands over his chest.

Nick's temper snapped. He grabbed the super, shoved him up against the mirror and held him there.

"Let go of me," Will shouted, beating his fists against Nick's arms in a useless attempt to break free.

Nick held him easily and, finally sensing his efforts were gaining him nothing, Will stopped fighting. "Okay, okay. You win. Just get me away from the mirror."

"I thought you said he couldn't get out," Nick echoed.

"That doesn't mean he isn't dangerous."

"Exactly my point," Nick said, pulling him away from the mirror. "Now what are we going to do about that? And by 'we,' I mean you."

CHAPTER NINETEEN

Mai and Sarah stepped forward. "Can you do that?" Sarah asked, uncertainty edging her voice. "Can you really get rid of the genie?"

Will seemed to drag his gaze from Nick's with effort and looked at her. "Yeah. Sure. I think."

Mai didn't think he sounded convincing. "How would you do it?" she asked.

"How?" He gave her a deer-in-the-headlights look as he seemed to focus his thoughts. "I suppose I would reverse the spell I used to summon him?"

"I think it's more complicated than that," Mai advised. She had seen both Lexi and Heather perform spells enough times to have picked up a basic understanding. "You'll have to destroy it."

Beside her, Sarah gasped and Mai felt bad for shocking her. "It's the only way," Mai told her gently.

"But what about the interdependency of the dimensions and all that?" Will asked.

"It could be lies," Sarah suggested, surprising Mai.

"If it's true, the worst that will happen is that your magic won't work," Mai said. "The balance between light magic and dark magic that protects the dimension will also protect the genie."

Nick listened to the exchange. "She's right, so let's do this. Get whatever you need."

Nick let him go and Will backed away slowly, moving in the direction of his living room. "I'm not sure I have everything here," he grumbled, opening the chest in front of the couch.

Nick said nothing, but it was obvious to Mai that he wasn't leaving until Will had performed his magic.

Will must have realized the same thing because he pulled out candles and several bottles, which he then carried over to the dining table. He placed each of the four candles at opposite corners.

"If everyone will gather around the table with me," he instructed. Mai exchanged uncertain looks with Nick, in essence asking if he was sure this was the right thing to do.

He nodded and gave her hand a gentle squeeze. Sarah had already moved to stand at one end of the table, as far from the mirror as she possibly could.

"Take positions on opposite sides," he instructed. As soon as they were in place, he picked up the knife he'd set before him and pressed its tip to the heel of his palm until several drops of blood fell into a bowl.

"I summon thee, genie."

Mai turned toward the mirror expectantly, but nothing happened. Will heaved a sigh, giving Mai the impression this had happened before.

"I call on Apep, the Great Destroyer; Set, God of Evil; and Am-Heh, Devourer of Millions. I offer my blood as sacrifice and pray you grant me this boon. I call upon your powers of darkness to be my strength." He turned back to the mirror. "Genie—I summon thee forth."

The glass of the mirror misted over and when it cleared, Mai saw they were looking down a long, dark tunnel. A shadowy form appeared at the far end and Mai tensed, wondering what would happen.

Will dipped his finger into the bowl of blood, then touched it to the glass. "I ask you to grant me the power of destruction that I might destroy all reflected—"

"Wait," Sarah interrupted urgently, drawing three pairs of eyes. "All reflected? Are you sure about that wording?"

She was right, Mai thought, glancing at Nick. *All reflected* could mean the four of them looking into the mirror. Will had already bungled things enough. "I have a friend who's a witch," she quickly offered. "Maybe I should call her to come perform this?"

"No." Will's face turned red, whether with embarrassment or anger, Mai didn't know. "I know how to do this," he snarled.

Mai looked at the others.

"How soon could your friend be here?" Nick asked.

Mai thought about it. How long had Heather said she'd be out of town? The conference had only been for a week. She counted the days in her head and realized with a start that Heather had been gone only a few days. Could that be right? It seemed to Mai as if she'd moved into her apartment months ago.

"It might take a while," she admitted.

At that moment, a keening sound erupted from inside the mirror, growing louder as the form moved toward them.

"I don't think we can afford to wait," Nick shouted over the noise. "Keep going," he told Will.

With a final glance at Sarah, Will focused on the black candle in front of him. Mai thought she saw him swallow nervously and she understood. They were all feeling anxious.

"I ask you to grant me the power of destruction that I might destroy that which exists inside the mirror," he intoned, casting another glance at Sarah, who nodded in approval.

He dragged the dagger across his palm again and held his hand high above his head. "What is dark, be filled with light. Remove this spirit from my sight."

An inhuman wail filled the room seconds before the dark figure in the tunnel burst into flames.

Mai watched in horror as the figure, waving his arms and screaming in pain, slowly burned.

Then the noise stopped and Mai held her breath. In the ensuing silence, the burning figure in the mirror toppled forward and lay still. The fire gradually died.

When it was over, there was nothing left. No body. No ashes. Nothing.

For a long minute, no one said anything. Then Sarah sighed. "It's over. Your spell worked."

"Oh," Mai gasped as the silver glass of the mirror reappeared. She couldn't help feeling enormously relieved.

Nick, however, still didn't look happy. "Now the question is—what do we do with you?"

Will's eyes grew suspicious. "What do you mean?"

"Sarah was kidnapped, Jenna was seriously injured and is still in the hospital and Mai has been terrorized." Will opened his mouth to argue but Nick cut him off. "You can't possibly defend your actions. Before you even think about casting another magic spell, find out what you're doing first. There are several agencies you can go to for training. I suggest you contact either the Coven of Light or the Academy of Magical Studies. They're both on the Internet."

For a full minute, the men stared at each other, waging a silent test of wills. Nick won and Will finally agreed to seek help.

"Let's go," Nick said to the ladies as he headed for the door. "Stay out of trouble, Will. I'll be watching you."

Leaving Will alone in his apartment, the three returned

to Mai's place. Nick desperately wanted a chance to speak to Mai alone. In the excitement of Sarah's return and everything afterward, he'd completely forgotten about his own discovery.

He watched her now, saw how tired she looked, how slowly she moved. She was exhausted and he wanted nothing more than to climb into bed with her and hold her while she slept.

The elevator stopped on the fourteenth floor and the small group stepped off. As they approached Sarah's apartment door, they slowed.

"I can't begin to know how or what you're feeling right now," Mai said to Sarah. "If you want to stay in your own place, I think you'll be perfectly safe. But you're more than welcome to stay with me for a while."

"Really?" Sarah asked eagerly. Nick could tell the offer appealed to her. Of course she'd rather be around people, he thought, but he couldn't help being a bit resentful. After all, he wanted Mai alone to himself.

Mai reached out and gave the girl's arm a gentle tug. "Absolutely," she said. "Come on."

Nick followed them in silence to Mai's door. "Mai, I—" He stopped when she turned to him and he saw the dark circles under her eyes. "You should get some sleep," he finished.

She didn't even argue with him. "I feel like I could use a few hundred hours of it," she agreed. "Thanks for being here."

He rubbed his hand against her arm in an attempt to comfort her. "Nowhere else I'd rather be."

"Yes, thank you for your help," Sarah echoed as Mai opened the door.

As they walked inside her apartment, Mai felt the excitement of the last couple of hours start to ebb. Fighting exhaustion, she tried unsuccessfully to stifle a yawn. She wanted to go to bed and sleep for days. She glanced at Sarah and thought the young woman wasn't looking much better. "Even though it's morning, I think we could all use a nap." She glanced at Nick. He looked exhausted, too, and she thought he'd probably want to go home. She didn't like the idea of him leaving, though. Maybe . . .

"You're welcome to stick around. Catch a few hours of sleep here," she offered.

His warm gaze felt like a hug as it swept over her. "Thanks. I'd like that."

He turned to look at Sarah, drawing Mai's attention to the young woman. She seemed to be glowering at Nick, and Mai couldn't understand why. Maybe after her experience, she was leery of all men. Who could blame her?

Mai considered the dynamics of having one bedroom and two guests. One person could sleep on the couch and her bed was big enough for two. The bigger question was—which two? Certainly not Sarah and Nick, but after his rejection of her earlier, Mai wasn't sure sharing a bed with Nick was such a good idea. She supposed that meant she should share the bed with Sarah, but for some reason, that idea bothered her.

Trying to convince herself she was being silly, Mai headed toward her bedroom. "I'll get some extra blankets and a pillow."

Sarah followed her into the bedroom and immediately started to undress.

"Do you want to borrow a nightshirt?" Mai asked.

"I'll sleep in this one," she said, pulling off her pants.

Mai grabbed the extra pillow out of the closet as Sarah pulled back the covers of the bed and climbed in. Mai sighed. That pretty much settled it.

She carried everything into the front room where Nick stood waiting for her. "Sarah was pretty tired," she said as she set about making up the couch for him. "I think she fell asleep as soon as her head hit the pillow."

She bent to tuck the edge of the bottom sheet under the cushion only to stop when Nick placed his hand on her arm. Straightening, she gazed into his face, waiting almost breathlessly for him to speak.

"Mai, I need to talk to you. It's why I came back tonight."

"Oh?"

"About what happened earlier today. Or rather, what happened yesterday."

She sighed. Her hallucinations and the lies she'd told him were the last things she wanted to discuss. "Could we maybe talk about this after we've both had some sleep?"

He saw the exhaustion on her face. She was ready to fall over where she stood. "Sure." He didn't want her falling asleep in the middle of what could possibly be the most important conversation of their lives.

She finished putting the pillowcase on the extra pillow and laid it on the couch. "I hope you'll be comfortable here. I guess I'll sleep with Sarah."

He heard the wistfulness in her tone and wondered if she'd even realized she'd spoken aloud. "Why don't you take the couch? You're too tired to stay on your feet much longer and the last thing you need to worry about is sharing a bed—with anyone."

"What about you?"

He looked at the oversized chair and ottoman. "I'll be fine right here."

"Are you sure?"

"I'll be asleep before you are."

She smiled, too tired to argue. "Thanks." She took off her shoes and stretched out on the couch. Nick resisted the urge to kiss her cheek when he covered her with the blanket.

Then he picked up the extra one she'd brought, kicked off his shoes and got comfortable in the chair. It really wasn't too bad.

"Good night, Mai," he said softly.

"Good night . . . Nick." He barely heard her response. He sat there listening to the sound of her breathing as it evened out and grew heavy. He scooted down in the chair so he could rest his head against the back of it and closed his eyes. He didn't let himself fall asleep, though. For what he was about to do, he wanted to be in control.

He freed himself from his corporeal body and entered the spiritual plane. A quick look around showed him Mai's green energy pattern. There was also a trace of his own energy pattern throughout the room, and Sarah's. He was about to move on but hesitated, wanting to study Sarah's energy pattern a little longer.

It still appeared like a pale blue light, but it was dimmer than he would have thought it should be. He wondered exactly what had happened to her in the genie's dimension and made a mental note to talk to Mai later about getting Sarah counseling. The girl was going to need it after what had happened to her and her sister.

He floated over to Mai's energy pattern and transcended the spiritual plane to reach the dream plane. As he moved into it, he assumed a corporeal dream form. He focused his thoughts on Mai and felt a compulsion drawing him forward. A door appeared before him, so he opened it and stepped into a bedroom. Mai was there lying on the bed. She was facing away from him, but as he entered, she rolled toward him and smiled.

"You came," she said, holding up her arms, beckoning him to her.

"I wanted to be with you," he said truthfully.

"Come lie with me," she invited.

"Not yet, love," he whispered, stroking the hair from

her face. Now that he knew who she was, he could see her features clearly. "Mai, we have to talk."

"Later." She looped her arms around his neck and drew him down to her. "I missed you."

She was impossible to resist, but he knew he had to try. He brushed his lips against hers because he wanted so badly to taste her and then pulled away. "Mai, do you know me?"

"Of course," she cooed.

He could see the way she looked at him, not really seeing him. He couldn't convince her that she was his spirit mate if she didn't even know who he was. It was much easier to pull her to a sitting position in the dream than it would have been in real life. He sat beside her and forced her to look at him.

"Who am I?" he demanded. "What's my name?"

She peered closely at him for several seconds. Then a slow smile spread across her face. "Nick."

He wasn't prepared for how that one word changed his world. That she recognized him meant she really was his spirit mate. His heart swelled with love and he gathered her into his arms. "You know me."

"Of course I know you," Mai said, returning his hug.

"I have something important to tell you," he said, and heard her sigh.

"It's about earlier. You don't think I'm crazy, do you?"

"No, I don't."

"I might be, you know." She let her head drop to his shoulder. "I see things that aren't there."

"You're not crazy," he said firmly. "And you're not alone. Not anymore. Not ever again. I'll protect you."

She raised her head and smiled at him. "From genies?"

He smiled back. "Yes, from genies."

"And demons?"

"And demons," he agreed.

"And the bogeyman?"

He heard the tremor in her voice. "Especially from the bogeyman."

"What about leprechauns?"

"Leprechauns? They seem pretty harmless to me."

"They are *not* harmless," Mai assured him. "One tried to turn me into a vampire once." She shook her head. "It's always the ones you least expect."

"Then let the leprechauns and the genies and all the others beware, because I will protect you with my life. I love you, Mai."

"I love you, too, Nick."

He kissed her brow. "Now relax and let me show you just how much I love you."

And he did.

CHAPTER TWENTY

When Mai woke up later that day, Nick was gone and the only evidence that he'd been there was his folded blanket. It was hard not to be disappointed, although after the dream she'd had, she might have been too embarrassed to face him. Throwing back her covers, she slid her legs off the side of the couch and sat up. She could think better if she was sitting.

It was perfectly natural that she would have an erotic dream of Nick, she reasoned. He was extremely good-looking, she'd had fantastic sex with him once and, in true hero fashion, he'd once again been there when she needed him. He was like her own private knight in shining armor. Yes. It was all perfectly natural.

But it *had* only been a dream, she thought with disappointment. The memory of his rejection came rushing back. Just then, her bedroom door opened, saving her from spending too much time wallowing in self-pity.

"Hello," Sarah said cheerfully as she walked into the living room.

"I hope you slept well." Mai guessed the girl had a right to feel so happy. After all, for the last several days, she'd been a prisoner in an alternate dimension. Escaping that prison was bound to put one in a good mood.

"I did," Sarah said. She came over to sit beside Mai on the couch. "How about you? I didn't mean to kick you out of your bed. We could have shared it."

Mai patted her arm. "I'm fine. Don't you worry."

Sarah looked around the room. "And Nick?"

Mai absently followed her gaze as if Nick might suddenly appear out of nowhere. "He was gone when I woke up. I guess he had something else to do."

"Oh." Sarah hopped up, clearly too full of energy to sit still. Mai watched her walk around the room, touching the books on her shelf and the various knickknacks. She stopped when she reached the framed picture of Darius, Lexi and the baby.

"Are these your friends?" she asked.

"Yes."

"I think I remember seeing them when you moved in. Do they live nearby?"

"No. They live in a place called Ravenscroft."

Sarah nodded as if she'd heard of the place, though Mai was fairly certain she hadn't. "Do they visit often?"

"I've seen them more in the last week than the past six months," Mai admitted. "The last time was . . ." She thought about the incidents leading up to Darius' and Lexi's last visit. "It was when I heard someone calling me just the other day. It was you, wasn't it?" Mai didn't need to see Sarah's nod to know it was the truth. "You were trying to get my attention."

"Sorry I scared you."

Mai smiled. "No need for *you* to apologize. I'm just sorry I didn't know it was you. Maybe I could have gotten you out of there sooner. As it was, I think my friends thought I was touched in the head."

"Invite them over. I'll be glad to tell them the truth," Sarah offered.

"Thanks. I appreciate that, but don't worry about it. I'll explain it to them the next time I see them."

Sarah looked like she wanted to say more, but just then, there was a knock on the door. Mai hurried to answer, hoping it would be Nick. Instead, she found Will. He looked sullen and Mai waited impatiently for him to tell her why he was there. After an extended period of silence, she grew impatient.

"What do you want?"

"I came by to see how Sarah was doing," he said.

"Why?"

"I guess I feel a little bit responsible."

"You should," Mai told him. "To answer your question, though, she's doing fine. Thanks for coming by." She started to close the door when he put up his hand to stop her.

"Would you mind if I talked to her myself?" he asked.

Mai wasn't so sure that was a good idea. She was on the verge of giving Will an excuse that Sarah was indisposed when the girl suddenly appeared at her side.

"You wanted to see me?" she asked.

"Yes." He studied her closely. "I wanted to tell you that I'm sorry for what happened to you and your sister. I promise that I would have destroyed the genie a long time ago if I'd known what he had planned. I—"

He stopped short at the sound of Sarah's laughter. Or was it crying? Mai couldn't tell.

Even Will appeared dumbfounded. "I'm sorry," Sarah apologized, wiping tears from her eyes. "I was thinking about the ritual and . . ." She made a hiccupping noise. "It was all so frightening. Excuse me."

Overcome with emotion, she covered her mouth and

hurried from the room. Will looked at Mai helplessly. "I didn't mean to upset her."

"I know," Mai told him. "Maybe you should go. I'll make sure she's all right."

"Thanks." She'd started to close the door when he put up a hand to stop her. "Can I ask you something? Has she been acting different?"

Mai tamped down on her growing irritation. "I don't know, Will. She was kidnapped and held hostage in another dimension by a genie. How's she supposed to be acting?"

He didn't have an answer for her, so after giving her a brief nod, he turned and left.

Mai closed the door and went to the kitchen to find something to eat. That's where Sarah found her a minute later.

"You think I hurt his feelings?" Sarah asked, coming in to lean against the counter.

Mai waved it aside. "After what he did? Who cares?"

Sarah nodded and smiled. "That's what I thought." She reached a hand into her pocket and pulled out a key. "Look what I found."

"Your apartment key?"

"Yeah. It was still in the pocket of my jeans. I'm going to run next door to shower and change clothes."

"Want me to go with you so you don't have to be alone?"

"No, I'll be fine. But if it's all right with you, I'd like to come back. Just for a little bit. As long as it's no trouble . . ."

Mai thought she detected a note of fear and hesitation in the girl's voice and hurried to reassure her. "Absolutely. It's no trouble at all. Whenever you're done, come on back. I'll be here."

Shortly after the girl left, Mai went back to the kitchen and opened a cupboard, hoping to find at least a package of crackers—or something.

Nothing. There was nothing to eat. Mai tried to remember the last time she'd been to the store. It had been a while ago. As soon as Sarah got back, maybe they could go out and grab a bite to eat.

A knock sounded at the door. It hadn't been that long since Sarah left and thinking her neighbor might have changed her mind, Mai opened the door. "Nick!"

"Hi. I just saw Sarah. She said you were awake." He snaked an arm around her waist and pulled her close. "How did you sleep?"

Her entire body came alive at the contact, but it was the memory of the dream that caused her to blush. "Fine, thanks. And what happened to you? I thought you'd still be here when I woke up."

"I wanted to take care of a few things at the office so I could spend the rest of the day with you. Didn't you get my note?"

"You left a note?"

"Yeah, in the kitchen."

She eyed him warily. "I was just in the kitchen and there was no note."

He frowned. "I wonder what happened to it. Well, I guess that explains why you didn't call me like I asked. Wow. I hate to think what you must have thought."

She felt like a huge weight had been lifted off her shoulders, though she was surprised. He was still holding her and it was causing her stomach to do somersaults. "I'm glad you came back."

He dipped his head and kissed her, taking his time to do a thorough job.

Wrapped up in the heady emotions he was creating in her, Mai took a minute to collect her thoughts. She broke the kiss and pushed him away. "I thought you were seeing someone," she accused.

"Not anymore." He sighed. "Look. We need to talk."

She folded her arms across her chest, feeling confused and a little sick. She'd expected him to break up with her, but now—she didn't know what to expect. "Okay."

He smiled. "Great, because I don't want to put this off any longer." He glanced around the apartment. "Actually, that's not true. I do want to put it off just a little longer—can we go someplace else to talk? Someplace where we won't be interrupted?"

Mai wanted nothing more than to get out of the apartment and spend time with him. She wasn't sure it was such a good idea, though. Her feelings for him were still raw. "I told Sarah I'd wait here for her. I'd hate for her to come back to an empty apartment."

"Leave her a note and tell her you'll be right back."

"I don't know . . ."

Nick came up to her and ran the back of his fingers down her cheek, awakening desires that she'd finally managed to get under control. "Mai, I'm begging you to come with me."

It was impossible to resist him. "Give me a second to find paper and a pen."

Will stood in front of the broken mirror in his apartment, wringing his hands. *Destroy* that *which exists inside the mirror?* He stopped. Was that right? Or should it have been *destroy* the genie *which exists inside the mirror?* Or *destroy* the evil *inside the mirror?*

He started pacing around the table, unable to shake the feeling that he'd screwed up. He just couldn't put his finger on how.

He went back over the words of his spell. *Destroy the genie of the mirror.* Yes. That's how it should have gone, but that's not what he'd said, was it?

He knew that spell, had studied it time and time again. He'd known he'd have to use it one day. The genie had been growing defiant, had started turning Will's wishes against him. Will had known there'd come a time when he'd have to give up the wishes and put the cork back in the genie's bottle. But when it came time to do it, time to utter the words to the spell, he'd messed it up. *Why? Why? Why?*

He felt like beating his head against the wall. It was important that he remember.

Someone knocked on his door, but he ignored it. He couldn't deal with tenants at the moment. It was far too important that he figure this out.

He started pacing another circuit around his living room when his visitor knocked again, this time more insistent.

"Will? Are you there?"

He recognized the voice and hurried to the door. "Sarah."

They stood staring at each other for several long seconds. Finally Sarah heaved a sigh. "Are you going to invite me in?"

"Yes, of course. Come in." He stood back.

She walked past him and when he turned, he saw her studying the mirror. He knew it must remind her of the time she spent behind it.

"I'm glad you came down," he began, wanting to distract her. "I wanted to tell you again how sorry I am for conjuring that . . . that monster. I should have found a better way to control him."

He thought she looked irritated and couldn't blame her. It was his fault she'd been taken. "I don't expect you to forgive me," he continued. "I just wanted you to know how sorry I am."

"You're a pathetic excuse for a man," she snapped, turning on him. "Do you really imagine that you were ever strong enough to defeat me?"

"Excuse me?" Will stammered, surprised by the vehemence in her tone. When she glared at him, it sent chills down his spine. "Sarah?" She simply stared at him, waiting until the truth slowly dawned. "You! Oh my God."

"Finally," the genie said with Sarah's voice. "I was beginning to think you were too stupid to figure it out."

"What have you done with Sarah? If you're in her body . . ." He glanced anxiously at the shattered remains of the mirror as the horrible truth came crashing down on him. "You killed her."

The genie laughed. "*I* didn't kill her. *You* did, with that idiotic spell of yours."

The entire episode replayed itself in Will's mind, the casting of the spell, the genie's wretched cries that hadn't been the genie at all. They'd been a young girl's last cries for help. "Oh God." Will fell to his knees. He'd cast that spell. He'd killed Sarah.

"Why?" he moaned. "She never hurt anyone." He didn't expect an answer, so was surprised when the genie gave him one.

"I never meant for her to get hurt. It was the other one I was after."

"Her sister?"

The genie gave him a scornful look. "No, moron. Mai. I was after Mai. Sarah looks like her. From the other side of the mirror, it was hard to tell the difference."

"But why would you want Mai? I don't understand."

The genie came toward him. "Try centuries of being magically chained to that damned wish dimension. Centuries of serving morons like you. There's only one way out for me."

Will thought he understood. "You wanted her to trade places with you. But why her?"

The genie threw up his hands. "I swear. With a mind like that, it's a wonder you can remember how to breathe. I only wanted her so I could lure my real target."

"Whatever your plan is," Will told him defiantly, "I'm not going to help you. I'll see to it that you pay for Sarah's death. I won't rest until I've found a way to put you back in that dimension."

"How noble of you," the genie said dryly. "It might almost be worth keeping you alive to watch you try."

Will stared in horror as the genie walked toward him, his eyes glowing with a reddish light. He was in big trouble. He thought about casting a protective spell about him, but he couldn't think of the words. The genie was almost to him. He tried to think, tried to recall a spell—any spell—but his mind was blank.

Will stumbled backward into the dining table, putting up his hands behind him to brace himself. "They'll stop you," he threatened, but the genie only smiled.

"I'm afraid I've already arranged for our friend Nick to have a little accident. Most unfortunate. You see, when the elevator cable suddenly gave out, he was trapped inside. Such a shame. He died on impact."

Will shook his head. "No. I can't let you do that."

"And what, pray tell, are you going to do to stop me?" the genie asked.

Will remembered seeing a serving knife on the table and blindly felt around for it. When he found it, he brought it forward, slashing the palm of his other hand. "I call on Apep, the Great Destroyer; Set, God of Evil; and Am-Heh, Devourer of Millions. I offer my blood as sacrifice and pray you grant me this boon. I call upon your powers of darkness to be my strength. Genie—I command thee stop."

The genie stopped and allowed a smile to touch his lips. "How many times do I have to tell you? Word choice."

Upstairs in her apartment, Mai got her light jacket and followed Nick to the door. "I'm ready."

"Let's hurry—I don't want any more delays." His words warmed her as much as they worried her. So far, he'd not given her any reason for changing his mind about their relationship—nor had he said anything about breaking up with the other woman he'd told her he was seeing. All of these questions needed answering before Mai was going to surrender her heart to this man. A part of her, though, thought it might already be too late.

They left her apartment and walked hand in hand down the hall to the elevator. Mai pressed the call button and the doors immediately opened so they stepped inside.

As the elevator began to descend, Nick pulled Mai into his arms. "There's something I've been wanting to tell you and I just don't think I can wait another second. Mai, I'm—"

The elevator car lurched, nearly causing them to fall.

"What the—?" Nick cocked his head to the side to listen.

"Nick?" She clutched him a little tighter.

"It's probably nothing," he tried to reassure her.

Mai wasn't reassured.

The elevator groaned again, and then stopped. They waited, neither of them daring to breathe, which is why the popping noise, when it came, sounded like a small explosion.

Mai yelped.

They heard another popping noise. Then the car started moving again. Faster and faster.

There was no screeching sound of safety brakes. Nothing at all to stop the elevator's free fall but the ground, twelve stories down and closing fast.

CHAPTER TWENTY-ONE

Mai knew they only had moments to live. The bright future she'd imagined for herself and Nick was never going to happen. The dream she'd had of him the night before was all she would get—and it wasn't enough.

Wrapping her arms around him, she thought of the ocean. She focused on the cool watery depths and pulled magic from the deepest recesses of her soul, praying to every deity she could that this time they grant her full use of the magic she had previously taken for granted.

As the screeching sound of the metal scraping metal filled her ears, Mai held tightly to Nick and willed them both to the crystal-blue depths.

The force of impact knocked the breath out of her and she fought for air, sucking in a mouthful of salty water instead. She spat it out as she thrashed about with her arms and legs to reach the surface. She felt as if she'd been hit by a Mack truck. Her entire body ached, but as her head broke water and her lungs filled with air, it occurred to her that she was still very much alive.

Nick. Panicked, she looked around. Had her magic worked to save him? Or had she only saved herself? Was he now lying beneath the crushed, mangled steel of the elevator?

A splashing sound behind her caused her to spin around in the water just in time to see a dark head appear above the surface. "Nick!"

He turned at the sound of her voice and she caught the flash of his smile. They hadn't landed that far apart and it didn't take them long to reach each other. Mai was so happy to see Nick that when she was close enough to wrap her arms around him, she did, nearly drowning them both in the process.

"That was one hell of a ride, baby. Are you okay?" Nick asked.

"I am now." She grabbed Nick to her and met his lips as they came down on hers.

Their kiss was both desperate and passionate. Seconds ago, they'd thought they were dying. Now they were alive. This kiss was as much about affirming life as it was a declaration of love.

Mai's thoughts came to a grinding halt. *Love.* It was the first time she'd used that word to describe her feelings for Nick and it was somewhat of a shock to realize the true depth of her feelings. It would have been more of a shock if she hadn't dreamed of him the night before. Obviously, on a subconscious level, she'd known all along.

The kiss ended and Nick released her only so they could both tread water. "I thought it was all over back there," he said. "I didn't see any way to avoid the inevitable, and all I could think about was how I'd never gotten the chance to tell you how much I love you."

"What?" Mai was sure she'd heard him wrong.

"I know we haven't known each other long and God knows that I never meant to get married, but that was before I met you."

"Nick, I—"

"No, before you say anything, hear me out. Do you remember how I told you that my people believe in spirit mates—a perfect someone for everyone—two spirits that find each other and become stronger together than apart?"

She nodded, remembering a conversation like that.

"Well, you're my spirit mate."

Her brow furrowed. "How do you know?"

"Because your spirit called to me in the dream realm and I came. I always will. That first time, I saved you from a Keltok when he attacked you—I know you remember it. And I've been coming to you in your dreams ever since."

Mai thought back to the erotic dreams she'd had in the last couple of days. Had the man she'd been having dream sex with really been Nick? "What about the other woman? The one you told me you were seeing?"

He smiled. "It was you all along, only I didn't know it at the time. I didn't realize the woman I'd been dreaming about was real. And then you described the attack and I knew she was."

"And when I told you it had happened to my friend," Mai said, filling in the story for herself.

"It wouldn't have been right to sleep with you knowing I had found my spirit mate." He smiled. "I was trying so hard to deny having a spirit mate so I could justify being with you that I never stopped to consider the friend didn't exist. Until last night. That's when I knew that you're my spirit mate, Mai."

"I don't know . . ."

"Look in your heart, Mai, and see me there."

"In my dreams?" She was still having problems grasping that one.

"I promised to protect you and I failed," he said. "I couldn't have saved you just now." He frowned. "But I think I would have done better against leprechauns."

"Leprechauns?" She stared at him openmouthed. The conversation she'd had with her dream lover the night before came back to her. In the dream, she'd known him as

Nick. Was it so hard to believe her dream lover and her real-life lover were one and the same? He was watching her intently, his heart in his eyes. She reached out briefly to press her palm against his cheek. "It *is* you."

He smiled. "Yes."

She leaned forward and kissed him. She wouldn't have thought this kiss could have been any better than the one before it, but it was. "Oh, Nick."

"Is that 'Oh, Nick, I love what you do to me'? Or 'Oh, Nick, this is too freaky for me, I need time'?"

"It's 'Oh, Nick, I love you, too.' How could I not? As corny as it sounds, you're the man of my dreams."

His laugh rumbled deep in his chest. "I know that after nearly dying, I shouldn't feel this great."

"Speaking of that," Mai said, "maybe we should get back to dry land? I'm not sure how much longer I can tread water. Besides, it's cold."

They both looked around at the miles of ocean surrounding them. "Where do you think we are?" Mai asked.

"You don't know? You teleported us."

"Actually, I was too scared to think clearly. I just visualized lots of ocean and both of us landing in it."

"I had no idea your magic was so powerful."

A wave caught and lifted her higher in the water. "Neither did I," she admitted. "This is the first time in more than a year that it's even worked."

"How did you know it would today?"

"I didn't. But the alternative wasn't looking so great. And I wasn't ready to give up without a fight."

He pulled her to him and kissed her. "That's my girl. What are the chances you can teleport us back?" he asked when they came up for air. "Because I have no idea where in the hell we are."

"I could try."

"Let's do that and if it doesn't work, then we'll go to plan B."

"Which is?"

"Ever been swimming with a dolphin?"

She smiled. Life with Nick promised to be interesting. She wrapped her arms around him and willed them back to the apartment building.

Mai was less surprised this time when her magic worked, but just as pleased. They stood across the street from her building watching the flurry of activity as policemen and firefighters hurried in and out of the building.

"What do you think caused the elevator to break?" Mai didn't really want to think about it, but knew they had to. It was too important. "And what happened to the emergency brakes? What are the odds of both of those happening while—"

"We're inside?" Nick finished her question. "I wouldn't think very good."

"Which means it was sabotage," she concluded. "But who wants us dead?"

Nick frowned. "You mean other than Preston and Will? I think we should leave Preston to the police, but it might be good to have another chat with Will."

"Not without me," Mai informed him. It felt good to have solid ground under her feet again. "After what we just went through, I've got a few things I'd like to say to him."

"I don't know, Mai. If he's responsible, then he's obviously more dangerous than we originally thought and I'm not happy with the idea of putting you in more danger." Before she could protest, he held up his hand to silence her. "I know I'd never convince you to stay behind, so at least promise me you won't go see him alone."

"I promise."

"Good." He turned his head, looking first right and then left. Holding her hand, he led her through the crowd until they reached the police tape.

"This is Mai Groves," Nick told the police officer. "She lives in 14-B. I'm Nick Blackhawk, her fiancé. Can we go inside?"

As the policeman spoke into a radio, Mai's attention was still focused on Nick's words. *Fiancé.* She stared at him in wonder. For the first time since the shock of their fall and Nick's confession, she stopped to think about the course of her life. There was a real chance that if she didn't do anything to screw it up, she could soon find herself married to Nick. After that, there would never be anyone else. She'd spend every day of her life with him. She'd never sleep with another man. Never know the feel of another man's arms around her. Never know the touch of another man's kiss. Never make love to another man. Ever. Suddenly, the rest of her life seemed very long and—she could hardly wait to start. Committing to a single mate and settling down might not appeal to most wood nymphs, but it appealed to Mai. Nick was all she ever wanted or needed.

"Mai."

Nick broke into her thoughts just as an officer escorted them past the tape and into the building. There, another man took them through the lobby where a team of firefighters used the Jaws of Life to pry apart the crushed metal.

He turned when they approached.

"Detective, this is Nick Blackhawk and his fiancée, Mai Groves, who lives in 14-B."

The detective studied Nick carefully. "You're Nick Blackhawk?"

"Yes."

"We had a report that you were on the elevator," he said.

"I was," Nick replied calmly.

"Mind telling me how you got out alive?"

Nick glanced at Mai, who shrugged. Nick gestured to Mai. "She's a wood nymph with the ability to teleport. As soon as we realized the elevator was falling, she got us out."

The detective didn't look comfortable with the magic explanation but considering they were standing in front of him with wet hair and clothes—for no apparent reason—he was at least familiar with magical beings and their abilities.

After a minute of deep thought and consideration, he seemed to make up his mind about something. "Mr. Blackhawk, can you think of any reason why someone might want you dead?"

"So the elevator falling wasn't an accident?" Nick asked, though they'd known it wasn't.

"No. Someone definitely tampered with it."

Mai listened in a half daze as Nick spoke to the detective. When they finished, he took Mai by the elbow and led her down the hall on the far side of the mailboxes.

"Where are we going?" she asked.

"The detective said there's a service elevator around here." They rounded the mailboxes and continued down the hall. Sure enough, there was a service elevator. She'd not had to use it when she moved into her apartment, thanks to Darius and Lexi's help.

Nick pressed the up button, but when the doors opened, they both hesitated. Then, as if resigned to their fate, no matter what it was, they stepped into the car.

"They didn't think you were with me," Nick told her.

"How did they know *you* were on there?" she wanted to know.

"Sarah told them."

"Sarah. Oh no. I forgot all about her alone upstairs," Mai exclaimed. "She must be worried sick."

The elevator stopped on the fourteenth floor and they hurried around the corner and down the hall toward Mai's apartment.

They found Sarah pacing inside. As soon as she saw Mai, she gave a cry of delight and ran toward her. "Where have you been?"

"I was on the elevator with Nick when it fell," she said.

Sarah stared at her with eyes round with horror. "You were on the elevator?"

"Yes. Nick and I were going to pick up some food," she improvised quickly.

Nick watched the exchange between the women. There was something about Sarah that bothered him and he couldn't ignore it anymore.

He freed his spirit to soar into the spiritual realm. Mai's green energy was glowing brightly all around her. Beside it was a dark, cold energy that definitely didn't belong to Sarah.

Nick looked around trying to find Sarah's blue light and found traces of it, so faint that it had to be old.

Alarm rippled through him. He'd suspected something wasn't right and now he had proof. What he didn't have were answers. Or a clear idea of what exactly was wrong.

When he returned to his body, it was to find Sarah and Mai standing beside the kitchen table with Mai reassuring Sarah that everything was all right.

"Mai," Nick said in a casual tone. "I need to talk to you in private—it won't take long."

Mai looked over at him in surprise. "What?"

He held out his hand to her, keeping a wary eye on Sarah. "Please, it's important."

"All right." Mai looked from him to Sarah. "I'll be right back." She took a step toward him, but Sarah grabbed her arm.

"No," Sarah growled.

"Let her go," Nick warned.

"Nick, it's okay," Mai said, clearly confused.

Then his gaze fell on the mirror. What had once been a shattered mess had been completely repaired. "Mai, teleport out of here—now!"

He saw her confusion right before she closed her eyes to comply. Her momentary hesitation, however, was all it took. Grinning, Sarah held on to Mai with one hand and waved the other in the air.

There was a flash of magic that temporarily blinded him. When his vision cleared, Sarah and Mai were gone.

CHAPTER TWENTY-TWO

Nick rushed to the spot where Mai and Sarah had been standing, but there was no trace of the pair. It was foolish to hope for a clue, he knew. The two hadn't run to hide in a corner of the apartment. They had gone into the mirror.

He looked into the increasingly cloudy glass and saw two dark figures moving within the mist. The smaller one struggled against a larger one and he knew instinctively that it was Mai.

He touched the glass of the mirror, praying his hand would pass through, but it didn't. He knew that breaking it was not the answer to reaching Mai. He'd have to find another.

He railed against the fate that allowed him to find his spirit mate only to take her so callously.

Vowing he would find a way to save her, he raced from the apartment, hating to leave Mai but needing to talk to the one person who might be able to help him.

By the time he reached the basement door, he had managed to get his thoughts together. He needed to remain calm if he was going to help Mai.

He hurried to Will's apartment and knocked on the door. There was no answer. He pounded on the door again, starting to lose his tenuous hold on his temper. As far as Nick was concerned, this was all Will's fault. If he hadn't conjured the genie, Mai's life wouldn't now be at risk.

When Nick still got no answer, his patience ran out. Lifting his foot, he kicked in the door, sending pieces of it flying.

Inside, an unnatural quiet permeated the place.

"Will!" Nick shouted. "Where are you?"

He received no answer. Storming into the place, he cast a quick glance in the kitchen on his way into the living room.

At first, the room looked empty and Nick wondered if the maintenance man had decided to move out. Then he saw a foot sticking out past the far end of the couch.

Nick hurried over and found Will lying on the floor. His body was twisted at an odd angle and his eyes were open, staring and lifeless. The carpet beneath his head was soaked dark with blood.

Though he knew it was pointless, Nick squatted beside the body and checked for a pulse. There was none.

Who had murdered him? Nick wondered. Sarah might have, but not the Sarah who had disappeared. The Sarah who murdered Will was the creature Mai had rescued from the mirror: the genie.

And now the genie had Mai. But why?

Nick knew that if he could figure that out, he'd know how to rescue Mai.

Mai was being dragged down a long dark tunnel lit only by floating threads of yellow light. When she looked more closely, she saw the threads were made of words written in every kind of language. At one point, they passed through one and Mai thought she heard the echo of voices. "I wish I could go to the . . ." "I wish he would call me . . ." *"Je voudrai bonne chance . . . " "Querro una Mercedes . . ."*

"Where are we?" she asked, struggling to sound calm even though fear clawed at her.

"In my world," Sarah said, still holding her arm.

"Your world? Inside the mirror?"

Sarah laughed and the unpleasant sound echoed around Mai. "The mirror is merely a portal. My world is the realm of wishes."

"You're not Sarah."

The creature impersonating Sarah came to a halt and met Mai's gaze. "No, I'm not." Sarah's image grew fuzzy and when it cleared, a red manlike creature with full horns and a tail stood before her.

"Are you . . . ?" Mai couldn't bring herself to finish the question.

"I am Rafe," the creature said, "the genie bound to serve this realm."

"You kidnapped Sarah," Mai accused. "I thought we killed you."

"Not me," he corrected. "Sarah."

The news hit Mai like a punch to the gut. The genie might have been lying, but she didn't think so. There'd be no point. It didn't matter that they had been tricked. It made her sick to think she'd played a role in killing an innocent woman.

As Mai allowed herself a moment to mourn Sarah, the genie pulled her deeper into the tunnel.

"What do you want with me?" she asked.

"Nothing."

The answer was surprising. "Then why did you kidnap me?"

He stopped and she nearly bumped into him. He stared down at her and then, in a flash, his hand shot out, closed around the lightning bolt necklace and yanked. The chain bit into the back of her neck, but wouldn't break. Mai remembered that Darius had used a special chain that would not come off unless she was the one to remove it. As the genie continued to exert his strength, she worried the chain would sever her head from her neck.

Then, to her utter surprise, it broke.

Rafe held the necklace in the air as they both stared at it.

"How did you do that?" Mai asked. "It's not supposed to come off unless I take it off."

The genie gave a snort of disgust. "Those kinds of enchantments don't work in here."

He held the necklace up so he could study it.

"Now that you have that, what do you intend to do with it?" Maybe she could trick him into throwing it. If she could summon Darius and Lexi, they might save her.

The genie looked at her from over the necklace. "I have waited centuries for a chance to be free." He smiled.

"But you were just out."

"A very temporary situation, I assure you. I once was a leech demon with the ability to take over another's body. This impressive body you see before you once belonged to the actual genie who served this dimension. In a moment of weakness—mine, not his—he switched bodies with me and escaped. Now it's time I carry on the tradition he started."

"Don't do this," she pleaded, afraid he meant to switch bodies with her. "We'll find a way to break your bonds."

"Haven't you been listening?" he roared. "This realm won't survive without a genie bound in service to it. This isn't a gesture I make to ensure the safety of the world. This is nature's law that will not be broken. There will be a genie bound to this dimension for all time! And I'll be damned if it's going to be me."

Mai gasped. "You want me to take your place?" She tried not to imagine what it would be like to live for eternity in service to the wishes of others.

"You?" Rafe gave a shout of laughter. "You have so little magic, you might as well be a null."

It was absurd, but she felt insulted. "Then why the *hell* did you kidnap me?"

"For this." He held up her necklace with the lightning bolt.

Slowly understanding dawned on her. "You want Darius?"

He smiled. "Of course. No creature in the universe has greater magical power than a son of the Mother Goddess. His spirit will be strong enough to replace mine in the tethers that hold me prisoner and in return, not only will I have his freedom, but I will have his Immortal body."

"Darius will defeat you. He's much too powerful."

He smiled. "Not in this realm."

Mai was already shaking her head. "No. I can't let you do that."

Before she could think what to do, he threw the necklace to the ground.

A burst of light exploded from it accompanied by a clap of thunder. Mai cringed and threw up her arm to protect her eyes. When the light faded and the smoke cleared, Darius stood there. Clad in leather pants, his bare chest and arms covered in tattoos, he was fierce—and the look he shot the genie was one of barely suppressed anger.

"Careful, Darius," Mai shouted. "It's a trap."

Darius' expression didn't change and his attention didn't stray from the genie, though his words were directed to her. "Are you hurt?"

"No. He isn't interested in me. It's you he wants."

"And now you're here," the genie gloated. "This is going to be easier than I thought."

"Don't count on it," Darius warned him.

The genie laughed. "You have no power here. Your magic is tied to the physical world; it won't work in this realm."

"Unless you plan to talk me to death, let's do this. Show me what you've got."

In the blink of an eye, the red devil flashed across the space separating him from Darius. He brought his great arm down in what had to have been a crushing blow. Darius barely staggered beneath it, grabbing the arm instead and falling back, jerking the genie off balance. As the monster crashed to the ground, Darius rolled out of the way. He was on his feet in a flash, bringing his elbow down on the genie's back. The genie howled in rage.

Darius backed off, giving the genie a chance to regain his feet. Mai wondered why Darius wasn't using his magic or his tattooed weapons—then remembered what the genie had said. Darius' Immortal powers wouldn't work here.

With a mighty roar, the genie attacked. Darius threw his fist, trying to catch the genie in the jaw. It was a glancing blow that didn't slow the beast's charge.

The meaty fist that struck Darius drove him back as Mai watched, feeling helpless. Against a foe as powerful as the genie, what could she do?

Darius fell to one knee under the next blow and the genie seized the opening, moving in close and laying his hands, palm open, on Darius' head and shoulder. Darius' body began to shake and she heard his groan of pain. The beast's body seemed lit from within, growing brighter until even the air around him glowed.

Leech demon. The words echoed in her head.

With growing horror, Mai realized that the genie was using his magic to trade bodies with Darius—and the Immortal seemed unable to stop him.

She had to do something.

She considered beating him with her fists, or rushing him like an inside linebacker, driving him to the ground—but knew the reality was that she would bother him about as much as a gnat bothered an elephant. Of course, maybe that's all it would take to break the genie's concentration and give Darius the break he needed. With a mighty yell, she rushed forward and delivered three rapid roundhouse kicks to the demon's head, snapping it back. *Thank you, Billy Blanks*, she thought.

The bright light faded and the genie turned his horned head in her direction, his molten lava gaze touching hers. She hit him in rapid succession with her closed fists in another of her exercise moves. It hurt like hell, but it worked because the glow around the genie was gone. She only hoped she hadn't been too late.

Then Darius was rising like the superhero she'd always considered him to be, strong and proud. He slapped a hand to his forearm and lifted the dagger tattooed there. It came away in his hand, the metal glittering in the otherwise dark arena where they fought.

"How?" the genie gasped, clearly stunned. "An Immortal has no powers here."

"But Los Paseantes de Espíritu do."

Mai's attention, which had been focused on the genie, turned sharply to Darius. "Nick?"

"No," the genie said, his tone full of disbelief. "It can't be."

"It can and it is." Darius' face blurred like a television picture going out of focus. When it cleared, Mai was staring at Nick—but with Darius' tattooed torso. "Two things you need to know about me," he said to the genie.

"What's that?" the genie snarled, rising to his full height, which was significantly taller than Nick's.

"First is that the dream realm and all those like it are my playground—and have been for a very long time. And second, no one—*no one*—takes my spirit mate from me and lives."

Nick stretched out his arm and pointed his finger at the genie. From the tip, a bolt of lightning shot forth. Mai didn't even have time to draw in a breath before it arced across the distance and scorched the spot where the genie had been standing moments earlier. Only he wasn't there.

Suddenly, he was standing before her. "Nick—?"

"Stay away, Mai," Nick warned her.

The genie backed up, his eyes fixed on Nick but his target Mai. Before he could take more than a step, Nick hurled the dagger. The genie roared in pain and anger. Lashing out, he grabbed for Nick and caught his arm. Almost immediately, the area around the point of contact began to glow.

"Don't let him touch you," Mai yelled. "That's how he transfers to another body."

The genie barely spared her a glowering look as he held tight to Nick.

Nick labored for breath. He felt his spirit slipping out of his body; saw the genie's spirit leaving his. He knew he couldn't let the genie complete the transfer and fought to bring his spirit back.

Using Darius' form had been helpful, but now Nick had to tap into his own resources. As the genie struggled to pull out the dagger, Nick shifted, taking on the mass and height of a grizzly bear. The genie was shocked enough to loosen his grip momentarily, and Nick used the split-second advantage to pull free.

He swatted once at the genie, ripping four deep gashes in his side. The red devil staggered back, clutching the dagger that still protruded from his chest. He was down, but not dead.

Nick shifted back to his normal form as he went to Mai, who fell into his arms. "I wasn't sure if I'd see you again," she said into his chest.

"You have to know that I would never leave you," he told her. He longed to hold her, to comfort her, but there was no time. "We have to go. The real Darius and Lexi are waiting in your room, by the mirror. I wasn't sure if we could get out without magical assistance." He cast a glance at the genie. "I think we'd better hurry."

"What about him?"

"I'll kill him if he tries to stop us," Nick growled.

"You can't," Mai said desperately. She quickly told him what the genie had said about the dimension always making sure it had its genie.

"Then let it keep the one it has." He grabbed her hand and pushed her ahead of him down the hall in the direction he had come earlier. When the genie had thrown the lightning bolt, Nick had been ready—having finally figured out why he'd kidnapped Mai. In that instant, he'd had to use his powers to slow the passage of time in the wish dimension long enough to explain to Darius and Lexi what was going on. He hoped that in the time he'd been gone they'd discovered a spell for sealing the realm. "Run, Mai!"

Looking back, he saw that the genie had finally succeeded in pulling the dagger from his chest and was now lumbering after them.

Mai's living room was a small dot of light up ahead. "There!" Nick shouted. They both raced toward it.

Their pounding footsteps resounded sharply in the darkness. As they drew nearer, Nick saw Darius and Lexi through the glass. He conjured a ball of light and hurled it forward, signaling them to action.

Nick and Mai had almost reached the glass when the genie shouted after them, oddly calm, "Espíritu, you only think you've won."

A blast of power hit Nick from behind and he went down. For a few precious seconds, he was stunned, unable to move. The genie raced past him and grabbed Mai about the waist. Nick watched him lift Mai off the ground as easily as if she were a doll, despite the way she fought to get free.

"Let her go," Nick threatened the genie.

"Or what?" The genie sneered. "You'll give me what I want?" One of his big hands wrapped around Mai's neck, easily encircling it. "I think you'll do that anyway."

He began to squeeze and Nick watched with impotent rage as Mai's face turned red and her eyes grew wide with fear.

"What do you want?" he asked, desperate to save Mai's life. "You know that I can't let you leave here. Even if you were to take my body, the instant you stepped out of the mirror, you're a dead man." He nodded toward the opening where Darius and Lexi stood, a lethal-looking duo biding their time until they could strike.

"No," the genie said resignedly. "I see now that I'll never be allowed to live among the humans."

"Then let her go."

"Not yet," the genie said. "There's still something I require of you."

"What's that?"

"Freedom."

Nick stared at the genie as his meaning came clear. "You want me to kill you?"

The genie smiled. "Yes. You're the only one who can do it—and it's the only way I'll be free."

With Mai's life on the line, Nick knew he was as trapped as the genie. "Okay," he said, understanding the consequences of his action. "Let her go."

The genie loosened the hand around Mai's neck and set her back on her feet. She coughed, trying to catch her breath, but the genie didn't release her.

"Mai?" Nick asked, worried about the pallor of her skin.

Her hand went to her throat and it took several tries before she was able to speak. "I'm okay."

"Listen to me, baby. I want you to go to the portal. Darius and Lexi are waiting there to help you out. They'll take care of you."

"You can't kill him," Mai pleaded. "It's a trick."

Nick looked from the genie to her. "I know what I'm doing, Mai."

The genie smiled. "It's the devil's choice. You can trade bodies with me and stay here in my place, trapped for all time. Or you can kill me and become the new genie, trapped here for all time."

Nick ground his teeth together. "Let Mai go first."

"No, I don't think so," the genie said. "She's my—how do you put it?—my insurance policy against you changing your mind. So I'll tell you what we're going to do." He jerked Mai to him. "I'm going to start killing her. If you want to save her life, you'll have to kill me. Since you're the dream walker, you're the one the dimension will claim as its own. The wood nymph will be free to leave."

It was a no-win situation. Either way, Nick was never going to be with Mai again. Saving her life was the least he could do. "I'm sorry, love."

He began to pull the magic around him, just like his father had taught him. He saw Mai's face turn red as the genie slowly squeezed her throat. She fought for her life and Nick knew she fought for his as well. Channeling the magic through his body, he hurled it forth in a bolt that hit the genie in that part of the chest visible above Mai's head. It blew a hole clean through him. The expression on the genie's face was one of surprise. Then he screamed as the hole expanded, burning away more flesh.

Then the screaming stopped. For a second, the genie stood glowing like a hot ember, his image wavering in and out of focus. Then he smiled—and vanished.

A sigh reached them, carried on a breeze—followed by an unnatural silence.

Then Mai was in Nick's arms. He held her tightly, knowing it would be the last time he could. "What have you done?" she cried. "What have you done?"

"I couldn't let him kill you." Nick begged her to understand. Something that felt like fingers played across his soul and though he'd never experienced the sensation before, he knew they were the tethers of the realm reaching for him.

"Mai, we don't have much time." He caught her face between his hands and kissed her, desperately. Finally he released her long enough to catch his breath. He wanted to tell her he loved her, but knew that it would just make their parting that much harder.

She grabbed his hand and tried to pull him to the portal. "Maybe there's something Darius and Lexi can do. His mother's a goddess. She has powers."

He went with her, not wanting to tell her that even a goddess could not alter the laws of the universe. This realm was not complete without its servant, and Nick would not jeopardize the rest of the universe for his own needs—though how he was to survive without Mai, he had no idea.

Outside the portal, Darius held Lexi's hand as she muttered incantations beneath her breath. The power of their love, Nick knew, gave them the strength to keep the portal open. He could see the strain of their effort in Lexi's face and knew she couldn't keep the portal open much longer.

"This is my fate," he told Mai.

"But I don't want to live without you," she whispered. "I love you."

The fingers of the realm tightened their hold on him.

"Come with me," she begged him. "Maybe the genie was wrong. Maybe he lied about what would happen to you."

"He didn't lie," Nick said. "You need to go now, Mai. Before you're trapped in here, too."

Her eyes lit up. "That's it. I could stay with you. We could be together forever."

It was so tempting, but he couldn't do that to her. "No."

He signaled Darius with a slight dip of his head and stepped back. "It's time for you to go."

Tears gathered in her eyes and Nick knew he was lost if she cried. "For God's sake, take her," he yelled at Darius. "And don't let her back in."

Mai tried to duck beyond Darius' reach, but he was too fast for her. Holding her tightly, he pulled her through the portal and to safety.

"Let me go," she shouted, struggling to break free. "I want to stay with Nick."

Darius shot him a questioning look and Nick shook his head. Darius might not understand why it had to be this way, but he would restrain Mai and keep her safe. Of that, Nick was sure.

The cloudy mist gathered as the portal began to close. Nick watched it with a sense of growing resignation.

He could see through to the other side, where Mai had stopped struggling and was openly weeping. Darius was no longer restraining her as much as he was supporting her.

"I love you," he told her, though she couldn't hear him.

When he could stand it no more, he turned and headed deeper into the dark tunnels of his new home. This, then, was his fate, to grant everyone else's wish but his own. As far as fates went, this one sucked.

CHAPTER TWENTY-THREE

Her world was collapsing around her. Darius held her in his arms as she wept and Mai was barely aware of him. Every thought was with Nick. She wanted to be with him. "Please," she begged of anyone who could help. "Do something."

She'd found the love of her life and in a cruel twist of fate, he'd been taken from her before she'd even had a chance to appreciate that love.

What was the point in going on?

"How is she?" Mai heard Darius ask as he came into Mai's bedroom.

It was a week later and Lexi was sitting in a chair beside the bed. "Still asleep," she said. "I'm worried about her. She's been out for days."

"It takes time," he said reassuringly. "How are you doing?"

Mai heard Darius' affection for his wife in his voice. *Lexi is lucky*, she thought. *Things have worked out for her*. She'd found her true love in the Immortal. It could have been a disaster—her growing old and him not. But they'd found a way to make it work. They would have eternity together, while she and Nick . . .

"I feel so helpless," Lexi said. "I don't know what to do to help her."

"Just be here for her," Darius replied. "The rest, time will have to heal."

"I don't know," Lexi said softly, her voice beginning to fade as Mai let herself slip into sleep. "Some hurts don't heal over time."

Mai didn't want to hear any more. Her heart ached and the only relief she found was when she dreamed.

"Your friends are worried about you," a familiar voice said. Mai's heart raced as it always did when Nick appeared.

"I'm fine," she said, moving into his arms. "As long as I'm with you."

The first time he came to her, she'd thought he'd found a way to escape—and in a way he had. He was a dream walker and they were spirit mates. As he'd told her once before, he'd always find her in her dreams.

"You can't sleep the rest of your life away," Nick chided gently even as he lay down beside her. She reveled in the rough feel of his hands against her bare skin. They created a delicious friction along the more sensitive areas of her body.

"Why not? If it's the only way I can be with you, then that's what I'll do."

"You have a life to live."

"My life has no purpose without you," Mai told him truthfully.

He paused in the act of trailing kisses along the column of her throat. "Maybe coming to see you was a mistake," he said, rolling onto his back and staring up at nothing in particular. "I wanted to be with you so badly, I didn't care how. But I don't think I can do this."

"What are you saying?" She turned onto her side to face him.

"I love you too much to let you waste your life away."

"Oh, please, Nick. Don't do this to me again," she begged. She'd thought she'd lost him before and it had been the most horrible thing in the world. Having him in her dreams wasn't perfect, but at least he was a part of her life this way. He was the best part.

"Mai, I—"

She laid a finger across his lips to silence him. "Sshh, no more talking. Let me show you how much I love you."

She kissed him then, silencing whatever words he would have uttered. She didn't want to hear them. All she wanted was to be with him.

For hours, it seemed, they cuddled, caressed and kissed, neither one of them in a hurry to finish. In her heart, she knew that this really was their last time together and she wanted it to last. When he finally rolled her beneath him and took her, she cried—for herself, for Nick and for their lost love.

Mai awoke the next morning carrying the memory of her dream with her. She kept her eyes closed, thinking she might fall back to sleep, but then changed her mind. Nick was right. She had to start living her life again.

Opening her eyes, she saw Lexi sitting in the chair beside her bed. She was awake and watching Mai closely.

"Thank you," Mai said.

"For?"

"For being here with me." She had to stop speaking as a wave of intense pain and loneliness washed over her. She took a couple of steadying breaths. "I appreciate everything you've done and I wanted you to know that. I also want you to know that I'm going to be okay."

Lexi didn't look like she was entirely convinced. "I

know you will, but how about if I stick around for a while anyway?"

Mai tried to smile, but found it harder to do than she'd expected. "One day. You can stay for one day, and then you and Darius need to go back to Ravenscroft. I have a godson who needs his parents."

"We'll see," Lexi told her. "Do you feel like getting out of bed?"

"No." Mai figured it was best to be honest because Lexi would know if she lied. "But I'm going to anyway."

Lexi seemed to visibly relax. "It'll get easier."

Mai nodded as she threw back the covers and sat up, swinging her legs over the side. She stayed like that for a few minutes, gathering her strength. She'd been in bed a long time and knew her muscles would be stiff.

Lexi stood ready to help her as she finally pushed off the bed to stand. She was unsteady on her feet, but soon got her bearings. At that moment, her stomach growled and she realized just how hungry she was.

"I don't suppose there's anything to eat?"

Lexi smiled. "Eggs and bacon, coming up."

"Great. Mind if I grab a shower?"

"Not at all," Lexi said, heading out of the bedroom toward the kitchen.

Mai brought some clothes into the bathroom with her. It took a great deal of self-discipline not to think of anything in particular during her shower, but she managed. When she got out, her gaze automatically flicked to the mirror, but there was nothing scrawled in the steam. She wondered again if that had been something the genie had done. As soon as she formed the thought, she cut if off. She didn't want to think about the genie. Or Nick.

Quickly dressing, Mai spent a little time doing her hair and makeup. There was nothing she could do for the dark circles under her eyes.

She went to the kitchen, where Lexi was still cooking breakfast. As she stood there, her gaze fell on the large mirror.

"Darius was going to destroy it," Lexi said, noting the direction of her gaze. "I told him to hold off. I wasn't sure if you wanted it around or not."

Mai gave her friend a grateful look. "Thanks. I think I'd like to hang on to it for a while." She looked around the room. "Speaking of Darius, where is he?"

Lexi smiled as she turned off the burner and picked up the skillet of eggs. "Sekhmet zapped him home to watch over Zach. But he left me a way to get in touch with him when you're ready to get rid of me." Her hand touched the lightning bolt necklace Mai had worn. "Turns out it's a good way to communicate between dimensions. Now— are you ready to eat?" She scooped eggs onto two plates and carried them to the table, where bacon and toast had already been prepared and sat waiting. Mai joined her and for the first few minutes, they both ate in silence.

"How's Jenna?" Mai asked finally, feeling a little guilty for not having remembered her earlier.

Lexi sighed. "She's awake. After we introduced ourselves, we had to tell her about Sarah. She didn't take it well, but at least now she knows that *she* didn't kill her sister."

No, Mai thought. She, Nick and Will had killed Sarah. Not that they'd known, but she still felt responsible. And poor Sarah.

It would be easy to blame the genie, but she wondered what she might be capable of doing had she been trapped there as long as he had. As long as Nick was going to be.

"What do you want to do today?"

Lexi's question was a welcome distraction from the direction her thoughts were taking. "I need to get in touch with Nick's father and tell him what happened. And then I could use your help with something."

Lexi shrugged. "Sure, what?"

"I need to find a couple of missing persons."

One day faded into the next until Mai wasn't really sure what day it was. Thanksgiving came and went. Though Heather had invited her over for the holidays, Mai went home. She hadn't seen her family in months and after these recent experiences, she felt a need to renew those bonds.

She had many things to feel grateful for—caring friends, loving family, her health and the firm offer from Tom to go back to work if she wanted it. She was still thinking about it, though she'd have to decide soon since she had bills to pay.

On top of everything else, she'd not had a vision or hallucination in weeks. Of course, she also hadn't seen Nick and it was hard to appreciate the good things when her heart ached with missing him. Every night that he didn't visit her in her dreams was a fresh reminder and so Mai found herself cutting back on sleep until she got so tired that when she fell into bed exhausted, she didn't dream at all.

"Why don't you come to the club tonight?" Ricco suggested when he called some weeks later. "I'll even pick you up so you don't have to come over by yourself."

"I don't know," she hesitated. "I'm not really in the mood."

"Come on. It'll do you good to get out."

"You're probably right, but I just don't feel like it."

She heard Ricco heave a sigh and since vampires didn't breathe, she knew how frustrated he must have been with her. She hated that all her friends were so worried. She injected some enthusiasm into her voice. "Tell you what. I need to do a little work on my next article, but if it's not too late when I finish, I'll come over."

"Call me and I'll come get you," he offered, probably knowing she had no intention of doing either.

"That won't be necessary," she assured him. "I'll teleport." *At least that's working*, she thought.

They talked a few minutes more, then said good-bye.

Afterward, Mai sat in her living room contemplating her next story. The Preston story had finally run and the buzz around it had exceeded Mai's expectations. Since her source was already dead, Mai had willingly shared her information and all her notes with the police for their investigation. Unfortunately, Preston had conveniently disappeared before they could arrest him.

In the world of investigative reporting, Mai had made a name for herself. Her next story would prove that she was either a serious player or a flash in the pan.

Mai's head jerked and she realized she'd fallen asleep sitting on the couch. It was late and she was clearly exhausted, so she headed off to bed for another night of dreamless sleep.

She felt like she'd only shut her eyes for a second when she heard someone call her name.

"Mai." It was just a whisper, but she recognized the voice.

"Nick?"

She'd wanted to hear his voice again so badly, she nearly cried with joy at the sound of it.

"Wake up, Mai. There's someone in the apartment."

It was the last thing she expected him to say. At the warning, her eyes flew up and she was instantly awake. Nick's voice was now only a shadow in her mind. She wasn't even sure if she'd really heard it.

Careful not to move or change her breathing, she focused on listening to the sounds around her, trying to determine if she really did have an intruder. As tired as she was, it could just as easily have been her mind playing tricks on her.

Then she heard the footsteps.

She eased out of bed, careful not to make any noise. She slipped to the floor on the far side of the bed, trying to hide from whoever might come through the open doorway.

She began crawling toward her purse, hoping to get her can of pepper spray. She had almost reached it when she sensed someone else in her room.

Fear skittered down her spine as she looked behind her. She experienced an eerie sense of déjà vu when she spotted the black-clad figure standing in the doorway. Before she could scream, he rushed forward and with a single hit, knocked her unconscious.

CHAPTER TWENTY-FOUR

Nick threw himself against the glass of the portal, hoping to shatter it. Mai was in trouble and he had to save her.

Movement in the hall caught his attention and he stopped long enough to see the figure reappear. He'd pulled off his mask and Nick recognized Bill Preston.

"Next time anyone sees you," he muttered, dragging Mai's unconscious body out of the bedroom, "it'll be when they drag your decomposing body from the river."

Hang on, baby. I'll find a way to save you.

Nick was so focused on trying to figure out what he could do that he almost missed the faint sound.

Nick.

It was Mai. Of course. Because she was unconscious, he could go to her.

He escaped his corporeal form and entered the dream realm. He found her standing in a dark room, looking lost. "Mai, I'm here."

"Oh, Nick. You came." She hurried to him and he welcomed her with open arms.

"Mai, honey. You have to wake up now."

"No. I want to be with you."

"You're in danger. The man who broke into your apartment is Bill Preston."

"Bill Preston. Are you sure?"

"I'm positive. Now wake up."

"It won't do you any good," Preston's voice boomed from much too close. Nick turned his head at the sound and saw the man standing there.

"How . . . ?" Mai asked, clearly confused. She turned to him. "Nick?"

"I see him," Nick said. "I'm guessing that in addition to being less than ethical, you're also less than human," he said to Preston. "Am I right?"

Preston laughed. It was a mocking, grating sound.

"In fact," Nick continued, "you're not human at all, are you?"

"What do you mean?" Mai asked.

"Mai, meet your hallucination. Preston is a Keltok demon. Or, in more familiar terms—he's the bogeyman."

Preston laughed. "So you've figured it out at last."

"I didn't think there were any who could leave the dream realm," Mai argued.

"Yeah, well, news flash," Preston sneered. "There's at least one of us."

"You're the one who attacked me in my old apartment." Mai sounded both surprised and shocked.

"Guilty, I'm afraid," Preston said. "You were asking too many questions. I had to stop you before you ruined my campaign."

"By killing me?"

"No." Preston sounded offended. "Well, not at first, anyway. I thought I might offer you a job. It never hurts to have a reporter on your team."

"I would never work for someone like you."

Preston shrugged. "So I gathered from talking to your therapist."

Mai gasped. "*You* killed my therapist."

"Yes, and just before he died, he was very forthcoming about your problems, the vivid hallucinations and your inability to teleport. I found them most useful."

"You almost killed her when you attacked her in the dream realm," Nick accused.

"I admit that I got carried away," Preston said without the slightest remorse. "And you are obviously the one I fought."

"Did you leave the messages in the mirror?" Mai asked.

Preston laughed. "A nice touch, don't you think? And very entertaining."

"But how?"

"That's simple," he said. "My natural form is invisible to the human eye."

She frowned. "And later. The hallucination about being trapped in a river of molten lava?"

"Yes, I'm particularly proud of that piece of work. Still trying to make an impression at that point, but we're past that now, aren't we?"

"I won't let you hurt her," Nick threatened, stepping forward.

Preston merely laughed. "You can't stop me." In a blink, he was gone.

Nick turned to Mai and saw her image beginning to fade. She was waking up. "Mai," he shouted, trying to keep her with him.

"Nick!"

He heard her cry long after she disappeared and his sense of helplessness was overwhelming. Trapped as he was, there was nothing he could do. Reluctantly, he returned to the wish realm and watched through the portal. Preston hefted Mai over his shoulder as if she weighed nothing and headed for the door. Right before he left, he cast a glance at the mirror and Nick could have sworn the man looked directly at him.

The moment passed before Nick could think what to do and a second later, Preston and Mai were gone.

In complete despair, Nick placed his hands against the glass and tried to resist the urge to bang his head against it. He had to exert great control to calm himself enough to think rationally.

As he leaned against the glass, it began to vibrate. For a second, Nick thought that New York might be experiencing a rare earthquake. He went to push himself away from the glass—and almost fell through.

Experimentally, Nick stretched out his hand and found that it passed right through the glass. He couldn't help getting excited. He leaned out farther, his pulse racing. If he went slowly, maybe he could escape.

He bent forward and found that his head slipped through as easily as his hands and arms. He knew he wouldn't be able to escape totally, but wondered how far he could go. He lifted a foot, wanting to see if he could step out, but the invisible tethers that bound him to the dimension tightened their hold. So that was it. He could touch the physical world, but that was all.

Frustrated, he turned and headed back into the wish dimension. Somewhere out there, Preston was going to kill Mai and there wasn't a damn thing Nick could do about it.

Mai.

Startled awake by the sound of her name, Mai looked around. As far as she could tell, she was alone in a dark room. Her head hurt like a son of a bitch and she couldn't shake the pressing feeling that there was something she needed to do—only she couldn't remember what it was.

Mai.

She looked around, trying to identify the source of the voice calling her name. It was familiar and yet, when she heard it, a sharp ache squeezed her chest.

Mai.

"Go away," she shouted. "Leave me alone. I want to be alone." It wasn't true. She was tired of being alone. What she wanted more than anything else was impossible—because Nick was gone.

The sense that there was more to it worried at her until the events of the evening came back in sharp relief. Preston had broken into her apartment, knocked her out and now she had no idea where she was.

She looked around to see if she recognized her surroundings but saw only darkness. A tremor of fear worked its way past the rest of her worries. Was she dead?

No, she hastily reassured herself. She wouldn't be able to think if she was dead, would she? So she was alive—and obviously awake—and possibly blind? Why else couldn't she see? And deaf, too, because when she tried to listen, all she heard was an eerie silence.

But there had been a voice, hadn't there?

Mai.

It came again—and she knew who was calling her name.

"Nick?"

Mai. Thank God you can hear me.

"Where are you? Why can't I see you?" To Mai, he sounded like he could be standing beside her.

I'm still in the wish dimension.

"But I can hear you," she said.

You hear my thoughts.

But she was awake, so how could that be? *I don't understand.* This time she thought it instead of saying it out loud.

We're spirit mates, he explained. *Our bond is spiritual first and physical second. No matter how far apart we are, we'll always be able to speak to each other on the spiritual plane.*

She wasn't alone. Knowing that helped ease her fear. *I*

still wish you were with me physically, she told him as the ache in her chest swelled.

Me, too. With all my heart.

They fell into silence as they both worked to conquer their feelings. *Where's Preston?* Nick finally asked.

I don't know. I can't see anything.

You have to stop him.

If the situation hadn't been so dire, she would have laughed at the absurdity of his suggestion. If she was capable of stopping Preston, didn't he think she would have done so by now? *No problem*, she thought with a healthy dose of sarcasm. *How do you propose I do that?*

Yes. How? Preston's voice intruded. Then he laughed. *I'm just as at home in this dimension as you are, spirit walker. Maybe more so.*

Leave her alone, Nick warned.

Or what? There was more laughter when Nick didn't reply. *That's what I thought. Say good-bye to your girlfriend, spirit walker.*

Sarah's mistake doesn't have to be yours, Nick said quickly, his voice fading. *I love you, Mai.*

Nick was gone and she was alone—except for Preston. Nick had tried to tell her something. Now she had to figure out what he'd meant. What mistake had Sarah made? When—

She bolted upright, sputtering for air as ice-cold water hit her in the face. Preston stood nearby, a metal bucket dangling from one hand.

"I just wanted to make sure you were fully awake," he said with a smile.

"What are you going to do to me?"

"Kill you—as promised."

His voice droned on and on as he told her just how he planned to kill her, but Mai had stopped listening. What had Sarah's mistake been?

The sound of the bucket scraping across the floor snapped Mai's attention back to the moment. "Time to go, princess," Preston said. "Get up."

"I don't know if I can," she said as she made a show of struggling. "My legs are stiff from lying on this cold floor so long."

"Good news for you, then, that you'll soon be too dead to care." Despite his words, Preston came over to her and grabbed her by the arm. As he hauled her up, she wrapped her other arm around him and held on tightly because she'd just figured out what mistake Sarah had made.

Then she teleported back to her apartment, landing in front of the mirror.

Nick was waiting beside the portal and the instant Mai and Preston appeared, he reached out and dragged the Keltok demon through.

The portal closed behind them, but Nick didn't let go of the demon until he had taken him deep into the realm. Above them floated the yellow threads of unfulfilled wishes, echoes of voices floating around them on the wind like the desperate moans of long forgotten ghosts.

"You can't keep me here," Preston growled, trying to free himself from Nick's hold.

"You may be right," Nick acknowledged. "But then, I wasn't planning to hold you prisoner."

Preston looked momentarily surprised, but then he gave a snort of laughter. "What? You think you can kill me?"

"I know I can." Using the side of his hand, Nick hit him across the throat in a move that would have killed a human. Preston fell back, coughing, but still very much alive.

Recovering almost as fast as the genie had, Preston launched himself forward, faster than any opponent Nick had fought before. Preston came after him, tackling Nick to the ground. Trapped beneath Preston, Nick struggled to turn himself. Using his legs for leverage, he flipped Preston into the air and over his head.

Instantly Nick was back on top, driving his fists into Preston's face. They fought viciously, tirelessly. Nick's entire body ached and he wondered how much more abuse he could dole out. Wondered how much more he could take.

As he struggled back to his feet for the hundredth time, he wondered if perhaps he'd overestimated his ability to hold Preston. Fear for Mai spurred him on. If he didn't kill Preston, then he'd failed his spirit mate and put her life in danger.

Another set of wishes floated by, this time lit with the deep, dark yellow of powerful desire. Its rumbling noise vibrated across the fighting men.

"I wish Nick were free."

"I wish for Nick to be safe."

"I wish Nick to be with me."

Accompanying these wishes was a softer litany of words running beneath them all. "I love him. I love him. I love him."

As Nick drew closer to the portal, the yellow threads of wishes grew into a large, dense cloud that expanded downward, settling over Preston.

"No." Preston's protest was faint as the thrum of the wishes grew louder. "No. Let me go."

Nick stepped away, unsure what was happening.

As he watched, the cloud took on the shape of golden coils. They wrapped around Preston like ropes and despite how he struggled, Preston couldn't break the bonds.

He was lifted into the air and carried by the yellow cloud back into the tunnels. Unsure what magic was at work here, Nick turned and watched him go. Once Preston was out of sight, Nick turned back to the portal. Mai was there, tears running down her cheeks, her lips moving in a silent prayer.

Nick moved closer and when he reached the portal, he reached out. Unexpectedly, the mirror opened at his touch and his hand slipped through. At the sight of him, Mai's lips stilled. On a soft gasp, she rushed forward, threw her arms around his neck and pulled him forward for a kiss.

She tasted like warm honey and he knew that he'd never experience anything sweeter than this moment. He wished with all his being that it could last forever.

He deepened the kiss, unwilling to let it end. How long he kissed her, he had no idea, but eventually Mai pulled back and smiled. "Welcome home," she whispered, her voice breaking with emotion.

"Home?" He was confused.

"You're free."

Startled, Nick looked around. She was right. He wasn't sure how it happened, but he was standing in her living room. Behind him, the portal had closed and the only faces he saw when he looked in the mirror were his and Mai's.

"It seems the dimension has a new genie." She smiled and kissed his cheek. Then she thought of something. "What if Preston starts haunting the apartment building?"

"We'll make sure he doesn't, starting by taking down all the mirrors. Then we can ask your Coven of Light friends to cast a spell to keep him inside the dimension." He hugged her to him. "But in any event, that's not something you're going to have to worry about."

"Why's that?"

"Because you won't be living here."

She looked up at him. "And where will I be living?"

"With me." He was dead serious and before she could say anything, he turned her so he could see into her face.

"Move in with me, Mai. Right now. We'll get married as soon as we can arrange for the wedding and live in my apartment with Dave until we can find our own place."

Mai leaned away so she could see his face. "You're serious?" She sounded surprised and that worried him.

He'd been so sure about how he felt that he'd just assumed she felt the same. Had he been wrong? "If you need time to think about it—"

"No."

"No?"

"Nick, while you were trapped in the dimension, all I had was time to think. I know my answer. Yes—I'll marry you. I love you."

At that moment, the phone rang. "Ignore it," Mai said, leaning up to kiss him. Nick's world tilted off its axis once again—but in a good way. In the background, he became aware of a man's voice coming across on the answering machine telling Mai he'd read her article on Preston and had a lead on a possible story if she was interested.

To her credit, she didn't answer the phone, but he could tell she'd listened to the message and had no doubt that they'd soon be chasing down the facts of a new story. Nick realized that with Mai, his life would never be peaceful and quiet, but he'd never be bored.

CHAPTER TWENTY-FIVE

"Are you sure you know what you're doing?" Dave asked Nick as they stood in the groom's dressing room a week later.

"You make it sound like I'm getting ready for my funeral instead of my wedding."

"I just don't want you to get hurt."

He didn't need to say the words out loud for Nick to know the rest of that sentence was "like me." "One day, you'll find her."

"Who?"

"Your spirit mate. The one worth risking your heart over."

Dave scoffed. "Been there, done that. Still have the burn marks to show for it."

"Lana was never your spirit mate," Nick said sharply, daring to bring up the name neither of them had uttered in years. He knew the memory of her was painful for Dave and he didn't want either of them to dwell on it tonight of all nights. "In the meantime," he continued, attempting to steer to safer ground, "there are plenty of women still out there. Not even you could've slept with all of them."

Dave grinned. "True. Did you see Mai's third cousin out there? She's hot."

Just then, the door to the groom's dressing room opened and Nick's father stuck his head in. "It's time."

"All right," Nick said. "We're coming."

Nick's father retreated and after the door closed, Nick turned to Dave. "How do I look?"

"Like a man who's found his purpose for living."

Nick smiled. "I have. Now let's get out there."

They stepped out of the room and walked the short distance to where Nick's father, who was performing the ceremony, waited for them.

Mai's extended family filled one half of the church while Los Paseantes de Espíritu filled the other half. Lexi and Heather had decorated the church with white and pale green ribbons, flowers and magically produced glittering lights that bathed the otherwise dark room in their warm glow like hundreds of lit candles. None of it took his breath away as the image of his bride did when she appeared at the end of the aisle and started walking toward him.

"Would you like to dance?"

Jenna looked up into the too-handsome face of Dave Runningbear wondering what his agenda might be. They'd sat beside each other at the table reserved for the bridal party and eaten an entire meal without saying a single word to each other beyond "pass the salt, please." Not exactly stimulating conversation. Now he was asking her to dance?

She knew better than to think he was trying to flirt with her. Maybe it was a pity dance because she'd been sitting by herself for some time now. She didn't like being anyone's charity case. "Thanks," she said. "But you don't have to."

He extended his hand to her. "I know."

It had never occurred to her that he might actually want to dance with her. She quickly squashed the thought. She'd seen who he flirted with and she was not his type.

Still, she placed her hand in his and let him guide her onto the dance floor. The music that was playing transitioned to a slow tune and when Dave pulled her into his arms, Jenna felt a moment of panic.

"Relax," he told her. "I don't bite." When she tried to put some space between them, he simply pulled her closer. "Just listen to the music. Feel the rhythm." He put his hand against her lower back and pressed her hips into his as he moved to the music. It was deliciously erotic and Jenna let him sweep her away in the moment.

When the music stopped, it took her a moment to realize that they had stopped moving and she was standing here with her arms around Dave with her eyes closed. She opened them and felt the blood rush to her face. Dave was staring down at her with a bemused, curious expression on his face.

"I should go," Jenna said, sounding breathless. "Thank you."

She pulled out of his arms and disappeared into the crowd. Under other circumstances, she would push the entire embarrassing episode from her mind and move on with her life. This time, she didn't have that luxury.

She went to find Mai and Nick, and congratulated them once more. "You leaving so soon?" Mai asked.

"I thought I'd try to get up early and start looking for a job."

"You know you're welcome to stay at the apartment with us for as long as you need to," Nick told her. "And don't worry about Dave, he won't mind."

"Thanks, you two. I appreciate all you've done for me. Now, go enjoy your reception and don't worry about me. Congratulations again."

She left them then and hurried back to her room. To-morrow was another day and she'd face it when it came.

"Finally, I have you all to myself," Nick said as he carried Mai across the threshold. They were spending their wedding night in a bed-and-breakfast not far from Nick's village in upstate New York.

At one point in the ceremony, Darius' mother, Sekhmet, had dropped in unexpectedly. Since Mai was godmother to Sekhmet's grandson, the goddess had a vested interest in Mai's well-being—which meant she was also interested in checking out the man who had won Mai's heart. Mai assumed she approved of Nick because she hadn't struck him dead.

The ceremony had proceeded smoothly and for hours afterward, Mai and Nick had visited with their family and close friends. Now it was late and Mai wanted nothing more than to be alone with her new husband.

Husband. She couldn't get over it. When she thought back to how lonely she'd been just months earlier . . .

"Why the frown, love?" Nick asked, releasing her legs so she could stand without letting her out of his embrace.

"I think about how lonely my life would have been if I'd never found you."

"That would not have happened."

"What do you mean?"

"Spirit mates are destined to find each other. When you were ready to be found, your spirit called me to you."

"I'm glad it was you," she told him.

"Me, too." He kissed her and when he pulled away, it was to slip the straps of her wedding dress from her shoulders. As the gown slid down her body, he trailed kisses along her throat, running his fingers through the silken strands of her hair. "You're so beautiful," he whispered. "And I'm so lucky."

"I'm the lucky one," she told him, running her hands up his chest and along his shoulders, pushing his jacket off as she did.

She'd worn nothing under her gown and now stood before him naked with the silk pooling around her feet. She saw the way his gaze heated when he looked at her and her pulse quickened in anticipation. She made fast work of the buttons on his shirt and then reached for the waistband of his slacks. The intensity of her hunger made her hands shake. She'd made love to him before, both in and out of her dreams, but it never seemed to be enough.

The hungry look in his eyes told her that his need was as great as her own. Before she could suggest they move to the bed, he scooped her up into his arms and carried her there. Soon they were lying side by side, Nick's warm body cradling hers.

Her entire body tingled with unabated desire. "Let's not ever leave," he whispered between kisses. "In fact, let's spend the entire day tomorrow in this room, in this bed, making love. When we get hungry, we'll order room service."

"Mmmmm, I like that idea," she said softly. And then she remembered why they couldn't do that. "Damn."

He stopped kissing her. "What?"

"I completely forgot. I sort of made an appointment to talk to someone tomorrow."

"You're working? Mai. It's our honeymoon. Can't you get out of it?"

"I'm sorry, but it's really important—and it's not work."

"Then what is it?"

"I'm going to talk to your mom—and your brothers."

He pulled back and it felt as if he'd put an ocean between them. "What?"

"Yeah." She spoke slowly, trying to gauge his reaction to her words. "I invited them to the wedding, but we agreed that after the wedding might be a better time to reconcile."

"Why would you do that?" His tone was sharp, blaming.

She'd thought she was doing the right thing, but maybe she'd been wrong. She hurried to explain before the entire wedding night was ruined. "You told me that your parents were spirit mates. Being one myself, I didn't understand how your mother could walk out on your father—or how your father could let your mother go. I thought there might be more to the story than what you'd been told. Plus, I wanted her to know the kind of man her son had turned out to be. She would be so proud of you." She waited for him to say something, but the silence got to be too much. "Nick, I'll cancel my appointment if you want me to, but I was hoping that you might want to go with me and see your mother and brothers again. They want to see you."

It seemed a long time before he slowly nodded. "All right. I'll go with you to see my mother and hear what she has to say. After that—we'll see. That's all I can promise."

"Thank you." She dragged him down for a lengthy kiss. "I love you," she told him when they came up for air.

She ran her hand down his stomach, intending to stroke and fondle him until the temptation to take her proved too much. For the first time in a very long while, she felt like a wood nymph, wanting to make love all night long. She moved her hand past his stomach, her goal almost in hand when he pulled her hand away.

"I can't do this," he said suddenly, throwing back the covers and climbing out of bed.

He was angry with her for contacting his mother. She shouldn't have interfered—but she'd only wanted to make things better. "Nick, I—"

"I'm sorry, Mai. I tried to ignore it, but I can't. It's driving me crazy."

"I'm sorry, Nick."

"Don't be ridiculous. It's not your fault," he told her,

pulling on his pants. He didn't bother putting on his shirt but walked across the room and grabbed the large mirror by its frame and lifted it from the wall. Going over to the door, he opened it and carried the mirror out into the hallway. Then he came back, locking the door behind him.

He quickly undressed and climbed back into the bed. "What?" he asked when he caught her staring at him.

"You were talking about the mirror?"

"Of course. Tell me you don't feel better with it gone." He shook his head. "I hope you're not going to mind that we don't have mirrors in our house for a few . . . years." He turned onto his side, raised himself onto one elbow and trailed a finger along the ridge of her collarbone, down along the length of her breast and around her nipple until it rose to a stiff peak. "Now—where were we? Oh yeah." He lifted himself on top of her and settled between her legs.

A long while later, they lay exhausted from a long day and replete from making love, not once, but twice. Mai snuggled against Nick, her head on his chest. She couldn't remember ever being this happy before in her life. "Nick?" she whispered in case he was asleep.

"Yeah, baby?" His voice was a husky whisper.

"I love you."

"I love you, too." He tightened the arm around her, giving her a gentle squeeze. His hold on her remained secure even though his breathing slowed as sleep stole over him.

Mai was content to listen. Being with him like this was so much better than the dream, she thought, as she slowly drifted off to sleep.

"What took you so long?" Nick's voice floated to her as he entered her dream and took her by the hand. Suddenly they were standing on a tropical beach with crystal-blue waters gently washing ashore. The sun was setting over the horizon, giving the sky a warm glow. Ahead of them, a large bed, draped in white sheets, stood waiting for them. Nick smiled down at her as he led her to the bed.

A short while later, Mai rode the crest of the most powerful climax of the evening. When it slowly ebbed away, she couldn't help but smile. The reality might be better than the dream, but the dream was definitely not bad.

☐ **YES!**

Sign me up for the Love Spell Book Club and send my FREE BOOKS! If I choose to stay in the club, I will pay only $8.50* each month, a savings of $6.48!

NAME: _____

ADDRESS: _____

TELEPHONE: _____

EMAIL: _____

☐ I want to pay by credit card.

☐ **VISA**　　☐ **MasterCard.**　　☐ **DISCOVER**

ACCOUNT #: _____

EXPIRATION DATE: _____

SIGNATURE: _____

Mail this page along with $2.00 shipping and handling to:

Love Spell Book Club
PO Box 6640
Wayne, PA 19087

Or fax (must include credit card information) to:

610-995-9274

You can also sign up online at **www.dorchesterpub.com**.

*Plus $2.00 for shipping. Offer open to residents of the U.S. and Canada only. Canadian residents please call 1-800-481-9191 for pricing information.

If under 18, a parent or guardian must sign. Terms, prices and conditions subject to change. Subscription subject to acceptance. Dorchester Publishing reserves the right to reject any order or cancel any subscription.